# A DISMAL HARVEST

## DAISY BATEMAN

SEVENTH
STREET
BOOKS®

*For*
*Mom and Dad*

# CHAPTER ONE

"**I** can't find the frog."

Claudia looked up from where she had been counting place settings and tried to get her mind around that sentence.

"Did you check in the tank?"

"I looked everywhere," Iryna said. "I don't know where he went."

"He was probably scared off by all the activity," said Claudia. "This is a lot more noise than he's used to hearing this time of day. I wouldn't worry about it. I'm sure he'll be back. Did the mini pierogies make it over okay?"

"Yes, they're fine. Carmen is putting them on the toothpicks now. I should probably go and help her."

Claudia agreed that sounded like a better use of Iryna's time, but she promised to keep an eye out for her friend. Watching her go, Claudia had the familiar feeling of wondering what she had gotten herself into this time.

Specifically, the answer to that question was that she was hosting a harvest dinner to benefit the local library, in her marketplace for sellers of artisan foods. Iryna and her wife Carmen were two of her tenants, owners of The Corner Pocket, Northern California's premier combination pierogi and empanada stand. Claudia liked and respected them both, even if Iryna was occasionally subject to flights of sentiment about unusual things.

The frog in question (Claudia suspected it might actually be several frogs, working in shifts) was a part-time resident of the marketplace's bathroom. He, she, or they had been identified as a common tree frog, and since this stretch of the wind-blown Sonoma coast wasn't big on trees, Claudia supposed he had settled on the bathroom as the next best thing. He was usually behind the toilet or the sink, though occasionally could be found hanging out stuck to the wall, like gravity wasn't really a thing, and in one unfortunate incident he had emerged from under the seat at a critical moment. After that, Iryna had hand-lettered a warning sign, which was now posted next to the one about not flushing paper towels. There were occasional conversations about relocating him to a more appropriate environment, but no one was sure exactly how to do that, and in the interim "going to talk to the frog" had become a standard euphemism among the marketplace tenants.

Coming back from her amphibianic musings, Claudia realized she had lost track of how many settings she had counted, or where she had stopped. Sighing, she put down the one she was holding and started over. In just over two hours the leading citizens of San Elmo were due to arrive, and she didn't want to be caught without enough forks.

Around her, the marketplace was a hive of activity. Long tables filled the central corridor, which was usually kept open for customers to stroll between the shops, or stop to eat an empanada and consult their guidebooks. In the stores, samples and appetizers were arranged on the counters and information about how the goods were made displayed on the shelves and walls. (Anything particularly portable that wasn't a sample had been put away, to prevent anyone from taking the self-serve aspect too far.) All of the vendors had stayed on after their usual closing time, to help with service and answer questions, but the bulk of the food was being handled by the catering staff, who seemed more than capable.

"Here, try this." Claudia's friend Betty materialized seemingly out of nowhere and handed her a spoonful of something green, which Claudia dutifully put in her mouth.

"Delicious," she said. "What is it?"

"Kale pesto. I'm trying to decide if it needs more cheese."

Betty, in addition to her day jobs of helping to run the guest ranch she owned with her husband, cooking all the meals for same, and raising three children, had recently started her own catering business, and Claudia knew this dinner was the biggest thing she had taken on so far. Which probably went a long way to explaining why her usually unflusterable friend was showing signs of stress, for the first time since Claudia had known her. (Not that anyone who didn't know her would have noticed. With her naturally effortless sense of style, Betty's "frazzled" would count as most people's "just spent an hour getting ready to go out.")

"I don't think it's missing anything," Claudia said, on the subject of the pesto. "But I'd never say no to more cheese."

Betty nodded in a way that made it clear she hadn't heard a word Claudia said, while her eyes followed one of the waiters as she overloaded a tray with water glasses.

"Okay, maybe I'll just grate some over the top. Thanks." Betty took the spoon back and flitted off in the direction of the next crisis, leaving Claudia with a handful of cutlery and no idea what number she had gotten to. She was about to start again when there was a shout and a crash from the pickle shop, and a stream of invective from Helen, the store's owner. Claudia looked at the place settings, then back at her marketplace, and it was clear where her priorities needed to be.

"May the forks be with us," she muttered, and went to see what the problem was this time.

One and a half hours and fifteen near disasters later and, improbably, the tables were set, the food was plated and waiting to serve, and everything was about as ready as it was going to be. Which was good, because the guests were already starting to filter in, thanks to whoever had forgotten the front door was propped open. Through it, Claudia could see that the parking lot was filling up, and the overflow was heading up the road, toward the tiny cottage where she lived and on to the much grander house of her nearest neighbor. A few months earlier, that would have been another cause for concern, but one of the results of the rather lively summer Claudia had had was that she and Nathan Rodgers were on much better terms than they had been.

Good enough, in fact, that he was there now, helping to set up the beer taps in the temporary bar. In his previous life (if a thirty-seven year-old can be said to have had a previous life), he had been the founder and owner of Fog Heart Brewing Company, a local brewery that had attained near-legendary status among beer nerds, until he got bored and sold it to a multinational conglomerate for what he would only describe as "a lot of money." The resulting leisure had left him at loose ends, which had originally been the source of some friction when Claudia moved in and opened the market, and now meant that he showed up at random times, to talk about his latest ideas or just to see if she wanted to get some dinner. Claudia wasn't sure what sort of relationship he thought they had, or even what she wanted, but she had come to like having him around.

And it certainly didn't hurt the attendance at the charity dinner when word had somehow gotten out that it would be the exclusive place to try the results of his latest project, an experiment with sour beers using locally grown fruit. Already, a number of men with ill-advised beards had come in and made a beeline for the bar, where they waited impatiently, clutching their drink tickets.

Thinking of bees reminded Claudia that she should probably check in on her newest tenant. Most of the shops in the marketplace were set up for food sales, with sinks and power for refrigerators, but there was one that had space for neither, and it had been a source of trouble for Claudia in the past. It had recently become vacant, and a determination on her part to be choosier about who could occupy it meant she had been without rent on the space for over a month. So it was a relief when one of her tenants mentioned they knew a beekeeper who was looking for a place to sell his wares, and more so when she met Eugene Royal and he turned out to be a preternaturally cheerful black man with a verifiable group of hives set on an old orchard property about ten miles away.

He had come to beekeeping after a career in corporate accounting, so Claudia wasn't concerned about him being overwhelmed by this relatively modest event, but she thought it would be a good idea to make sure he hadn't run into any unexpected trouble.

She needn't have worried. Eugene's shop, In the Honey, was doing steady business, and its proprietor was clearly in his element. Betty had made a special appetizer using his lavender honey and mascarpone from the cheese shop, sprinkled with jewel-like pomegranate seeds on a slice of dried pear, and as Claudia cut the line to steal one, she reflected it was nice to be around people who knew what they were doing.

"Not bad, eh?" Eugene detached himself from a group of visitors as Claudia licked honey off her fingers. "I wasn't sure about the chips, but a-pear-antly they're going over pretty well."

He laughed, and Claudia chuckled along. At some point in his transition to full-time beekeeper, Eugene seemed to have decided that what he needed was an extensive repertoire mostly of bee- and honey-related jokes and puns. They were uniformly terrible, but Claudia appreciated his dedication.

Not everyone shared her point of view. Jeannie, Eugene's teenage daughter, who had been labeling the sample tray with careful calligraphy, looked like she would like to turn herself inside out.

"Dad—"

"I know, I know. I need better material." He shook his head in mock exasperation. "My toughest critic. But I guess you're stuck with me, right?"

This time Jeannie didn't say anything, but the suffering in her eyes was plenty familiar to Claudia. It was a good twenty years now since she had lived in horror of her mother's inclination to randomly burst into song, but she knew the feeling.

"Actually," she said. "I was just coming over to see if you could spare Jeannie for a bit. A couple of Orlan's people didn't show up and he's short-handed right now. Would you mind?"

It wasn't entirely a lie, since the young workforce of the vegetable market wasn't always the most reliable, and there were almost never enough of them on hand. But mostly, Claudia thought Jeannie might be ready to have some time around people her own age.

From the speed at which her offer was accepted, it appeared Claudia had guessed right. (Though from the way Jeannie ran her hands over her hair and checked her face in the reflective surface of the sign on her father's shop, it occurred to Claudia that she might not have guessed the complete reason for the girl's agitation.)

Her father watched her go with affectionate bemusement.

"They grow up so fast, don't they?"

Claudia, who had no children, agreed on general principle. She might have said something about feeling the same way about her dog, but she was save from that particular faux pas by an elderly couple in matching purple suits who approached the table with questions about organic means of controlling mites in a bee colony. Eugene launched into a passionately opinionated response and, figuring her value here was limited, Claudia headed off to see what other kinds of trouble she could get into.

For the first hour of the party, the guests circulated through the market, eating Betty's canapés and asking the shopholders the same questions over and over. Then, at the appointed time, Julie Muller—who, in addition to being the chair of the Friends of the Library, was also the co-owner with her father of Dancing Cow Cheese, the marketplace's marquee tenant—rang an antique cowbell and made a speech about the goals for the evening. Which essentially boiled down to "how about you give us some money," but phrased in a way that caused Claudia to reflect on why Julie was a beloved leader of the local charity scene, and she was not.

Still, if she had wanted to make people like her, Claudia decided she could do worse than to start with Betty's cooking. The first course to come out was a warm salad of roasted butternut squash and chickpeas in a garlicky tahini dressing, garnished with slivers of prosciutto (omitted for the vegetarian option). After that, there was an amuse of a deviled quail egg topped with a sprinkling of the tiniest chives Claudia had ever seen, and a short break for the guests to take pictures of it with their phones.

As the owner of the marketplace, Claudia supposed she might have expected to be seated at the VIP table. The fact that she was instead tucked in a corner with the members of the local mime troupe, however, she took as less of a slight than a sign that Julie knew her well enough to know where she would rather be. Out of costume, the mimes were a chatty bunch, and over the course of the dinner, Claudia learned more than she ever would have thought possible about face paints.

She had been planning to dress for the event in her best jeans and a sequined top, both left over from her earlier life as a programmer in San Francisco, where variations on that outfit had constituted her "going out" look for the better part of two years. But trying it on, she had realized that the style was both dated (those two years were three years in the past now) and simply wrong. Who she had been then wasn't who she was now and, frankly, San Elmo wasn't a sequins sort of place. So she had reached into her closet for her only "nice" outfit: a jersey wrap dress in a shade of green that made her brown hair look less mousey, some fashionably ugly (and surprisingly comfortable) platform shoes, and a chunky glass necklace made by a local artist that had been Betty's present on her last birthday.

Part of her had worried about looking like she was trying too hard, but now that she was here, listening to an argument about whether the invisible window-washing sketch was a classic or just unbearably cliché, she was glad to have made the effort. She was aware of eyes on her, and the occasional finger pointed in her direction by people she hoped were just talking about who owned the marketplace, and she felt better knowing that for once she was dressed with some amount of appropriateness for her thirty-six years. Although, as the food kept coming, she was starting to regret the body-shaper.

The main course of the meal was served family-style, and as Claudia helped herself to a mini stuffed eggplant with red pepper sauce and some ravioli filled with braised pork belly, she thought about the irony of a harvest-themed meal in California in October. The truth was, with the exception of the wine grapes, very little was being harvested at the moment, and for most things the season was either ending (tomatoes, sweet corn) or not yet started (citrus, crabs). There was no freezing winter to dread, just ongoing conversations about when the rains would come. (When the state quarters were being designed, someone had suggested that California's should be the local version of the four seasons—flood, fire, earthquake, and mudslide.)

She understood that it was traditional, but partisan enough to be annoyed that they had to be bound by the traditions of another place. Next year she would suggest to Julie that the party be held in June, when the peaches and tomatoes were rolling in, and the green beans and cucumbers were just hitting their stride.

Then again, she thought as she watched her friend and tenant listening to some long-winded explanation from the town's only dentist, maybe she wouldn't. Julie seemed to have enough people telling her things right now.

And she had to admit, it was nice to have the boost to business at this time of year. The weather in San Elmo might not exactly have seasons, but the tourists certainly did, and in the three years she had owned the marketplace, she had already learned that for the stretch between Labor Day and Christmas, sales could be few and far between. Part of Julie's pitch for her to host this event was to build connections with the local community, with the idea that the people who lived in San Elmo might be inspired to start doing at least some of their shopping among the marketplace's gourmet cheeses and small-batch pickles. Claudia wasn't so sure about that, considering that the average income in the former fishing town didn't tend to run to five-dollar-a-pound tomatoes.

But averages weren't populations, and Claudia had to admit that most of the guests at the fundraiser looked like they could spring for the occasional fancy ham. They were, she supposed, what counted as the small town's leading citizens, the doctors and lawyers and full-time resident retirees. She even spotted the new chief of police, who had only been hired a week earlier. She was a tall woman in her mid-fifties, with black hair gone mostly to gray and lines around her eyes like she spent a lot of time outside without sunglasses. Her previous job had been running the police department in a larger town in the Central Valley, and according to Julie (who knew these things) she had been looking to make a move to somewhere quieter once her youngest left for college. Claudia had avoided meeting her so far, and she thought she would try to continue with that policy. Not that it had exactly been her fault that the former chief had been forced to resign in disgrace, but in Claudia's experience, cops tended to stick together, and she had a feeling it would be a good idea for her to keep a low profile for a while.

As she was thinking this, she was unconsciously staring at the new chief, who chose that moment to look up from her plate and directly into Claudia's gaze. Claudia froze, and was in the middle of deciding between a casual cough or pretending she had something in her eye, when the party was interrupted by a cry from the back of the room.

Seventy-five heads turned to see where it had come from, including Claudia's, though she thought she already had a pretty good idea. Sure enough, the door to the bathroom opened and the vice mayor came out, looking confused and mildly distressed.

"Excuse me," Claudia said to the mimes as she folded her napkin and set it on the table. "I need to see a man about a frog."

# CHAPTER TWO

Fortunately, the frog incident didn't result in the diners leaving en masse, or demands that someone call the health department. In fact, once word got around that there was no actual emergency, most of the guests seemed to find it a good joke, and a line formed at the bathroom of people wanting to see for themselves and discussing what he should be named. (Davey Croaker was an early favorite.) The vice mayor himself insisted that everything was fine, though he would give no specifics of the encounter, except that he was "startled."

Not for the first time, Claudia was glad to have made her life in a place where eccentricity was de rigueur, even if it did mean it could be hard sometimes to find a muffin without flaxseed in it.

If anything, the disruption seemed to have loosened up the party, and it became livelier as it went on. (Though the fact that Nathan's new beer clocked in at thirteen percent might also have had something to do with that.) By the time the desserts were served (a goat cheese ice cream on individual apple galettes), order had almost totally broken down, as guests dropped in at neighboring tables, wandered in and out of the shops, and took pictures with their friends. Claudia considered trying to do something about it, but she couldn't think of what, and besides, her ice cream was melting. So she just applied herself to her plate and hoped nothing would happen that they couldn't clean up later.

Later, Claudia was prying out a fork that had gotten wedged behind one of the light fixtures when Betty approached, looking tired but satisfied.

"I'm going to run a carload of stuff back to the ranch, are you going to be all right on your own here for a while?" she asked.

Claudia looked around at the marketplace, where all of Betty's servers, most of her own tenants, two-thirds of the Friends of the Library board, and Nathan Rodgers were wiping surfaces, folding chairs, packing up the bar, and generally getting in each other's way with attempts to be helpful.

"I think I'll be okay," she said. "Why don't you just get some rest? You must be dead on your feet. We can bring the rest of it over in the morning."

"Oh, no, I'm fine. Roy's taking the kids riding tomorrow, so I'll be able to get some rest then. And we've only got a couple of guests at the moment. Actually, one of them was asking about the marketplace today. A guy named Nguyen—he seems like a pretty serious foodie, and I guess you made it onto his radar. It sounded like he might want to plan an event here or something."

"Really? That's nice." After seeing how much work had gone into the dinner, Claudia wasn't sure she wanted to do any more event hosting, but she didn't want to say so, with Betty just starting to get her catering business going.

"If he's that into food, it's a shame he wasn't here tonight," she said, trying to change the subject. "Honestly, Betty, you outdid yourself. I don't think I've seen a speck of ravioli left on any of the plates."

"Oh, well . . ." Betty looked like she was about to say something self-deprecating, but then broke into a smile. "It did all turn out pretty well, didn't it? Damn good thing, too, considering how much work I put into it."

Betty headed for the door, and Claudia wished she'd thought ahead to have something on hand for some post-event celebratory toasts.

Maybe she would see if Nathan could come up with something for that when Betty got back. She turned to look for him, but her view was blocked by the sudden appearance of one of the young employees from the produce market.

"Ms. Simcoe?" the girl said, with a worried look that promised something worse than some flattened avocados. "I think you need to come and see this."

"Well," Claudia said finally. "That's interesting."

She was standing in the corner of the produce market, in front of what she had thought, up until then, was a perfectly ordinary wood-paneled wall, just like all the others in the marketplace. And it was, except for the part where a section of one of the panels was standing open, revealing a hidden cupboard behind it.

"You didn't know that was there?" Nathan asked. He, along with everyone else on the cleanup crew, had stopped what they were doing and come to gather around behind Claudia.

"No idea," Claudia said. "Nobody mentioned anything like this when I bought the building. I don't even know how it opens."

"It looks like there's a keyhole. See, right here, in this knot in the wood." Helen, the pickle shop owner, had worked her way to the front of the crowd and was pointing with a pair of discarded sunglasses.

Claudia could feel the crowd pressing in as she moved to take a closer look at the spot in question. Sure enough, what looked like an ordinary flaw in the wood concealed an opening for a tiny key, which connected to a small but sturdy-looking latch. Claudia wasn't an expert in vintage locksmithing, but from the look of the metal, neither had been made in the current century, and she wasn't too certain about the previous one.

"You mean this thing has been here the whole time and no one ever noticed it?" It had been a long day and Julie must have been tired, because she wasn't usually that short with people. Though, to be fair, Claudia was a little annoyed herself.

"Well, somebody must have, or it wouldn't be open now." She turned to the produce market employees, who were huddled in a nervous cluster near their boss, Orlan Martinez. "Did any of you come over here tonight? Or see anyone else who did?"

There was a chorus of nos, and Orlan looked around at the group, with their unanimous expressions of ignorance, and then back at Claudia.

"None of us had any idea that door was there," he said, with an air of finality. "If anyone had noticed it, it would have been me. I had been thinking for a while I should maybe hang a poster or something in the corner here, because it's so dark, but I hadn't done it yet."

It was true; the wall where the cupboard was located was in the farthest corner of the shop, back where Orlan kept the extra produce bags. Claudia doubted that she herself had been back there since she had first toured the building, which she felt like might have been a good time for the owner to have mentioned any secret compartments. She was starting to get angry, some of which she recognized as the result of being tired herself, but also because of what she had been through in the summer had left her feeling like she had had quite enough of mysterious goings-on at her fledgling business. Which, in fact, was what got her to a solution.

"Well, there's no point standing around here talking about this all night," she said, stepping away, but leaving the cupboard open. "I'll just go and check the recording."

One of the consequences of Claudia's previous adventure was that, having had her fill of nasty surprises, she had gone out and bought a video surveillance system. Everyone who worked in the marketplace knew about it, but she hadn't advertised it widely, which had more to do with not wanting customers to feel uncomfortable than any concern about criminals trying to evade it. She knew there had been some grumbling at the time when she installed the cameras, and Claudia had had her doubts as to whether they were worth the expense, but she was ready to take that all back now.

"Okay," she said as she sat down in front of the computer in her minuscule office and opened the application that ran the system. "Let's see what we have here."

It took a few tries to find the right camera, and for the first ten minutes of fast-forwarding nothing of interest happened. The office was really only big enough for one person, and though Helen had managed to wedge herself in behind Claudia's chair, while Julie and Nathan jostled for spots in the doorway, no one else was able to get much of a view. Because of that, and lacking evidence that there was going to be anything worth seeing, the rest of the audience drifted away, to finish their tasks and talk about how they should be getting home soon. Claudia would have liked to be heading bedward herself, but she wasn't going to sleep before she figured out who was popping open walls in her building.

On the screen, the party flew by. Guests arrived, gathering into groups that separated and reformed and separated again, while the servers rocketed around the room with their trays. Claudia noticed that Julie was paying particular attention to the socializing, occasionally making interested noises when some particular combination of people appeared. Under other circumstances, Claudia might have asked what it was about, but for the moment her only interest was in the back wall of the produce market and the people who came near it.

Which, for the most part, they didn't do. The crowd got into everything else, from knocking over stacks of onions to leaning too heavily on a pumpkin, but as the high-speed night wore on, the far corner of the produce market remained largely ignored. It wasn't until the evening was almost over, during the post-dessert milling-around period, that a figure detached itself from the crowd and moved, casually but deliberately, toward it.

"Who is that?" Helen asked, as Claudia reversed the recording to play it back at normal speed. "What is he doing?"

The figure was a Caucasian man, sporting a gray suit over a rounded belly and a bald spot made particularly noticeable by the overheard camera angle. Which would probably have been a fairly good description of about half of the men in that room, so Claudia tabled the "who" question for the moment and focused on the "what."

That part was significantly more clear. As poor as the lighting was in the corner, it wasn't hard to see the man approach the wall, look around, and then in a quick series of movements, open the panel and pull out a long, light-colored rectangle that he hid in the coat he was carrying over his arm. The entire operation took no more than about ten seconds, and no one else at the party seemed to notice at all.

"Wow," said Nathan. "Seriously?" And Claudia had to agree. Even though it was about what she had expected—if the door was open, then someone must have opened it—the brazenness of the action was stunning.

"I can't believe no one saw him. And why would someone do that?" Claudia had a lot more questions, but those were the first two on her mind.

"And what did he take out of there?" asked Helen, coming in with the close third.

Claudia played back the recording a few more times, at even slower speeds, expanding the screen to get the best possible look at what was happening and freezing it for the moment the object was in view.

"It's not big enough to be any significant amount of money," said Nathan, who had what might be considered a nonstandard view of how much money was significant. "Maybe it's gold?"

Helen pressed right up over Claudia's shoulder to get a better look.

"No, the way he's holding it in one hand, not heavy enough. It could be a small painting."

"But why would someone hide a painting in the wall? And why come get it now?" said Claudia.

"More likely a legal envelope." Julie had been quiet since the discovery, and she spoke with a funny tone to her voice. "If that's who I think it is, he should have plenty."

Everyone stopped studying the screen and turned to look at the cheesemaker.

"You know who he is?" Claudia asked.

"I'm not positive, but I remember seeing Clark Gowan carrying his coat like that toward the end of the evening. I remember because I hoped he was leaving."

Claudia played the recording again, and now that she had a name she thought she did recognize the lawyer, from the ad he had been running in the local paper every Thursday for as long as she had lived in San Elmo, and from her own dealings with him.

"He was the lawyer the former owner hired to help manage the sale when I bought the marketplace. Which I guess would explain how he knew the panel was there," Claudia said. "But not much else."

The crowd around the doorway had grown again, and everyone who was left in the cleanup crew craned in to have a look. The consensus was that it was definitely Mr. Gowan, and a check of some of the other camera angles where his face was more clearly visible confirmed it. At that point, the theories started flying, each more arcane than the last. Claudia participated for a bit, until Iryna suggested that maybe there were more treasures hidden in the walls, and she realized she needed to shut the speculation down before somebody got a crowbar.

"Enough," she said, holding up a hand. "There's one person who can answer all our questions, and I'm going to go and talk to him tomorrow. Once he finds out we have him on camera, I'm guessing he's going to have to come clean. Until then, there's no point in speculating."

"And what if he doesn't tell you?" asked Iryna, who clearly felt like she had more to contribute in the speculation department.

"Then I'll go to the police. I've had enough of mysteries around here."

Claudia hoped that would at least temporarily put the subject to bed—where she very much wanted to be herself—but even as people were gathering their things to leave she overheard snatches of conversations about pirate maps and secret microfilms. Which were normally things that Claudia would have been more than happy to speculate about, but not when the obvious next step was for people to start treasure hunting in her walls. She needed to put a stop to that, and it needed to happen soon.

But not so soon that she couldn't get some sleep first. (Claudia had firmly rejected all offers to accompany her to go to Mr. Gowan's house and demand immediate answers, on the grounds that she wasn't that crazy.) Whatever it was he had taken out of the compartment in the wall had obviously been there for some time without Claudia knowing about it, and she could deal with a few more hours of ignorance.

But she did think it might be useful to know a bit more about the man she was going to have to confront with her accusation. Claudia had met Gowan a few times when he was working for the former owner of the marketplace, helping to deal with some of the more complex aspects of its sale, and she hadn't formed much of an opinion of him. On the other hand, from the way Julie had been talking it was clear that she had some more specific thoughts about him, and it seemed like it would be in Claudia's interest to learn more about that.

She caught up with Julie as her tenant was locking the cheese case and double-checking that she had everything in her bags.

"Heading out?" Claudia asked, somewhat unnecessarily.

"Just about," Julie said. "I'm exhausted. Can't do these late nights anymore, like you young people."

Claudia wasn't sure what ideas Julie had about her social life, but she didn't want to get into that now.

"Before you go, is there anything you can tell me about Mr. Gowan? From what you said earlier I had the impression you knew him."

"We've met a few times. My ex-husband hired him when we split."

Claudia didn't know much about Julie's long-finished marriage, except that from what she had heard it hadn't ended well. But she was confused about how a property lawyer would have fitted in to it.

"How was Gowan involved?" she asked. "Is he also a divorce lawyer?"

Julie's expression darkened. "No. He's not."

She started for the exit, and Claudia hesitated for a moment before falling in behind her. It was clear this wasn't something Julie wanted to talk about, and normally Claudia would have respected that. But she was getting progressively more worried that a can of worms had been opened in her wall, and on top of now having a really gross mental image to deal with, she didn't like the feeling that she was missing some critical information.

So she pressed.

"What happened? Is there something I should know about him?"

Julie stopped just short of the door and rubbed a hand across her face. "It's a long story and I can't get into it now. Let's just say that what-ever Gowan was up to tonight, it wasn't to do anyone any good."

And with that, she went out into the parking lot, leaving Claudia to wonder, again, what sort of trouble she was getting herself into this time.

# CHAPTER THREE

Planning her errand for first thing in the morning had seemed like a good idea when Claudia set her alarm, but less so by the time it went off. Groggily, she reasoned that lawyers' offices didn't open that early anyway, and gave herself another twenty minutes, which somehow turned into an hour. Then there was coffee to be made and drunk, her dog to be taken outside, a shower and the question of what in her wardrobe could make up an outfit suitable for confronting a lawyer about stealing from her walls, before she made her morning stop by the marketplace to make sure everything was ready to open for the day. None of it took very long (with the exception of the outfit thing), but the time still managed to pass, and the upshot was that it was midmorning before she pointed her car down the winding road that led from her home to what passed for San Elmo's downtown.

However little she was looking forward to her errand, Claudia had to admit it was a nice day to be doing it. Autumn was one of the best times of the year on the Sonoma coast, when the fog held back and the winds died down, and Claudia drove on under a bright blue sky, with only the occasional wisp of cloud. Out her window she could see the Pacific—ominous some days and terrifying on others—sparkling like a drag queen's gown, and for a moment she considered just forgetting the whole thing and heading to the beach.

But that wasn't really an option, so she settled for picking up an iced coffee and a fresh donut at the Breakers Cafe, and looking in the windows of the tourist shops on Main Street while she thought about what she was going to say to Gowan.

The law offices of Gowan and Finley were just off Main, in a converted Victorian house. Claudia had only been there once before, but she remembered being surprised at how much of the interior had been left intact, down to the linen closets (now holding office supplies) and the hand pump in the kitchen. It had made her nervous about how much preservation she was expected to do at the marketplace, but it had never come up and she assumed that old barns didn't have the same historic status as houses.

She hadn't made an appointment, but if Gowan kept his website up to date, someone should have been there. So she rang the bell and, getting no response after a decent interval, then tried knocking, which was equally ineffective. Which left Claudia with a dilemma. She didn't want to leave without getting some kind of answer, but there was no convenient place to wait in front of the building. She was also concerned about the amount of gossip that was probably already swirling about the last night's discovery—enough people had been there to see it that the news had probably already made it around town twice, picking up some embroideries along the way. There was a good chance that some helpful person had already mentioned it to Gowan himself, which was why he wasn't answering his door.

Or maybe the doorbell just didn't work. Claudia pressed it again, and heard no answering chime from inside. Now that she thought about it, she wasn't even sure she had waited to be let in on her last visit, or if she had gone straight in to a reception. Maybe this was like standing outside a dentist's office, waiting for someone to come and greet you.

She tried the door and found it unlocked. Feeling more than a little foolish, Claudia opened it and went in, hoping that whoever was inside hadn't noticed her standing on the doorstep for the last several minutes, looking like she was expecting an engraved invitation.

As it happened, that was not something she needed to worry about.

There was no reception, just a hallway with stairs going up on one side and two doors on the other, ending at the old kitchen. The first door led to the former parlor, which had been converted to a meeting space, with a conference table and video screens. From there she could see through the open double doors into the dining room, now an office. Claudia had some vague memory of seeing a secretary there when she had visited before, but it was empty now and looked like it hadn't been used in a while. Gowan's office, she recalled, was upstairs, and having come this far, she figured that she might as well go up and see if he was in it. If he wasn't, well, she would deal with that later.

He couldn't accuse her of sneaking up on him, at least. Every step in the staircase seemed to have its own unique creak or groan, and walking up them reminded Claudia of the giant toy keyboard she had wanted as a child, only creepier. At the top of the stairs, there were three doors to choose from, all closed. Claudia picked the one she thought she remembered as Gowan's office, but it turned out to be the bathroom. Her next choice was locked, so she was left with only one option, before she was going to have to give up and try to find another way to get her questions answered.

The final door wasn't latched. In fact, as Claudia got closer she realized it was slightly ajar. Which made her feel a little better about opening it—going through an open door seemed less like snooping, and she was fairly sure by now that there was no one in the building. But she was wrong about that. As Claudia tapped on the door and pushed it open, she could see the desk from across the room, with its chair turned to the side and a hand resting on the armrest. She was sure this was the right room now—the collection of Wild West artifacts in cases on the walls, and the mounted grizzly bear head over the window were hard to forget. It was less tidy than she remembered, with drawers hanging open and papers scattered across the desk, but maybe Gowan was the sort of person who only cleaned up if he knew someone was coming. Which was all the more reason to think her intrusion wouldn't be a welcome one, but there was no turning back now.

"Mr. Gowan? It's Claudia Simcoe, from the marketplace. I wonder if I could just talk to you for a moment?"

Then she came through the door and got a better look at the figure in the chair, and it was clear that, however much Claudia wanted to talk, Mr. Gowan was not going to be listening, to her or to anyone. There was a hole in the middle of his forehead, and from the looks of the chair, another one at the back, and lines of dried blood ran down his face, past blank, staring eyes.

"Oh no," said Claudia.

She backed out into the hallway, fumbling through her bag to try and find her phone. Her rising gorge reminded her of the donut she regretted having eaten, and she thought about going to make her call from the bathroom, just in case. But she probably wasn't supposed to be touching anything, and when the police got there they would want to know why she was messing around in another part of their crime scene. Claudia had recently been introduced to what it was like to be a suspect in a murder investigation, and she wasn't keen to repeat the experience, so she stayed where she was, clenched her teeth, and tried to think good thoughts as she dialed 911.

By the time she had finished delivering the basics of her message, she felt like she could probably manage the stairs. No one could blame her for that, and as she made her way down, clutching the bannister with one hand and her phone with the dispatcher still on speaker mode in the other, she found her capacity for rational thought returning. Of course she wasn't going to be involved this time. She had barely known the man, had no connection to him at all. She hadn't even recognized him when she had seen him on the video taking something out of a secret compartment in her marketplace last night.

Claudia paused to steady herself on the last stair, which creaked ominously. Okay, that was probably going to raise some questions. Questions Claudia herself would have liked to have the answers to, which didn't seem likely to happen now. But the two things didn't have to be related, did they? People probably stole mysterious packages all the time without someone showing up and murdering them.

Assuming he was murdered, of course. The way that hole had been positioned in the forehead didn't look like it could have come from suicide, or an accident, but Claudia was hardly an expert in such things. Fortunately, according to the dispatcher, those experts were already on their way, and should be arriving in five minutes or less. (There were aspects of small town living that Claudia was not fond of, but this wasn't one of them.) Claudia thanked her, and said she would be waiting outside. And she would have been, except that she opened the door just as another woman was about to put her key in the lock.

"Who are you? What are you doing here?" the woman asked. She was short, barely coming up to Claudia's shoulder, with permed gray hair, on which a pair of tortoiseshell reading glasses was resting. The tote she carried over her arm said "Welcome Gravenstein Festival," but there was nothing festive or welcoming about her expression.

"I'm Claudia Simcoe. I, um, came to see Mr. Gowan and—"

"Do you have an appointment?"

"No, but—"

The woman tried to push past her into the building. "Then you're going to have to leave and come back when you have one. Excuse me."

"No, you can't—" The woman gave Claudia a look that could freeze time, and she realized she was going to have no choice but to go with the awful truth.

"Mr. Gowan is dead. He's been shot."

Claudia meant to follow up with an apology for delivering the news in such an abrupt and insensitive way, but she didn't get a chance, because the woman screamed and hit her with her tote.

"And you have no idea why?"

"I assumed she was upset."

Claudia had been anticipating answering questions when the police arrived, but her expectation was that they would be about the murder victim, rather than assault by a (less than) deadly tote bag. But the patrol car had pulled up just as Claudia's assailant was winding up for another blow, and in throwing up her arms to protect herself, Claudia had inadvertently knocked her backward down the front steps. So, while his colleagues went upstairs, followed by the paramedics and, later, the coroner, the most junior member of the local force was left to deal with the situation out front.

"I didn't mean to hurt her," Claudia went on. "I had no idea the step sloped down like that. I just told her what happened and she kind of lost it."

The young policeman (who, to Claudia's jaded thirty-six-year-old eyes, looked about twelve) nodded seriously. "That's what the dispatcher thought it sounded like."

In all the excitement, Claudia had completely forgotten she had still been on the call. She vaguely remembered that it had sounded like there was someone else shouting when she was trying to catch the falling woman, but she had other things on her mind. In fact, now that she thought about it, she didn't know where her phone was. She patted her pockets and started looking around, and it must have been obvious what was on her mind, because the cop pointed at the bushes that flanked the building's front door.

"I believe you dropped it into the shrubbery," he said.

"Oh, thanks. You're probably right. I'll go take a look for it later."

Since he was being helpful, Claudia thought maybe she could get in a question of her own. "Who was she, by the way? I never did get an introduction."

The policeman paused, like he wasn't sure he was supposed to be telling her things, but he must have decided there was no harm in this one.

"The other individual was a Ms. Kathy Finley. I believe she is one of the partners in the business here."

"Oh, of course." Claudia remembered seeing the name on the sign— it made sense that Gowan's law partner would be the next person to arrive for the day. Possibly, she would have been a good choice for someone to help Claudia solve the mystery of what Gowan had been doing in her marketplace, though the whole knocking-off-the-stairs thing had probably made it less of an option.

"The next time I see her, I'll be sure to apologize," she said, trying to sound like the sort of person who wouldn't push someone down the stairs on purpose.

She had also hoped this might signal the end of this interview, but there was no luck on that front.

"And according to you, she struck you first?" the policeman asked, turning over another page in his notebook.

"Yes, but I don't want to make a whole thing out of it. There's a lot going on right now," Claudia said. But she did feel the need to make one clarification. "Also, it wasn't really 'first' because there was no second. I wasn't hitting her back, I mean."

Claudia thought that question had already been settled, but the officer just nodded again and made another note on his page.

"Okay, I'm just going to have you wait here for a few minutes to see some other people. They'll let you know when it's okay for you to leave."

Claudia didn't like the sound of that, but then, she could hardly have expected them to run a murder investigation for her convenience. It occurred to her that she had better call someone at the marketplace and let them know she was going to be out for longer than she had expected, but then she realized she would need her phone for that.

"Can I—?" she started to ask, but the young cop was already gone, and a crime scene technician was approaching.

The crime scene tech then wiped Claudia's hands with a pad that was put away in a plastic bag, then took her fingerprints and let her go. This time, no one seemed to be paying attention to what she was doing, so she took the opportunity to go find her phone, which was indeed in the shrubbery, stuck in the ground like a less-demanding Excalibur. It took a few tries to find someone in the marketplace, but Claudia finally managed to reach Helen, who was manning the pickle shop that day, and who promised to pass on the message to anyone who was looking for her.

She also gave a brief outline of what had happened, since she could hardly avoid it, and no one had told her not to. Helen was suitably shocked, and agreed that of course she wasn't going to spread it around, which Claudia didn't believe for a second. Like her, the Pak family were recent arrivals to San Elmo, but Helen had adapted more easily to the local customs, particularly the one about not holding onto a piece of interesting gossip for any longer than it took to find someone to tell it to.

Although, Claudia thought as she hung up the phone, that was pretty much what she had just done. Maybe there was hope for her yet.

It was getting on for midday and Claudia was still waiting. She wasn't complaining, exactly, because the experience she had had in the past with being interviewed by the police on the subject of a suspicious death hadn't been pleasant, but she was starting to wonder if she'd been forgotten, and what she should do if that was the case. The spot she had found to sit, on a decorative rock on the lawn in front of the office, was all right for the short term, but her leg was falling asleep and the sun was getting uncomfortably warm. She was just starting to feel sorry for herself when the front door opened and three men from the coroner's office came out, supporting a gurney with its passenger in black plastic.

That was enough to bring her down to reality, and Claudia was straight back in the scene she had found in Gowan's office. She had been avoiding it so far by thinking of pretty much anything else, but watching his body being loaded into the van forced the image to the front of her mind with a vengeance.

At least he must not have suffered much, she thought. The way he had been sitting in the chair had looked natural, almost relaxed, not like someone who had spent any time on the agonies of dying. He had probably been in pretty much that position when whoever had shot him (still assuming he hadn't done it himself) had walked up and pulled the trigger. It must have been someone he knew, Claudia thought, knew and wasn't afraid of. She had just learned firsthand how hard it would be to sneak up on someone in that house, and there had been nothing about the body that suggested he had done anything but sit there and let himself be shot.

Not that it was any of Claudia's business, anyway. She had simply been unlucky enough to have come in at the wrong moment and found him. She hadn't even stopped to look around and see if the package he had taken from the marketplace was anywhere in his office. Because this wasn't her problem. The important thing was to remember that, and hope that other people would too.

Like, for example, the new chief of police, who was approaching Claudia now. Up close, she was taller than Claudia had realized and her shirt, clearly a men's style, hung loose on her frame. Her black and silver hair was pulled back into the same style of ponytail it had been the night before, and if she was wearing any makeup, it wasn't obvious.

"Ms. Simcoe," she said, in an abrupt but not unfriendly way. "I'm Chief Elena Weaver. Would you mind stepping inside with me for a minute? I'd like to ask you a few questions."

The chief led her back into the office building, which was another surprise for Claudia. She had assumed the whole building would be off limits for the foreseeable future, but that didn't seem to be the case. The downstairs conference room had clearly been converted into a temporary headquarters for the investigation—backpacks and equipment boxes were lined up against the wall and there were several notebooks and a half-empty water bottle on the table.

Chief Weaver must have sensed her surprise.

"The crime scene appears to be limited to the room upstairs," she said casually, as though she and Claudia were friendly coworkers. "Of course, if you're not comfortable talking here, we could always go back to the station."

Her smile was neutral and pleasant, and Claudia was very concerned.

"I don't mind. Here is fine." She tried to return the smile, and was aware that it came out watery and unconvincing.

"All right then. Let's take a seat and get started. At what time did you arrive at the office?"

Claudia took her through her morning, explaining as best she could why she had decided to go into an apparently empty office where she didn't have an appointment. She kept her eyes on Weaver's face the whole time, trying to determine how her story was going over, but the chief's expression gave nothing away.

"You're sure the door was unlocked?" she asked, when Claudia had finished her first time through.

"Yes. That's what made me think I should just let myself in."

"And you didn't see anyone on the ground floor before you went upstairs?"

"No. I didn't exactly make a thorough search, but I'm pretty sure there was no one in either of these rooms, at least." She waited for the chief to make some comment about the inappropriateness of her actions, but none came. They went over her time on the second floor again, which doors were open and which were locked, finally coming around to Claudia's discovery of the body.

"Are you're sure you didn't touch anything in the room?"

Claudia was ready for that one. "Positive. From where I was standing in the door, it was pretty clear there was nothing I could do to help him. And I've gotten some education in police procedure lately."

She wasn't sure why she had said that, and Claudia regretted the words as soon as they were out of her mouth. She had no reason to want to remind Weaver of her previous encounter with law enforcement, and the desire to get some kind of reaction was not one she could afford to give in to.

Fortunately (or was it?) the new chief wasn't easily baited. Holding her impassive expression, she finished what she was writing, and then turned the notebook page.

"You said you had been here before?" she asked.

"Only once, a couple of years ago. Mr. Gowan was handling some of the legal work for the seller when I bought the marketplace building. I came to the office to sign some papers and that was it."

Claudia hoped Weaver wouldn't ask her to provide any details as to the nature of those papers. She had been getting better, but the early days of her decision to buy the marketplace had been marked more by enthusiasm than shrewdness.

"Were you aware of anything in the office being different than the last time you were there?" asked Weaver, who didn't seem very interested in Claudia's business sense or lack thereof.

Claudia was about to make a reference to the fact that Gowan had been a lot less corpse-like during her last visit, but she managed to refrain.

"It was messier than I remembered," she said, trying to look like a serious person. "But I wasn't there long enough to get much of a look around."

Claudia thought that might be it, but they still had to go over her call and the trip down the stairs again, with Weaver asking for clarifications on what seemed to be insignificant points. She offered no explanations for her questions, and Claudia was torn between thinking she had some secret detective reasoning, or was just messing with her.

"You said that Ms. Finley was trying to unlock the door as you opened it?"

"That's what it looked like. Is she okay?"

"She's fine, the paramedics just took her in as a precaution." It was the first piece of information that Weaver had actually shared with her, and Claudia found that hopeful. Maybe she wasn't going to be in so much trouble after all.

"Now, can you explain to me again why you came to see Mr. Gowan?"

"You weren't aware of this wall compartment before then?"

"Not at all. It looked like it's been there a long time, though. Probably since the building was built."

Claudia had already talked Weaver through the discovery of the open cabinet, and showed her the video of Gowan on her phone. She had downloaded it to use in case the lawyer had tried to deny his actions, and she was glad to have it with her now. The further she got into telling her story, the more ridiculous she realized it sounded, and despite the fact that she had a whole roomful of witnesses who would back her up, it made her feel better to know she had incontrovertible evidence that something shady had indeed happened.

Weaver had watched the clip a few times, commented that it did look like Gowan, and asked Claudia to send it to her email, which Claudia agreed to do. Then, she turned a page in her notebook, wrote something on the top, and started in with another round of questions.

"And the seller didn't mention it when you bought the building?"

"No, I'm sure he didn't. And it wasn't in the disclosures either. I double-checked them last night." Claudia hesitated, not sure how she wanted to share the unsettling fact she had discovered before she had finally given up on the project and gone to sleep. But there was really no reason not to. "Although, there was one thing. I hadn't noticed before, but there's a page missing from the disclosure packet. It says on the first page there should be thirteen pages, and there are only twelve. But they're all numbered, and the last page ends halfway, so I'm not sure if it could be just a typo or something."

"Or something," Weaver agreed. "I think I'd like to see that too, if you don't mind."

"Sure, I can make you a copy. They probably have it on file here, too," she added helpfully.

"Yes, well, that might have some complications. I would appreciate it if you could get that to me."

It hadn't occurred to Claudia that there would be limitations on what the police could do with the dead man's papers, but she supposed lawyers had special rights for that sort of thing.

The sun had moved so that it was pouring through the window behind her, and Claudia was starting to get uncomfortably warm. The doors to the conference room were still standing open, and the members of San Elmo Bay's small police force (and the county services that were supporting them) passed by regularly, nearly all of them looking in for at least a moment. Claudia wondered what she looked like, the person who found the body sweating away as she was interviewed by the chief of police. She didn't think she was making the best possible impression.

"As far as this package goes, you don't know what might have been in it? Nothing that fits that description is missing from the marketplace?"

The possibility that she had been robbed hadn't even occurred to Claudia before now, but after a moment's consideration she rejected it.

"No, I don't think so. There were a few things that wandered off during the party, but they were more like pens and cups. And a ceramic pig with the butcher's cuts painted on it." That had been taken from Robbie, the impressively mustachioed owner of the charcuterie shop, who had been particularly annoyed; it had been a gift from his wife to commemorate the sale of their five-hundredth salami. "But nothing that would have gone in that kind of package."

The question must have been mostly a formality, because Weaver barely acknowledged her answer before moving on.

"And no one else who was there had any thoughts about what it was?"

Claudia thought about some of the wilder theories that had been floated the night before, and smiled.

"People had a lot of thoughts. But I don't think anyone actually knows anything. If they did, they didn't say so. One person did mention that it looked about the right size to be a legal envelope." Claudia didn't think it was necessary to bring up Julie's belief that anything Gowan was carrying must have a nefarious purpose. Having been on the receiving end of unnecessary police suspicion herself, Claudia wasn't about to subject anyone else to that experience.

Besides, he was a lawyer. Of course people didn't like him.

"Do you have any idea why he would have chosen to get whatever it was during the party?" Weaver asked.

"I've been thinking about that. The only thing that makes sense is that he must have decided recently that he needed to get whatever it was out of there. Before this summer, our security wasn't exactly tight—I hadn't even changed the locks since I bought the place. But since then I've had new locks put in, and there are alarms on all the windows, and outdoor cameras around the building."

"I see. So someone who might have been able to come and go fairly freely before, would find it more difficult now."

"A lot more difficult," Claudia agreed. "I'm not saying it's Fort Knox there, but I'm pretty confident that someone without professional burglary experience wouldn't be able to get in. Especially if they didn't want anyone to know they had been there."

"And the reason he didn't come in during business hours?" Weaver prompted.

"Well, to be honest, we're not often that crowded. The corner where the cabinet is is kind of out of the way, but it's visible from the rest of the produce shop. It's hard to imagine a time on a regular day when he could have gotten in there unnoticed."

"So you think he was using the crowd at the dinner as cover?" The chief sounded dubious, and Claudia didn't blame her.

"It's the best I can come up with. It seems pretty risky to me, but maybe he felt like he didn't have any other options."

"Mm hmm. According to your theory, then, he must have been pretty desperate to get this thing, whatever it was."

Claudia wasn't sure she was qualified to have theories, but that sounded about right to her.

"He must have been," she agreed. "Even if he didn't know about the cameras, the chances of being seen were pretty high. And then what was he going to say? Oh, don't mind me, just taking my secret envelope out for a walk?"

That almost got a smile, which emboldened Claudia enough to look around and do some thinking of her own. Her eyes went to the ceiling, where Gowan's office must have been right above them.

"If it was a legal envelope, then what better place to hide it than a law office, right? Do you think it's here somewhere?" she asked.

"That's a very good question." Weaver put her notebook away and held out her hand. "Thank you, Ms. Simcoe, you've been very helpful. Is there a number where I can reach you if I need to follow up?"

# CHAPTER FOUR

Claudia was almost all the way back to her car before the shock hit. It came over her in waves, starting deep in her chest and spreading outward through her body. Her stomach swirled, her fingers went numb, and her head felt like it was trying to leave the party entirely. Stumbling the last few feet to where her hatchback was parked, she gripped the edge of the roof and hoped that no one she knew was watching her. What would she tell them? "Oh, it's okay, just dealing with a little delayed reaction to finding a dead man. I'll be all right in a minute."

On the other hand, she *had* found a dead man, and been questioned by the police, and gotten into an accidental slapfight. Maybe she ought to take it easy on herself for once.

Claudia got into her car and leaned back in the driver's seat. Her head was still spinning, and her stomach felt like it belonged to someone else, but at least her heart rate was starting to come down, to the point that she felt like she could hear over the sound of her pulse. After a few deep breaths, she found that she was even able to think about what had just happened without the feeling returning, so that's what she did.

And, honestly, what had happened? In terms of the actual events, Claudia felt like she had them pretty well understood; she had explained them enough times to the police at least. But in a more general sense it made no sense at all, and that had her worried. A man she had barely known stole (retrieved? acquired?) something from a secret compartment she had never seen before, and before she could ask him about it, he was murdered. Could someone have known she was coming? It was certainly possible. She had even been worried about Gowan knowing, considering how many people heard her say she was planning to. And then what? Did the killer walk into the building, just like Claudia had, only when they got to Gowan's office he was alive, at least briefly? But Ms. Finley had clearly expected the door to be locked when she arrived. Had the killer made an appointment? That seemed like it could cause some trouble for them down the line. The clever criminal generally tried to avoid getting their name on the victim's calendar.

Or maybe she should leave the theorizing to the professionals. It was a nice thought, if not a very realistic one. Claudia wanted to believe there was no way she or her property were involved in Gowan's death, but then, she wanted a lot of things. Whether or not there was any relationship there, it was going to look that way to a lot of people, and she was going to have to be doing a lot of talking about the subject. Which meant that at some point she was going to have to come up with at least some answers that weren't "I don't know."

Though, if she was being honest, that was mostly an excuse. Claudia didn't like not knowing things, especially things that seemed like they had something to do with her. And there were a lot of things she didn't know right now.

But, as she sat up straight and put her hands on the steering wheel, only to be hit by another round of dizziness, she realized that there was one thing she knew for sure. She definitely was in no shape to be driving right now.

"Thanks for coming to get me."

"Of course, any time. Are you sure you don't want to come back to the ranch? I can send Roy with one of the guys to pick up your car."

Betty had responded to her call in under twenty minutes, pulling up in the Tyler Ranch SUV and handing Claudia a thermos of creamy tomato soup before she had a chance to say anything. Aside from the two car seats and the slight smell of horse, the truck was spotless, but she still apologized for the mess as Claudia fastened her seat belt.

"You can sit in the kitchen and keep me company while I make the pies for tonight," Betty went on. "It sounds like you've had a heck of a day."

Claudia thought it sounded that way too, and the offer was tempting, but she knew where her responsibilities lay.

"Unfortunately, the day isn't over yet," she said. "When I left this morning, I said I'd be back in an hour or so, and that was, I don't know how long ago that was. The news about what happened must be making the rounds now, and I have a feeling it's going to be all hands on deck."

"Well, I hadn't heard anything about it yet. That new police chief of ours must be keeping a pretty tight lid on things." Betty hadn't quite reached Julie's level of gossip connections, but she was making a strong play for the crown. If she hadn't heard about the murder yet, then it was a good sign that the story hadn't spread very far.

That also reminded Claudia of another question she had.

"Do you know anything about this Gowan guy? I only met him the one time, and he didn't make much of an impression, but Julie said some things that made me think she didn't like him very much. Something to do with her divorce."

"That's weird," Betty said, as they turned off the main road onto the street that went up to the marketplace. "I didn't think he was a divorce lawyer. And no, I don't know much about him. The only thing I can think of is I seem to remember there being some issue between him and the other members of the historical society. He tried to strong-arm them into buying a bunch of weapons or something, even though it didn't make any sense for what they were doing with the museum. That was his thing, old guns and stuff. I'd never even been to his office, but after the incident, everyone knew about the collection he had there."

And that was the thing Claudia had been trying to remember about Gowan's office. The bear head had made the immediate impact, but what had really shocked her was the case on the wall by the door, full of old guns. Historic, she supposed, whatever that meant. She hadn't noticed them on her most recent visit, for obvious reasons.

"That must have been why Weaver was asking me if I had seen anything in the office. I wonder if he was shot with one of them?"

"Probably. Isn't that Chekov's rule of guns? If you have a gun you're going to get shot by it, or something?" asked Betty, whose knowledge of Chekovs ran more to spacecraft than stagecraft.

"Something like that," agreed Claudia, not bothering to correct her. "But he wouldn't have had the ammunition for them, would he?"

They passed the marketplace, which appeared to be doing more than the usual amount of business, and Betty turned up the driveway to Claudia's cottage.

"More than that," she said. "He kept them loaded. Or he used to, at least. That was the incident I was talking about. Some guys were doing work on the building and one of them got hold of one of the guns, shot a hole right through the window. He claimed he thought there was no chance it would be loaded, Gowan tried to have him arrested for theft and vandalism, it was a whole thing."

"Wow. He sounds like he was quite a guy." Claudia realized that sounded bad, and backtracked a bit. "Still, it was terrible what happened to him. I wouldn't wish that on anybody."

"Almost anybody," Betty agreed as she parked in front of the cottage. "Anyway, give me a call tonight if you feel like coming over. We've got a couple of guests at the moment, but we can always find a spot for you."

"Thanks, but I'll be okay. I think the worst is over now."

Claudia made it about three steps in the door before she was nearly knocked over by a furry brown and black projectile. Teddy was a German Shepard mix, with an emphasis on the mix, who had shown up at Claudia's door a couple of months earlier and decided she was her dog. There had been some initial adjustment pains, mostly to do with when and where it was acceptable to go to the bathroom, but by now Claudia couldn't imagine life without her.

Teddy usually spent her days in the marketplace, where she was very popular, greeting customers and generally serving as mascot/cleanup crew for any spilled food. Lacking that outlet, she had clearly spent the morning building up a tremendous surplus of energy, which she now directed at Claudia.

"Okay, yes, hi. I'm happy to see you, too. No, down, down. Down doesn't mean try to jump on my shoulders."

After another minute of negotiations, Claudia managed to extract herself and got them both outside for some much needed play time. The land around her property wasn't very well fenced, but there was little to no traffic on the road (which only went as far as Nathan's house at the top of the hill) and Teddy had never shown an inclination to run off, so Claudia had no worries about leaving her off the leash to charge around the hillside to her heart's content. Claudia's home was separated from the marketplace by a field, empty except for a pair of highly territorial geese living in an old doghouse. At one time, Claudia had thought about trying to move them along, but since then they had proved their worth, and she now delivered them regular treats of leftover vegetables from Orlan's shop.

Thinking about that brought her back to the marketplace, and its latest mystery. So, while Teddy communed with nature in her own way, Claudia made a few calls to let people know she would be back soon and give a bare outline of what had happened, and find out how things were going.

The first person she reached was Carmen, who was handling sales that day at The Corner Pocket. Helen had already told her and everyone else in the marketplace about Gowan's death, but Carmen was appropriately shocked to hear the (expurgated) details Claudia provided. But she professed to be uninterested in any aspect of the story except for Claudia's own well-being, and of all her tenants, Claudia believed her. The empanada specialist was a petite, taciturn woman whose only interests were her pastries, her wife, and her nieces and nephews, and the San Elmo gossip scene had always been a little beneath her.

Claudia thanked her and said she would be there soon to help hold down the fort, but Carmen insisted that everything was under control, and Claudia didn't argue the point. She wasn't ready to do a lot more talking at the moment anyway. All she wanted right now was to sit for a while and stare at a nice blank wall.

She was on her way back to the cottage, ready to put her plan into inaction, when she heard the sound of a familiar footstep on her gravel driveway. By the time she got around the corner, Nathan was waiting at her front door, with a growler bottle in his hand and an expression on his face she couldn't quite read.

"Hi," he said, once Teddy was done with her more enthusiastic greeting. "I heard what happened. Thought you could use a little pick-me-up."

"Oh, thanks." Claudia hadn't been thinking about day drinking as a palliative for what ailed her, but now that he mentioned it, it didn't sound like such a bad idea. She was curious, though.

"How did you hear about it?" she asked as she let them into the house. "I didn't think the news had gotten around yet."

"Betty called. She thought you might like some company."

"Of course she did." Claudia should have known her friend would make sure she wasn't spending the time alone. She also suspected that Betty was trying to do some matchmaking with her and Nathan, who had at one point made a list of the most eligible bachelors in Sonoma County, to his enduring dismay.

When they had first met, he had, in his own words, been "going through some stuff," and his personal style and grooming had suffered accordingly. Now, with a fresh trim to bring his unruly black hair under control and a wardrobe that featured more skinny jeans and fewer pajama bottoms, he looked less like an overgrown college student, and more like the young ex-CEO he was. Which Claudia didn't disapprove of at all, but having seen some of the other women who had shown up to pursue him made her uncomfortable in taking on that role herself.

Leaving her guest in the living room, Claudia went to get some glasses from the kitchen. This required no interruption in the conversation, because the two rooms were essentially the same. Claudia's home was about five hundred square feet total, including a bedroom that just about fit her bed, a bathroom with the convenient feature that you could reach both the doorknob and the shower tap from the toilet, and the main living/dining/working space where they were at the moment.

The cottage was one of a pair that had come with the marketplace building when Claudia had purchased it. They had been built in the fifties and used on and off as vacation rentals and/or storage, so what the furnishings lacked in coherent style, they made up for in poor condition. Claudia sat on the loveseat, one of the few things she had brought with her, while Nathan made the less optimal choice of the armchair with one wonky leg.

"So, what's the latest project? Another sour beer?" Claudia asked, forcing her voice to be as cheerful as she could.

"No, this is a cider. Well, technically a perry. But, um, are you okay?"

"Sure, I'm fine," Claudia responded automatically. After some thought, she decided she needed to qualify that statement. "Maybe not totally fine. A little shaken up to be honest. Or maybe a lot. I'm not sure. You know how it is."

"Not really." He hesitated, searching for the right words. "Do you want to talk about it?"

"Not really." That didn't seem like quite enough, so Claudia added,

"I'm kind of talked out right now. Later? I feel like this is something that's going to be on my mind for a while."

"Right, I can see that."

Nathan wasn't the most socially adept person at the best of times, but even for him things seemed off. Claudia was about to probe him on what was going on—had he known Gowan well?—when he made things a little clearer.

"You know, you could have called me. I would have come to get you."

Claudia didn't know what to say to that. The truth was, it hadn't even occurred to her to call Nathan; if Betty hadn't picked up, she probably would have started with Julie and then worked her way through the marketplace tenants. Of course, if she and Nathan had been dating, that would be different, but they weren't. Were they? Did he think they were, and was that why the tone of his voice sounded slightly hurt? Or was Claudia just imagining things? If so, could she not manage a more exciting fantasy life than that?

If there was one things Claudia did not need more of in her day, it was questions. So she decided to take the offer at face value and see where it went from there.

"Thanks, I'll remember that for next time. If there is a next time, which I hope not." That had sounded better in her head, before she said it.

"Right, I hope not too. And probably not, right? What are the odds?"

They both laughed, but it didn't clear the air. The awkwardness that was radiating off Nathan was starting to affect Claudia as well. She felt like she was wandering through an unfamiliar forest, and every time she said anything she ran into another tree.

It wasn't like she hadn't dated before. Claudia's social life had never been that vibrant, but she'd had what she considered a normal number of boyfriends. But they had all been guys she met the usual ways—through friends, or on an app, or at a statewide math competition. (She wondered if she should stop counting that one. High school was a long time ago.) She had never had to negotiate a potential relationship with her only near neighbor, who until recently had been running a letter-writing campaign to get her parking variance revoked.

Moving forward into a relationship with Nathan was fraught with risks, not the least of which was what would happen if it all went wrong and she ended up with an ex who could see her every time she took the garbage out. (Which was often, because her kitchen trash can was, like everything else, tiny.) He could make her life miserable, and vice versa, for as long as they were sharing this windswept hilltop, and Claudia, for one, had no intention of going anywhere soon.

On the other hand, there was something awfully appealing about the look he was giving her, and how his hair curled down over his fore-head, and the way his long fingers played with the tag he had affixed to the neck of the growler.

She realized she was staring, and Nathan had noticed. She could have laughed it off, claimed to have spaced out in his general direction, but she didn't want to. And what was life if not an opportunity to take chances?

"I still have to go back to get my car," she said. "If the offer still stands, maybe you could drive me?"

Nathan was almost comically relieved by the suggestion. "Oh, sure. No problem. Do you want to go now?"

"Not really," Claudia said, parroting herself. "I'd rather stay out of the area for the moment, and they aren't going to ticket me there for a couple of days. Besides, I'm curious about what you brought. What did you call it?"

"Perry. It's like cider, but it's made with pears. I've got some apple cider going too, but those are harvested later, so it won't be ready for a couple of weeks." Beads of precipitation had been forming on the bottle while they talked, and as he twisted open the cap and poured it into the mismatched pint glasses Claudia had provided, a cool scent of fruit wafted out into the room. "The sours are interesting, but some of them are so harsh and funky, I just wanted to make something that would be easy to drink. Plus, I had a contact who knew a farmer who had a surplus he was selling cheap."

"Local?" asked Claudia, who found herself asking that a lot these days.

"Pretty much. These are from Lake County. They're further inland, so they get the heat you need, and the cold in the winter." Nathan was in full enthusiast mode now, his awkwardness forgotten as he held the glass up to the light and examined the streams of bubbles.

"Most of what's grown around here are eating pears, not for perry. I mean, it works, but it's too sweet. I have a batch of straight Bartlett that I'm going to try to make a kind of dessert wine out of. That, or I might distill it. But, anyway, I was able to find a couple of farms out there that have some heritage varieties that give it a nice acidity. What do you think?"

Claudia was starting to feel the way she sometimes did when she went wine tasting—like she'd sat down for a drink and ended up at a midterm. But she knew from experience that Nathan wasn't testing her palate or knowledge, just honestly wanted to know what she thought. So, she told him.

"It's nice, you can really taste the fruit. But maybe too much acid? For me at least. I've always thought pears were best when they're just on the edge of being too sweet, right before they go mealy." She thought about her experience with the fruit and added, "Which is about twenty minutes after they're completely unripe and hard as rocks."

"Pears are jerks," Nathan agreed. "But I see your point. Maybe I'll try barrel-aging this batch, see if I can't round off some of those edges."

The first time Claudia had visited Nathan's house she had been surprised to discover a door in the hillside. She had briefly been concerned that it would be some kind of dungeon situation, but it turned out to be nothing more than a wine cave, dug for the house's previous owner, that

Nathan was now using for whichever of his current experiments needed some time in a cool, dark place. Of course, thinking about mysterious doors brought up another topic, one she would have liked to forget but didn't seem to be able to avoid.

"Do you think Gowan's death could have had something to do with the marketplace?" she asked abruptly.

Nathan returned to staring into his glass, this time without looking like he was seeing anything.

"I don't know," he said at last. "It's a hell of a coincidence, isn't it? And, you know, coincidences do happen. But I don't like it."

"Me neither," said Claudia.

They finished the growler talking about the most bizarre coincidences they had each experienced, and it wasn't until Teddy went to the door and started whining to go out that Claudia realized how late it had gotten.

"Oh wow, I wasn't paying attention to the time. I was supposed to go back to the marketplace this afternoon. People will be wondering what happened to me."

"I think they'll understand. You've had a rough day."

Claudia sighed. "This was only one day? Feels like more. Anyway, I should at least go over there and check in on things."

"Mind if I come with you? I'd really like to have another look at that compartment."

They headed to the marketplace the short way, over the field, with Teddy romping ahead, and all three of them giving the geese plenty of room as they passed. The day was still clear, but the sun was getting low in the sky and the temperature had dropped noticeably. Dry grass crunched under their feet, a relic of summer that would last until the first rains came, hopefully in the next couple of weeks.

"What did you think of the new police chief?" Nathan asked. "Did she give you any trouble about finding the body?"

"No, not really. She's a lot sharper than Lennox was, that's for sure." San Elmo Bay's former chief of police had been a man notable for the way he had combined confidence with incompetence, and Claudia had very nearly paid the price for his failures. "Honestly, I don't know what to think of her. She's hard to read, to put it mildly. But very methodical, and nothing she said to me seemed unreasonable. I think she'll do a good job."

"I hope so," said Nathan as they crossed into the marketplace parking lot. "The last thing we need is a bunch of unsolved murders happening around this town."

# CHAPTER FIVE

They arrived in the marketplace just at closing time, and Claudia went to help Helen ring up a last-minute surge of sales in the pickle shop while Nathan wandered over to the door in the wall. Once the last of the customers were gone, Claudia joined him, followed eventually by several of the marketplace vendors as they finished up, stopping to look in on their way out.

"I can't believe this was here the whole time and I had no idea," Claudia said as she leaned in to take a closer look. Without the key, they hadn't been able to fully close and latch it, and it stood slightly ajar, an invitation to curiosity. "I wonder why it was built in the first place?"

"How old do you think it is?" Robbie's wife Emmanuelle asked. She ran a beautifully manicured finger down the edge of the door and poked her nail into the latch. "This looks like it's made of brass."

"Definitely brass," agreed Nathan, who had been examining the mechanism with a small magnifying glass he just happened to have in one of his pockets. "Looks like it's old, but it hasn't been exposed to the air very much."

"Here, let me see. I've got some experience with locks." Iryna took the glass from Nathan without waiting for a reply and applied her own eye to the keyhole. "It is a standard pin tumbler design. Nothing to date it from that."

Claudia was less interested in the nature of the lock than how a woman best known for her pierogies was able to analyze it, but the conversation moved on to whether there was any information to be derived from the shape of the screwheads, and she decided to leave it for another time. But it was her marketplace, after all, and as she leaned in to join the group that was clustering ever more tightly around the cupboard, she tried to think of something useful to contribute. But all she could come up with was that the air in it smelled slightly of apples, which probably had more to do with the stock in the produce market than any aspect of the mystery.

So she backed away again, while the investigative team of Robbie, Emmanuelle, Nathan, and Iryna got into whether or not anything could be learned from the variety of the wood, or the tightness of its grain. (To Claudia's eyes, it looked exactly the same as the timber in every other part of the building.) Casting around for something else to do, she noticed Eugene standing at the edge of the crowd, looking worried.

"This is all really something, isn't it?" Claudia said, for lack of anything better to open the conversation.

"It is that," the beekeeper agreed. "How are you doing? I heard you were there when that man's body was found."

Claudia confirmed the basic accuracy of that statement.

"It was definitely a shock, but I think I'll be all right. I didn't exactly know him, so I can't claim to be seriously bereaved."

"Sounds like a lot of people weren't."

Claudia looked at him curiously. As far as she knew, Eugene was even more of a newcomer to the area than her, and she couldn't imagine how he had managed to find a lawyer to hate in such a short time.

"Did you know him?" she asked.

"Me? No, I never met the guy. But I've been doing some accounting work on the side while I get the honey business up and buzzing, and one of my clients mentioned some trouble about him."

Claudia was intrigued, and also impressed that even in a conversation about a dead man, Eugene had managed to get in a bee pun. She wondered if he would be able to stop if he tried.

But that wasn't the main thing she was wondering.

"What kind of trouble? I'm not just curious—he was involved in the marketplace sale when I bought it, and all this talk about him being dishonest is starting to get me worried."

She had been half-hoping Eugene would laugh it off and tell her she was being foolish, but he looked unusually serious and shook his head.

"I didn't get all the details, but the basic issue as I understood it was that he was the guy you went to if you wanted to move some property around and not have your name attached to the transaction. My client hadn't encountered him directly, but he was looking to get into business with someone who had, and he hired me to go over the books before he pulled the trigger." He winced at the sound of that phrase, and looked apologetic. "Metaphorically speaking, of course. He didn't end up doing the deal, for other reasons, so I can't imagine he'd have anything to do with that."

"Of course," said Claudia who, regardless, was suddenly desperate to know the client's name, for no reason she was willing to say out loud.

"So, did you actually find any evidence that Gowan was doing these things?" she asked, grasping at straws. "Maybe it was all some rumor that got blown out of proportion?"

Eugene shook his head.

"I didn't come up with anything I could have taken to the IRS, if that's what you mean. But there were enough irregularities that I would have told my guy not to go for it, even without any real proof. It never came up, though, because around that time he got his identity stolen, and that put all the business plans on hold for a while."

"Actually," he rubbed his nose and looked around thoughtfully. "I'm not one for conspiracy theories, but I did think it was a little convenient, how that happened. Of course, that sort of thing's not uncommon these days, but it did make me wonder, like maybe somebody wanted to make sure he was too distracted to look into things any further. Crazy thinking, right?"

Claudia didn't think it sounded so wild, and she would still like to have known the name of the client. But before she even could come up with a bad pretense for asking, Jeannie came through the front door and made a beeline for them. (Now she was doing it.)

"Da-ad," Jeannie said, somehow managing to give the word at least three syllables. "Are you done yet? We're supposed to be at the gym at seven and I've got to change."

"Okay, okay, I'm coming. Just have to close up here." He gave Claudia a wave as he headed back to his stall. "I've got to buzz off now. Good luck with the mystery!"

He had meant the question of the secret compartment, of course. It wasn't Eugene's fault that she couldn't get it out of her head that Gowan's death was somehow related to her property, and as she sat in her cottage, contemplating the possibility, she became more and more uneasy.

As usually happened when she had a question, Claudia's first thought was to turn to her computer. It didn't take her long to learn that Gowan had been running his business in San Elmo for just over twenty years, had graduated from a midrange law school, and lived in one of the newer developments further inland. As far as she could determine, there was no one else at that address, and none of the news items that had already appeared about his death mentioned a spouse or partner. There was probably more out there for her to find, but it occurred to Claudia, as she skimmed through the legal notices and pictures of local events, that she had access to a potentially much more interesting source of information about what Gowan was doing very shortly before his death.

The last time she had reviewed the security camera footage, Claudia had only been interested in the compartment and who might have opened it. Now she wanted to know what else he had been up to, before and after his adventure with creative storage solutions. She had already set up her laptop to connect remotely to the computer in her office in the marketplace, and even with her lamentably slow internet it was a matter of minutes before she had the dashboard for the cameras open in front of her.

She started with when Gowan had accessed the compartment, and worked out from there. First, she went backward in time, hoping to see him interact with someone, or make some sign of what he was planning. But she was disappointed. Until he headed for the produce market, Gowan appeared to be strictly interested in his meal, and the conversations he had appeared to be brief and casual. There was a short period when she thought he was trying to break into one of the cases in the butcher shop, but when she backed up the recording and played it at half speed, she realized he was just using his reflection to try to get something out of his teeth.

So she wasn't feeling very optimistic when she got to the part with the compartment and moved past it to find out what had happened later. The process was long and tedious—even watching the recording at five-fold-speed, there were hours of footage to get through, and she kept having to keep switching cameras when Gowan passed out of the view of one to another. Her neck was stiff and her eyes were getting blurry, but she felt like she needed to finish the project, if only so she could be sure there was nothing she was missing.

As Claudia had expected, Gowan became even less social after he had picked up the package. The awkward way he was holding his coat to cover it might not have been immediately obvious to the casual observer, but an extended interaction could have made someone curious. At least, that was what Claudia assumed he was thinking as he circulated around the room, apparently marking the time until he could leave without drawing any attention to his movements.

Or maybe not. Claudia thought Gowan had been heading for

the door, and had slowed the playback down accordingly, in case he dropped some last clue on his way out, when he suddenly changed course and passed out of the view of her current camera. Claudia was getting pretty good at this by now, so it didn't take her long to find him again, though the camera with the best angle on his new position only gave her a view of the back of his head. On the other hand, she had a very clear view of who he was talking to, and Claudia was surprised to see that it was Julie.

From what Julie had said after the theft was discovered, Claudia hadn't gotten the impression they were on good terms, and the half of the conversation she could see showed her nothing to contradict it. Gowan must have been doing most of the talking, because Julie's responses were brief—no more than one or two words at a time—and her blankly polite expression made it clear she would rather be anywhere else. But she held it together, even managed a forced rictus of a smile as he took his leave. But once he turned away, the mask slipped, and the look Julie gave to Gowan's retreating back was one of pure, unadulterated fury.

Claudia sat back in her chair and let that sink in for a minute. Julie hadn't mentioned anything about talking to Gowan, even when the subject came up, and Claudia would very much have liked to know why. She supposed she would have to ask.

But not right now. The sun had long since set, the block of cheese (one of Julie's Gruyères, in fact) she had been eating in lieu of dinner was nearly gone, and it was past time for Teddy's last outing of the night. (It was one of the first things she had learned about dog ownership—no matter what else you might have going on, there were some aspects of your daily schedule that you had no ability to change.) So accepting her role in this relationship as being primarily service-oriented, she went through the going-out routine, and as Teddy did what she was going to do, Claudia wandered up to the crest of the hill and looked down at the marketplace building.

It was a clear night, and the quarter-moon was setting over the ocean. Below her, the marketplace sat in its pool of security lights like a museum display, the black eyes of its windows staring back at her. She looked into them for a while, thinking back through the last few years and what they had meant for her, and forward to what she might hope for her future in this place, when she caught a glimpse of movement in the shadows by the back door.

Claudia froze, uncertain if she had seen what she thought she had seen, and what she should do if she had. An innocent explanation was possible; raccoons and skunks had been known to stop by to check for scraps, and there had even been some mountain lion sightings in the area. As quietly as she could, she called Teddy back and held the dog close to her, while she peered into the darkness and waited until she saw it again.

It didn't take very long. Raccoons might look sharp in their masks, and skunks could have a formal style all their own, but Claudia was pretty sure neither had ever been known to go out in a black T-shirt and a baseball cap. She would have liked to get a better look at the wearer, who had only appeared momentarily from behind the dumpster. But aware that there had just been a murder, and of her own limitations when it came to hand-to-hand combat, and as much as she loved her marketplace, there was nothing there that couldn't wait until the police arrived. So she retreated back toward her cottage, trying to keep to the shadows and making sure she was out of sight before going for her phone.

She did stop to look back, though, just in time to see the figure grab a section of the exterior siding and start to pull.

"Oh, hell no," Claudia said.

The police arrived fairly quickly, all things considered. Unfortunately, by the time they did, the only evidence of the intruder were some scrapes on the siding and paint on the lenses of the security cameras. Claudia answered the responding officer's questions as best she could—no, she hadn't recognized the person, no, she didn't know what they might have wanted, no, she wasn't aware of there being anything in that part of the wall. Even the electrical panel was on the other side of the building, which Claudia had to show to him, as he didn't seem to believe this was something she would know. She was demonstrating that the cover was locked and undamaged when an unmarked car pulled up and the chief got out. She had changed out of her uniform, and into a near-identical outfit of a boxy short-sleeved shirt and straight-leg jeans.

Claudia wondered for a moment if Weaver had chosen a career in law enforcement because it suited her taste in clothing, or the other way around.

"Evening," she said, dismissing the officer with a nod. "I understand you've run into some more trouble here."

"Yes, I mean, it seems that way." Claudia tried to look like someone who did not go around looking for trouble to get into, and only partially succeeded. "Nothing much was damaged, though."

"Right, well we're going to take a look around, just in case. Did you see or hear any cars, coming or going, this evening?"

Claudia thought about that. The marketplace wasn't too far off the main road that ran through town, but it wasn't on a through street and therefore got very little traffic of its own. It was a quiet evening, and normally she would have been aware of the sound, but Claudia had to admit that she had been distracted, and said so.

"Sure. He also could have used a bicycle or something. You say you thought it was a man?"

"That was my impression, yes. He seemed kind of tall for a woman and, you know, man-shaped." Claudia hoped this was not something she would be expected to repeat in a court. "But I really didn't get a very good look," she repeated.

"What about your neighbor? Any chance he might have seen something?"

That got Claudia's attention. She hadn't even thought about Nathan since she had gently booted him and the rest of his historical research team out of the marketplace, so she could close up and go home. There was a time when he had kept a very close eye on everything that happened in the neighborhood, back when he was looking for ways to get Claudia and her business out of it, but now, as she looked up at his home, she could only see one light on in the kitchen, and no sign that he had even registered the arrival of the police.

Not that she had any reason to expect him to be watching her now, but Claudia found herself wishing he had, and that he was coming down the hill now, hopping over the rough ground in the way he did when he was in too much of a hurry to use the road.

That got her thinking about what she would have liked him to do when he got there, and at that point Claudia recognized that she was getting into deep waters here, and decided to just answer the question.

"I don't know," she said. "He could have, if he was looking. You'll have to ask him."

"Mm-hm," said Weaver. "Okay, I think that's all for now. Why don't you go home and get some rest. I'll make sure a patrol car comes by here every once in a while to check on things."

"Thanks, I appreciate that." Claudia hadn't even gotten around to thinking about whether she herself could be in danger, and for a moment she thought about calling Betty and taking her up on her offer of a guest room. But nothing that had happened so far had made it seem like it had anything to do with her, personally, it was all about the marketplace building and the things that might or might not be or have been in it.

And besides, if anyone did try to break into her cottage, Teddy would be there to protect her, if by that you meant lick them and check their pockets for treats.

Assuming the interview was over, Claudia got up from where she had been sitting, on the bench of one of the picnic tables at the edge of the marketplace parking lot. She was surprised when Weaver didn't rise as well, but stayed seated and reached for something in her pocket.

"You've had quite a day," she said, looking steadily into Claudia's eyes. "I don't want to alarm you, but I have a feeling there may be some more things yet to come."

Claudia couldn't think of anything to say to that, so she didn't. Weaver took out a business card and wrote on it.

"Here's my home number. Keep it handy, just in case."

And with that, she left, leaving Claudia to wonder, as was often the case, how much there was that she didn't know.

Without much to investigate, the other officers left not long after the chief, and Claudia walked back to her cottage alone. She was tired, unsettled, confused about a lot of things, and surprisingly hungry. Nathan's pear cider seemed like it had been a long time ago, and while in theory, Claudia didn't approve of alcohol as a coping mechanism, she didn't think she would have argued if someone else suggested it.

Thinking of that someone else brought her back to her neighbor, and what he might be doing to not notice a flurry of police activity outside his window. Maybe he had gone out, or he had someone there with him, and what might be happening in Claudia's general vicinity wasn't of much interest to him at the moment. Not that it was any of her business. They weren't even dating, and if she had misinterpreted his about-face decision to become a good neighbor as something more, then that was her problem. And honestly, with everything she had to deal with, what sense did it make to be thinking about this now?

But she couldn't resist glancing up the hill toward Nathan's house, or being disappointed when there was no movement behind the one illuminated window.

Back in her house, Claudia closed her own blinds, fed Teddy her dinner, and set about making one for herself. At least, that was what she intended to do when she sat down on the sofa with one of Robbie's pepperoni sticks (to help her think) and woke up forty minutes later with Teddy licking her fingers. Taking that as a sign, she decided she finally had had enough for one day, and went to bed.

# CHAPTER SIX

"**A**re you sure you're okay? You look terrible." It was Claudia's least favorite kind of question, and the third time she had gotten it that morning, so it took a heroic effort on her part to recognize the concern in Iryna's voice, and bite back the snide response that was on the tip of her tongue.

"I'm okay, thanks," she said through clenched teeth. "Do you need anything?"

"Nope, just checking in," Iryna said blithely. "Some people were asking questions about the building and the death, and it made me think of you. I guess that man really was murdered, wasn't he?"

"I guess," Claudia said, wondering where Iryna's certainty was coming from. Despite being a relative newcomer to San Elmo Bay, her tenant was no slouch when it came to picking up on the local gossip, but she was also someone who believed there was no need to let facts get in the way of a good story. "How do you know he was murdered? I thought there was still a chance he killed himself."

"Oh, definitely not. I was at my sunrise Pilates this morning and everyone was talking about it. Louise Ranson's daughter is a paramedic, and she said there was no gun near the body when they got there. So he couldn't exactly have shot himself, could he? And Phyllis Smeeth said she saw the police out there most of the afternoon and evening, searching around the building. Did they search you too?"

Claudia had to admit that she had been allowed to leave the scene without being thoroughly checked for hidden weapons, which seemed to disappoint Iryna. But she perked back up when she heard about them wiping her hands.

"For powder residue, of course. Well, that makes sense. If you had held it, they would have known." Nearly all of Iryna's knowledge of police procedure came from television shows, so Claudia wasn't sure how reliable it was, but she hoped she was right this time.

"Anyway," Iryna went on. "It must have been murder. That package he took out of here, I bet he had some plans for it. Why go to all that trouble if he was just going to kill himself?"

"We can't know what he was thinking," Claudia argued, though she didn't necessarily disagree. She did think, though, that she had a pretty good idea of what Iryna's contribution to the gossip rounds had been. "I hope there aren't a lot of people thinking he was killed over what he found here," she said, hoping the hint would go through.

It didn't.

"Well, it's certainly come up," Iryna said, looking pleased with herself. Claudia considered trying to explain to her tenant why it wasn't a great thing for the business to be associated in people's minds with violent death, but Iryna's feelings were easily hurt, and she wasn't sure how much good it was going to do at this point, anyway.

Still, every minute spent talking to Iryna risked increasing her supply of gossipable material, so Claudia looked around for an opportunity to make her escape. She had been meaning to talk to Julie, to ask her about her encounter with Gowan at the party, but she was nowhere to be seen, even though this was one of her regular days in the cheese shop. In fact, to Claudia's practiced eye, it looked like they were shorthanded behind the counter, though business was currently slow enough that it wasn't causing too many problems. But it was still a surprise, given that the Dancing Cow's co-owner was almost legendarily reliable.

"Have you seen Julie today?" Claudia asked abruptly, interrupting Iryna's account of the trouble one of her friends was having after someone stole her credit card (how this related to their current problems wasn't clear). Briefly thrown, she took a moment to recalibrate to the change of topic before diving in.

"I don't think so. No, I haven't, because I was going to ask her about how many guns she thought Gowan had, because I think she knew him? But she hasn't been around. Why? Is there something you need from her?"

"Nothing important," Claudia said, as she made a decision that directly contradicted her words. "Would you watch Teddy for me for a while? I have to run some errands."

Her car was still parked downtown, and not being sure of the status of Nathan's offer to take her to get it, Claudia opted to beg a ride from Robbie, who was making a delivery of his home-cured bacon to the cafe, where they used it in a calorically-record-setting scone. Between the coolers full of product and the stack of magazines about pig husbandry, getting into the cab of his truck was a bit of a squeeze, but they managed to sort it out, with Claudia spending the short ride downtown balancing bacon in her lap.

Conversation on the ride was blessedly free of the topics of murder, secret compartments, gunpowder, or lawyers. Instead they stuck to Robbie's plans to introduce a new variety of heritage pigs into his herd (which Claudia learned was called a drove) and the difficulties his wife Emmanuelle was having with some of the members of her extensive social media following. Claudia agreed that fame clearly had its price, and was noncommittal toward Robbie's offer to visit with his latest pigs. She had learned not to fear seeing how the sausage was made, but she still had some problems with meeting it before the fact.

Robbie dropped her off at her car, which Claudia was relieved to see remained unticketed and untowed. It also started, which in its increasingly advanced age was never a given.

On her way out of the downtown she had to pass Gowan's office, and it was not in her power to resist slowing down to look. For the most part, there was very little to see. No crime scene tape blocking the door, no flags in the lawn marking the locations of important clues. Just an old building that had once been a house, and was now an office, which happened to be closed on this bright autumn day. The only indication that there might be anything out of the ordinary about it was the sheet of paper taped to the front door, presumably explaining why there was no one in at the moment.

The drive to the Dancing Cow headquarters was a short one, by San Elmo standards—just twenty minutes down a narrow and approximately paved road that wound away from the coast, through the first line of hills that separated the ocean from the inland valleys. Here, the effects of the lack of rain were even more apparent; away from the foggy coast, the land looked parched and tired, and the golden tones of the summer hillsides had faded to a color that even a partisan like Claudia had to admit looked a lot like brown.

The shift in the view when she arrived at the farm was subtle but noticeable. The scrubland that had lined the road up to that point gave way to fields, not exactly green, but looking like they might have been. The buildings were bright and clean, freshly painted where they weren't newly built. The Mullers had been putting a lot into the business lately, betting on a market for their cheeses that only seemed to be growing. Claudia hoped it was a gamble that was going to pay off, for their sake as well as for hers.

She parked in the paved lot next to the creamery/visitor center. (There had been an attempt by a branding consultant to convince them to spell it "centre," categorically rejected by Julie's father Elias, a giant of a man who had immigrated from Switzerland in the sixties and never looked back, except to bring up the quality of the cheese in his adopted homeland.) Part of their promotion strategy involved regular tours, sometimes arriving in the kind of giant buses that had a tendency to block the driveway, and Claudia was relieved to see that things were quiet at the moment.

That peace did not last. Claudia had barely gotten out of the car when Elias came bursting out of the creamery building. He must have been working in the cheese caves, because he was wearing the white coat he kept especially for that purpose, and a hair net was sliding precariously off the back of his head. In one hand he held a small round of cheese, with which he was gesturing more wildly than usual.

"Claudia! Thank the goodness you came. Did they call you? We have to go and get her!"

"Get who? From where?" Elias had a well-earned reputation of being excitable, but even for him this was a lot. His voice echoed off the farm buildings, startling some of the cows on their way to the milking shed (Claudia didn't think it was even possible to surprise a cow) and his accent, which he typically only played up for interviews, had become thickly German. Even so, Claudia didn't have much trouble understanding the next thing he said.

"Julie! The police have her. They're going to try to say she killed that man!"

It took some doing, but eventually Claudia was able to get a few more details out of Elias, with the help of the farm manager, who had come out of the silage barn in double-quick time at the sound of the shouting. Apparently, Julie had been working in her office in the house, where she tended to go when she had something to do that required her full attention, away from the distractions of the creamery and, frankly, her father. The police chief had pulled up in an unmarked car and gone straight in, and about ten minutes later Julie had called Luis, the assistant head cheesemaker, and told him she was going to be out for a while, and she might not be reachable for the rest of the morning. Then she had gotten into Weaver's car and left before the message had time to reach Elias.

That was certainly concerning enough on its own, but Claudia was having trouble seeing how Elias had gotten from there to the idea that Julie was about to be accused of murder. Unusually for him, he was reticent on that point, and it was only when the farm manager had left to deal with some new crisis that was brewing in the breeding pens that he started to unbend.

"I'm not supposed to say this," he admitted at last, in the face of Claudia's persistent questioning. "But Julie did not like that bastard very much."

Claudia wasn't sure if his use of the epithet was a reflection of Elias's own hatred for Gowan, or if he had just forgotten the man's name. But she was confident that neither counted as probable cause for murder.

"From what I've heard, plenty of people didn't like Mr. Gowan," she pointed out. "That doesn't mean anything."

"Yes, well, the police didn't come and take any of those people away, did they?" was all he would say, and while there was an aspect to the argument Claudia found compelling, she remained unconvinced.

She was at least able to talk Elias out of his plan to have her drive him down to the police station and demand Julie's release, on the grounds that they had no idea what they would be releasing her from, but if he was that sure, then he needed a lawyer, not a marketplace owner. They compromised by going back to Elias's office and calling up the only lawyer whose number he could find, a retired intellectual property attorney who was part of Elias's bi-monthly mahjong game.

There wasn't a lot of space in Elias's office, so while he explained the details to his confused friend, Claudia wandered out into the hall, where a set of long windows looked into the cheesemaking room.

In addition to the visitor center, Dancing Cow's recent renovations included a demonstration kitchen for visiting chefs, a separate aging cave for cheeses from other creameries, and a patio area for receptions and small weddings, but most of the money had gone into the cheese-making room. Gone was the concrete-floored shed with the equipment Elias had been able to scrounge from auctions and hold together with duct tape and hope; in its place was the gleaming sanctuary of a temple to cleanliness.

The room was about twice the size of the average Starbucks, completely white from its linoleum floor to its acoustic-tile ceiling. Along the far side were the vats where the milk went through its initial heating, big round tubs with pipes that ran into them straight from the milking shed. Giant arms stirred them like the world's largest and slowest stand mixers. Down the line, workers sliced through the freshly set and drained curds, gently lifting and folding them to press out the excess whey. Julie had explained to her once why this process was important, but Claudia couldn't remember the details, only that the renovations that had brought Dancing Cow into the top level of craft cheesemaking had cost them plenty, and their ability to pay off the loans depended on an aggressive marketing strategy, and no small amount of luck. An arrest in a murder case, if that was what had happened, was definitely not part of the plan.

And that was a big if. Elias had a way of taking the darkest possible view of things, but even for him the assumption struck Claudia as extreme. Granted, she couldn't think of another reason off the top of her head for Julie to have left in a police car, but that didn't mean there wasn't one. Julie obviously had something against Gowan, which didn't seem to be a secret, but unless there was something she didn't know, Claudia stood by her earlier assertion that people didn't get arrested for disliking someone.

Unfortunately, Claudia was starting to suspect there were a lot of things she didn't know.

Elias was still talking to his friend, so Claudia went to get her own phone from the car, where she had just realized she had left it. (There was virtually no signal out here, but she still felt naked without her constant companion.) She was just checking to confirm that she had no bars when a patrol car pulled up and Julie got out of the passenger seat.

Julie looked around like she was hoping no one would see her, but on spotting Claudia, she gave a little shrug, clearly resigned to her fate.

"Did Father call you?" she asked, after they exchanged greetings.

"No, actually I came over on an unrelated issue." Claudia thought about that for a moment, and then amended, "Maybe not that unrelated. This is obviously a bad time, though. I'll catch up with you later."

"No, it's okay. I wouldn't mind having someone to talk to right now." She looked with regret but no bitterness in the direction of the patrol car vanishing down the driveway. "What's he up to?"

Claudia interpreted the question to mean Elias, and answered accordingly.

"Calling some lawyer friend of his to come down to the station and—I believe 'spring' you was the term he used. I'm not sure the guy was convinced."

Julie laughed. "That'd be Harold, I bet. Well, trying to explain things to him is bound to keep Father occupied for a while at least. Which is fine by me, don't think I'm quite ready for that conversation yet." Looking a little more relaxed, she gestured toward the house. "Want to come in for some coffee? The stuff they had at the station was just awful, and I need something to wash the taste of nondairy creamer out of my mouth."

Even if she hadn't been hoping to find out from Julie what exactly was going on, Claudia had a policy to never turn down coffee.

The farmhouse kitchen, despite being undeniably a kitchen in a farmhouse, didn't quite live up to the real estate fantasy of the name, lacking as it did an apron sink, stone countertops, or any form of tastefully rustic backsplash. Instead, it was a small but comfortable space, where the green-painted breakfast table teetered very slightly on well-worn slate floors, and a bunch of bright purple asters filled a jug that spoke of a midlife ceramics hobby.

The coffee was little stale for having sat through Julie's ordeal, but Claudia wasn't complaining, particularly not when her host brought a jug of fresh cream out of the refrigerator and poured generous doses into each mug. The molasses cookies she served with it were from a package, but not so much the worse for that, and Claudia followed Julie's lead to soak one in her drink, before getting down to business.

"So, what happened? Did they actually arrest you?"

"Oh, no," Julie said, already on her second cookie. Stress did that to some people, Claudia thought. "It's just that people are in and out of here all the time, and I didn't really want to have someone coming in on the police chief when she was asking me questions. So when she asked if I would come down to the station, that seemed like the best option."

Claudia considered that answer, and came to the obvious conclusion.

"In other words, you didn't want Elias to show up and start doing his thing where he says whatever comes into his head at the moment," she translated.

Julie smiled. "Something like that. So, yes, I decided I would be better off on neutral ground. It's not like anything was going to stop the gossip machine from firing up, anyway."

"Why? What was it you had against Gowan?"

Julie paused, staring into her coffee cup like the little bit of congealed cream floating on the surface might be a tea leaf she could read.

"You know I was married, right? To Beryl's father?" she said, her voice carefully even.

Claudia confirmed that she had heard those basic details.

"Well, Jonas, that was his name, he turned out to be a real piece of work. I supported him for years, all the way through dental school, the whole time he was getting his practice set up, everything. I was working full time as a paralegal, coming in to help dad with the farm evenings and weekends. It was a pretty intense time, but I always figured it was only temporary, and once he got himself established, I would be able to step back and do some more of what I wanted." She paused and smiled ruefully at Claudia. "Stop me if you've heard this song before. Anyway, I always knew he wasn't the most faithful guy, but I knew his hygienist and his receptionist, and I was confident in both of them."

"But you were wrong about them?"

"No, they were great. We still exchange Christmas cards. They were the ones who told me about the patient he was having an affair with, and how she had announced to the office that they were going to get married after the baby was born, because she didn't want to look fat in her pictures."

"Wow."

"My thoughts exactly. Anyway, by the time I got off the phone with my lawyer, Jonas had already emptied our shared accounts. I don't know where the money went, but I do know that he and Clark were golfing buddies from way back, and sometimes when he had had a few, Jonas would talk about how Clark was someone who could "fix" things, if he ever needed it. And before the divorce, he started taking a lot of meetings at Clark's office. Not that it proves anything, but for a guy with no money for alimony or child support, and a woman who never worked a day in her life, they didn't have much trouble buying a nice big house down in Anaheim."

"You think Gowan helped him hide his money? How would he do that?"

"I don't know, but I have some ideas. There've been a number of his clients who have had judgements against them—lawsuits, divorces, bankruptcies—who suddenly seem to have no money to pay up when the courts come calling, and then turn around with some amazing luck a few months later. People have been talking about it for years, but what can you do? Nobody around here has the kind of resources to hunt down that sort of thing."

Claudia had heard enough at this point about Gowan's alleged shadiness that she should have been ready for the details, but it still threw her to hear them spelled out. She knew she should be focusing on Julie's problems right now, and for the most part she was, but she couldn't help but flash back to the first time she had been in Gowan's office, signing a giant pile of papers she barely understood, and that missing page in the disclosure documents. If a property lawyer had been in the business of managing some kind of shady deals, was everything he touched suspect? Did Claudia even own the marketplace at all, or was it, and her money, about to disappear into a web of lawsuits that would last the rest of her natural life? They might have been selfish and unreasonable concerns, but that had never stopped her before.

Fortunately, Julie didn't seem to have noticed Claudia's distraction. She was on her fourth cookie now, transitioning from a dunking strategy to alternating bites and sips as the level of coffee dropped lower in her mug.

"You know, I should really be grateful. Jonas never believed in the farm or the creamery, or any of what we were trying to do here, and I let his doubts hold me back. Once he left, and I had to sell the house and move back in with dad, I felt like the business was all I had, and I really put everything into making it work. I never would have done that if it wasn't for him."

"That doesn't mean what he did wasn't terrible," Claudia argued, pulling her head out of her own problems for a moment. "Just because you were able to make the best out of it, he didn't do it for you."

"No, of course not. But it's important for me to frame it like that, in order to give myself permission to let go." Julie laughed. "At least that's what my therapist says. And I pay her enough, so I figure I'd better at least try it."

They both laughed, and Claudia was relieved. She must have been wrong, and Weaver was just talking to everyone with a reason to dislike Gowan, and if what Julie was saying was true, that list was bound to be long. So she took another cookie for herself and sat back a bit more, trying to think of ways she could find out more about how Gowan was running whatever scam he had going, and whether it could impact her.

"Did you tell all that to Weaver?" she asked. Despite her recent experience, Claudia didn't know much about talking to the police, but she suspected she had been doing it wrong.

"Well, I kind of had to. She knew a lot of it already, actually. But mostly she wanted to know what I was doing in his office that night after the party."

# CHAPTER SEVEN

Claudia sat bolt upright in her chair, her freshly dipped cookie slowly turning to mush in her hand.

"Wait—you were—what?" Unable to comprehend the possibilities behind that statement, Claudia's brain gave up and froze, leaving her mouth to its own devices.

Julie acknowledged her shock with a resigned sort of shrug.

"Not my most brilliant idea, I'll admit it. But there's no point in trying to keep it a secret, not the way they found out."

"Which was how? And why? You, I mean, not them." Claudia thought she had a pretty good handle on why the police would be interested in someone visiting a murdered man's business directly before he was found dead.

"Because of the package, of course," Julie said, answering her last question first. "As soon as I saw it was Clark on that tape, I knew there must have been something important in there. And for him to take that kind of risk to try and get it during the party, he must have needed it for something soon. So I thought I'd beat him at his own game. If he can break in to places and take things, why not me? He's certainly taken enough from me as it is. And if that happened to be the evidence of how he helped Jonas rip me off, well, then pretty much any risk would be worth it. At least that's what I thought."

"So, did you find it?" It was far from the main question Claudia should have been asking, but she had to know.

"No, not a trace. And honestly, it was a dumb idea from the start. Even if he did leave it at his office, instead of taking it home or hiding it somewhere else, how was I going to find it? There can't be a better place in the world to hide a bunch of papers than a lawyer's office. Anyway, I poked around a bit, until it was clear I wasn't going to find anything, and then I thought I heard something and panicked."

Julie was clearly in a bad way, and it seemed unfair to press her, but Claudia did have one question to ask. (Okay, she actually had a lot, but at least one she couldn't avoid.)

"Did this have anything to do with what he was saying to you after the dinner? I saw it on the recording," she explained in response to Julie's horrified look.

"Of course. I was hoping no one would have noticed. Yes, that was part of it. I usually try to avoid him, and I thought he was happy to do the same, but that night, I don't know what got into him. I suppose it must have had something to do with that thing he got from the wall there—he probably had it by then."

Claudia confirmed that that was the case.

"Well, that explains some of it, I guess. He just came up to me with the most horrible grin on his face, making snide comments about justice, and how life's winners and losers weren't always who you think they should be. Ostensibly, it was about the library not getting the funding it needs, but I knew he was trying to get at me." Julie made a face. "He was not a subtle man. Anyway, once I saw him on the video, I figured that must have had something to do with this great victory he was expecting to have, and I just thought, maybe this time I can do something about it. And if that meant breaking into his office, then fine. That's what I was going to do."

"But someone saw you?" Claudia had always thought of Julie as one of the most practical and level-headed people she knew; finding out that she had gone in for a spot of light burglary was like meeting your kindergarten teacher at a beer pong tournament.

"Sort of," Julie said. "One of the houses across the street had a camera, and when the police got the footage they were able to identify me."

"That must have been quite a camera." It was far from most relevant point, or even the top ten, but Claudia's interest in technology was enough to distract her from a lot of things. (And a household security camera that could positively identify a person at night from across the street was exactly the sort of thing she was interested in.) But the answer was simpler than that.

"Maybe. But it probably helped that I drove there in the van," Julie admitted.

"Ah. Well, yes, that might have done it," agreed Claudia.

The official vehicle of Dancing Cow Farmstead Creamery was an oversized white van, decorated on both sides with their logo, a tutu-clad bovine captured midpirouette, and across the back with a list of their famous cheeses. It was distinctive, to say the least. And it probably wouldn't have been Claudia's first choice of transportation options if she were planning something in the criminal line.

Her thoughts must have shown on her face, because Julie acknowledged them with a shrug and another sigh.

"Father might have noticed if I had taken the truck, and Beryl had gone in the wagon to go see a friend's band play at a brewery in Santa Rosa. And how was I supposed to know he was going to get murdered?"

Claudia admitted that she had suffered from a similar lack of foresight on that point.

"But he wasn't killed that night, right? I mean, you couldn't have done it then?" From the way he had looked when she found him, Claudia had assumed Gowan must have sat down to start his workday when someone had come in and shot him. But she hadn't exactly stopped to examine the condition of the body, and it occurred to her that she had no way of knowing how long he had been there.

"No, of course not. There was no one in the building when I got there," Julie said. "But it turns out breaking in to an office makes the police pretty interested in you when the guy turns up dead there."

"So they were treating you as a suspect? But they didn't arrest you?" Claudia was starting to think that Elias's idea of finding Julie a lawyer, however badly executed, might have been the right call.

Julie must have been thinking the same thing.

"They didn't, but I'm pretty sure at least some of them wanted to. The chief was the one who was talking to me, but there was another officer there who kept saying things I knew were lies. Like, that they found my fingerprints on the gun, or they had a witness who says they heard me confess. So finally I said I wasn't going to answer any more questions without a lawyer, and they let me go." She sighed again. "Now I just need to find one, and figure out how I can afford them. I don't suppose you know any who will work for cheese?"

"A sort of a pro queso attorney? Can't say I can think of anyone off the top of my head." Claudia took it as a sign of Julie's fragile mental state that she laughed as hard as she did at that. Hoping to distract her further, she cast around for another topic to talk about.

"Do you know anything about the other lawyer in the practice? A woman, her name's Finley or something like that. She and I had a little encounter after I found the body, and I'm wondering if I should get in touch and try and smooth things over with her before she makes some kind of complaint about me."

"Oh, Kathy? I'm sure you can talk to her if you want to, but I doubt she's out to cause you any trouble. I actually had her help me straighten out my taxes a couple of years ago when someone filed a false refund in my name. She's a really nice lady, as much an accountant as a lawyer, I think. I don't have any idea why she would share office space with someone like Clark."

"No accounting for taste, I guess." Claudia winced, and hoped Julie didn't think she had intended that pun. "You said Gowan had been pulling his scam on a lot of people around here. Do you know who any of the other ones were?"

"Let me see . . ." While Julie paused to remember, Claudia helped herself to another cookie and tried to convince herself that her interest in the answer was just normal curiosity.

"I think the first one was when Mr. Newman left town so suddenly, and it turned out he owed pretty much everyone money," Julie said. "And when a few people tried to collect, they couldn't get anything. That was when the rumors started, and I'm not sure it wasn't Clark who started them. Because now everyone knew that if you had some money you wanted to hide, he was the man to see." She took a sip of her coffee and looked grim. "After that, things just kept happening. There was the Cramer divorce, where she tried to put a bunch of money in some fake business in Paraguay, but Mr. Cramer found out and got it stopped by customs. And when old Mrs. Glenn died, her children found out that all of her property had somehow ended up in one of their cousins' names. I think that one is still in court, but you get the idea. It was never big stuff in the grand scheme of things, but enough to make a mess out of people's lives."

"Wow," said Claudia. "I'm amazed he was able to keep his business going like that. You'd think in a small town like this, he would have been made persona non grata years ago."

"Well, no one could ever prove anything. Plus, there were always people like Mr. Tolman, buying the marketplace, who had just come into the area and had no idea. Clark could always put on a good show if you didn't know him." They had both finished their coffee, so Julie got up to refresh their mugs from the pot. On her way, she stopped and looked out the window, at some distant reminder of something unpleasant. "Also, some people just love a con man, as long as they're not the ones getting conned."

Claudia couldn't argue with that. In fact, she had some personal experience along those lines. But she would rather not get into that now.

"How much of his business do you think it was?" she said, hoping to change the subject. "Like, was this how he paid his bills, or more of a sometimes thing?"

"Hard to say. If I was going to guess, I'd say it was a service he offered occasionally to special clients, and he charged enough to make it worth his while. I think the latest one was Martin, actually. He's our vet—you know him, right? A couple years ago he won a lawsuit against a former business partner who had been siphoning off money from their practice for years. Martin found out about it, and called him on it, and then the guy ran out and stole a bunch of his equipment on the way. So Martin took him to court and won, but when it came time to pay the judgement—" She held her hands palms-up, indicating emptiness. "The lost money, plus all the lawyer and court costs nearly bankrupted him. After that, he was pretty vocal about Clark being a part of it, and how he wasn't going to be allowed to get away with it for much longer, but he calmed down about it recently. Maybe he's in therapy, too. Or—"

The implications of what she had been saying hit Julie almost immediately after the words were out of her mouth. She flushed and looked stricken.

"I didn't mean, of course, he would never. Oh, hell, there must be a dozen people out there who hated Clark just as much as he did. Me, for example. Oh, God, Claudia, what am I going to do?"

Suddenly, the iron structure that had always seemed to hold Julie up melted away, and she collapsed on her kitchen table, a tired, middle-aged woman who couldn't take it any more. Claudia wished she could help, or at least come up with some magic combination of words that would lift some of the weight, convince her that things weren't as bad as they looked and it would all be solved soon. But she had never been a very convincing liar.

Instead, she opened her mouth, and the last thing she expected came out.

"Don't worry," the insane person who had taken over her power of speech said. "I'll figure out who killed him."

There wasn't much time to discuss Claudia's lunatic proposal, because it was right about then that Elias, having realized they were in the house, came bursting through the front door, full of concerns, theories, and an idea for a new washed-rind cheese using apple cider. (It wasn't clear where that last one came in, but it sounded good.) Claudia took the opportunity to make her escape, because Julie was going to have her hands full dealing with one crazy person, and she didn't want to think about what would happen if Elias got wind of her proposal to play detective on his daughter's behalf. He would probably get her one of those hats with the earflaps.

She doubted Julie was going to bring it up with him. The cheese-maker had seemed as surprised as Claudia had been by her proposal, and there was a good chance that if Claudia never mentioned it again, neither would she. It would just go down as another of the many odd, awkward things Claudia said when she was trying to be helpful, and she would try, and fail, to learn from the experience.

Except Claudia didn't want to give it up. As annoyed as she was with herself, and as mystified by her impulsiveness, Claudia realized she wasn't interested in going back on her offer. Ever since she had seen that open door in the wall of her marketplace, she had felt unsettled by the feeling of being immersed in something she didn't understand, surrounded by information that was always just out of her reach.

There were practical considerations too. Julie was the one in real trouble, and Julie was the heart and soul of Dancing Cow Cheeses. Which, in turn was the biggest draw and the best moneymaker for the entire marketplace. Claudia didn't think Weaver was going to be sloppy or unfair, but the facts were what they were, and those facts did not look good for her star tenant.

(There was, of course, the chance that Julie had actually killed the man, but one thing at a time.)

And, after all, it wouldn't be the first time Claudia had taken on an unofficial murder investigation. Granted, her previous experience hadn't exactly been an unqualified success, in the sense that she had almost, but not quite, identified the killer in time to keep them from making an attempt on her own life, but she had ultimately made it out alive, and anyway, practice makes perfect.

And then there was her own angle on the problem. Thinking back to when she had bought the marketplace, Claudia tried to remember if there had been anything that seemed suspicious. The problem was, having come from a background as a computer programmer, who bought the business when she was looking for a way to change the direction of her life, she didn't have a lot of context for what it was supposed to look like. Most aspects of the deal had been handled by the realtor, a bright, professionally intense woman who mostly stuck in Claudia's memory for the way she had ended nearly everything she said with a sharp "huh?" and a laugh. Claudia hadn't seen her recently, but she thought it might be a good idea to pay her a visit.

In fact, she thought as she glanced at the clock on her dashboard, there was no time like the present. True, her recent experience in unannounced visits to local professionals wasn't great, but what were the odds of something like that happening twice?

Having made up her mind, she changed her goal from the marketplace to back toward downtown, an impulse which required a less-than-thoroughly legal u-turn, because she had just missed the turnoff.

Once she had her directions sorted out, Claudia turned her thoughts back to the problem. What had she known about the seller of the marketplace building, when you came down to it? Claudia had only met him on a few occasions, since by the time he had decided to sell he had already moved out of the area. Mr. Tolman had been an unimpressive man in his late fifties who, despite his obvious relief at finally having found a buyer for the property, still made it clear that he had his doubts that Claudia was the right person to take it on. (Which, to be fair, Claudia had too.) His idea for the business was roughly in line with what she had done with it, though his plans had included a hotel to be built on the still-vacant lot, an event space, and several other things the county planning commission was never going to approve.

Her impression of him, from what little she knew, had been of a man whose dreams had overreached his resources, who still thought he knew better than anyone even though he had failed. Not someone she would normally hang out with, but you didn't have to be friends with someone in order to buy a building from them.

And, as she couldn't help remembering, at the time he was selling the property, he had recently gotten divorced.

Which didn't have to mean anything, Claudia argued with herself. Many, if not most, divorces involved little to no financial fraud, and Gowan must have at least occasionally done some legitimate work.

It was a perfectly good argument, but Claudia remained unconvinced.

The realtor's office shared space with a nail salon and a dry cleaners in a bland low-rise building at the edge of what passed for a downtown in San Elmo. The windows were stocked with photos of vacation homes and ocean-view lots, some with prices as spectacular as their vistas. It had been one of the things that had tempted Claudia into buying the market in the first place; as tiny as her cottage was, how else would she have been able to live where she could see the Pacific from her windows?

She opened the door to find the office empty, and for a moment Claudia had a horrible sense of déjà vu. But then a door at the back of the room opened and a woman's head popped out, fortunately attached to the rest of her body.

"Hi, can I help you?" She was a slim woman about Claudia's own age, with carefully sculpted brows and highlights in her hair that she didn't get in San Elmo. But her outfit was casual, jeans and a mismatched cardigan and shell combination that made Claudia wonder if she hadn't been expecting to see anyone today.

"Hi, I'm Claudia Simcoe. I was actually looking for Florence Bell, is she here? She handled the sale of a building I own, and I wanted to ask her some questions about it."

The woman nodded. "The marketplace, of course. I'm afraid Flo isn't in at the moment. She's actually out for the rest of the week, so I've been holding down the fort. My name's Amy Mills, by the way. Do you need me to try and reach out to her?"

"I don't know, maybe you can help me? I'm not sure if you heard, but we've recently had some, um, excitement over at the marketplace." Amy's expression suggested that she knew exactly what she was talking about, so Claudia didn't elaborate. "Anyway, I'm trying to find out more about what happened, and I came across an inconsistency in the disclosure packet. So I was wondering if you might have a copy here that I could look at?"

She didn't want to have to explain about the missing page that might not really be missing, because every way she thought of describing it sounded less credible than the last. Fortunately, Amy's desire to be helpful (or her curiosity) was enough to overcome any lack in the detail department.

"Well, sure, that shouldn't be a problem. We aren't usually supposed to share client files, but seeing as it's your property, I think we can make an exception."

Amy hadn't said she had heard about the incident at the harvest dinner, but she didn't have to. The speed with which she was moving through the files was enough evidence of her interest, and Claudia had already accepted that whatever she managed to learn here would be making the gossip rounds before she even got home.

What she didn't expect was for there to be nothing to share. But Amy looked through the files, then looked through them again, then tried another drawer, and another. She didn't say anything, but the way she was looking progressively more confused was enough to tell Claudia that something wasn't right.

"I don't understand it," she said at last. "We have all of the disclosures for sales going back over eight years. Yours definitely should be here."

"But it's not?"

"No, and I checked everywhere I could think of. If we had it, I should have found it."

"Huh," said Claudia.

"It could be just a mistake," Amy said, but she didn't sound very convinced.

"It could be," Claudia agreed, and even as she said it, she felt her last bit of hope that her marketplace wasn't tied up in Gowan's death slipping away. "But that's quite a coincidence."

"Yeah."

They stood in silence for a while, stuck on the obvious conclusions and the consequences they would have for each of them. Claudia was about to thank Amy for her time and go home to regroup when, for one of them at least, inspiration struck.

"I wonder if there's anything about it in the historical files," Amy said, suddenly brightening.

"The what?" asked Claudia.

"It's a project that Flo has had me working on for the last few months. She's very into local history. And she's got this idea that we should position ourselves as the go-to agency for any historic building to be sold in the greater San Elmo area. So, now anything she sells that's more than twenty years old needs some kind of background historical information and since I'm the new kid in the office, coming up with the raw material is my job."

She didn't sound upset about it, but Claudia couldn't help but notice that the corporate polish had faded off her speaking style, replaced by a twang that owed more to the Central Valley than middle management. As she spoke, Amy moved on to a smaller, less well-maintained filing cabinet in the back of the room. She flipped through the folders there, and this time it was only a few minutes before she came up with one.

"Here it is! I thought I had done yours already." The file she pulled out was slim, and she opened it to reveal a short stack of printouts with some indistinct, black-and-white pictures. In some of them, Claudia recognized the outline of a building that looked like her marketplace, but it was hard to tell, with the dirt roads around it and the crates of apples stacked around the wide barn doors. The only familiar thing about it was the mustaches on the men, who could have been any assortment of Robbie's friends.

"Where is this from?" Claudia asked, flipping through the sheets as she tried to place the different angles.

"The library, mostly. Their local history collection is really quite good. It just takes a while to find things, because it's all on microfilm, and nothing is searchable. Sometimes when I've been at it for a few days, I go to bed and close my eyes, and I can still see the pages going past on that little screen."

"I had the same thing when I got addicted to Tetris," Claudia said. Amy just looked confused, though, so she didn't follow up with a question of how whether this was really the sort of work Amy had gotten into realty for.

Instead, Claudia thought back to the fundraiser she had just hosted.

"I wonder what it would cost to do a digitization project," she said. "I should ask Julie about it."

"That would be great," Amy agreed. "And you'd be surprised how much demand there is. It seems like every time I'm in there, there's at least one other person trying to find something."

It was an appealing idea, and Claudia was about to get carried away with it when she remembered why she was there.

"Do you mind if I make copies of these? I'd like to look over them more closely, and I feel like I've probably taken up enough of your time."

Copier usage was agreed to, and one cleared paper jam later, Claudia had a set of the documents she could examine at her leisure.

# CHAPTER EIGHT

She still had a lot of questions, but as curious as Claudia was, and despite the damage she had done to Julie's cookie supply, she was also hungry, and the ride with Robbie had left her with an almost unreasonable hankering for bacon. The cafe was an option, but their tables were small, and at this time of day, competition for one of them could be fierce. So Claudia opted instead for San Elmo's only other all-day establishment, the Seagrass Diner, where the eclectic menu of breakfast and lunch classics had slowly been giving way to modern demands, and it was now possible to get a side of gluten-free toast to go with your free-range eggs.

(Claudia opted for a standard English muffin with the avocado scramble, extra bacon.)

The owners of the diner had never met a holiday they didn't like, and at the moment Halloween was in in a big way. Normally, it was one of Claudia's favorite holidays, style-wise, but she had to admit that looking up from her menu to see a skull grinning back at her from the artificial flowers was a little jarring to her current state of mind.

Unsettled, Claudia picked up and moved, switching herself and her thick white mug of very average coffee to the other side of the Formica table, where she could read through the file under the watchful eyes of a cardboard spider.

The barn, which she was able to recognize now as definitely her building, was identified in the accompanying documentation as belonging to the Satler family farm and used for apple storage and processing. That surprised Claudia. She knew that apples had been a cash crop in

Sonoma County for a long time—one of the biggest, until the wine industry had taken over and orchards were torn out by the dozens to make way for vineyards. But they had never been grown this close to the coast, where the salt winds and fog made it inhospitable to any fruit, and ranching was the only viable form of agriculture.

But the cartloads of apples in the photos were undeniable, and as Claudia read on her understanding improved. The Satlers had indeed had their farm further inland, where at one time they had grown apples on over a hundred acres, spread out across different properties. Unlike most of the farmers in the area, who generally sold apples to be eaten fresh, or to be canned as sauce, the Satlers' business model had taken a more libertine slant, and the majority of their produce had been processed into cider, probably not too unlike whatever Nathan was trying to make at the moment. Claudia thought she would mention it to him the next time she saw him, if he wasn't off doing something with someone, neither of which was any of her business.

Annoyed with herself, Claudia shook off the thought. Could a guy not go to bed early without her turning it into a federal case? Some people, she reflected, managed to stop being overdramatic teenagers by the time they reached their thirties.

At that point, her food arrived, and for a little while Claudia was spared from having to make any decisions beyond which of the four hot sauces on the table she wanted to use on her eggs. (She went with the bottle with the Mexican lady on it.) The eggs were actually fine by themselves—bright yellow yolks in a loose scramble with chunks of smooth avocado, topped with crumbled fresh cheese—but the spice and vinegar tang of the sauce put them over the top, and helped Claudia avoid admitting to herself that she had just eaten three consecutive pieces of bacon.

Around the sixth piece (the Seagrass's servings were nothing if not generous), it was getting harder to hide her choices behind bites of egg, so she turned her attention back to the printouts. The bulk of the information seemed to have come from a set of articles in the local paper marking the farm's centennial celebration in the midseventies, in which it was mentioned that the current owner, the sixty-five year-old Herb Satler, was unmarried with no children, and seemed to have no plans for the future of the business other than a vague hope that an "energetic young person" might someday want to take it on.

That hope seemed like it must have been unfulfilled, because the next, and second to last, sheet carried an article about the fight between the developer who had bought the "former Satler Farms property" and local anti-development interests. The outcome wasn't included in the piece, probably because it hadn't happened yet, but Claudia deduced from the lack of a six-story luxury hotel with two eighteen hole golf courses in the vicinity that the developer's plans had been at least partially scaled back.

Neither article had any further mention of the barn, who else had owned it, or how or when it had acquired the cottages, though there was a winking reference to "the Satlers' popular coast-side operation," which Claudia supposed she might have understood if it was fifty years ago and she was a longtime local. But since it, and she, wasn't, there was little she could do but to resign herself to following in Amy's footsteps, and devote what little free time she had to hunting through the depths of the library for more clues.

She had one more page to go, but she was also out of coffee, and priorities being what they were, Claudia took a break from her reading to try to get the attention of one of the Seagrass's legendarily disinterested waitresses. It didn't go well, and she was five minutes in and about to give up and try sneaking behind the counter to grab one of the pots for herself when a familiar figure blocked her view.

"Hi! Can I sit down?"

Nathan looked cheerful and pleased to see her, and not at all like someone who had spent the last sixteen hours avoiding her for unspecified reasons. (He also looked like he might have been wearing the same outfit from the day before, but it was difficult to tell, owing to his habit of buying clothes in lots of ten.) Claudia welcomed him to her table, and within moments the most senior of the servers was there with a mug and a fresh pot of coffee. She gathered up and put away the papers while Nathan placed his order from memory, and wondered how many magazine articles would have to be written about her before she got VIP diner service. (At the rate things were going, they would probably be about all the murders, but it might be worth it, for the coffee.)

"I figured you'd be here, because the cafe is so crowded this time of day," Nathan explained, once he was done measuring a precise eighth of a teaspoon of sugar into his mug. "I heard you had a prowler at the marketplace last night?"

"I guess you could call it that. I'm surprised you didn't notice." That was as close as Claudia was going to get to admitting she had been wondering about him, but Nathan didn't seem to find it unusual.

"I know," he said, sounding regretful. "That's what the police said too. They're the ones who told me. The problem was that I was down in the cellar until—actually, I'm not sure how long. I was working on the cider project, and then I had a thought about maybe using wild yeast from the apples to make a new beer, and then . . . I guess time kind of got away from me. I'm sorry I wasn't around to help." He brightened up. "But I think the beer is going to be pretty good, at least."

It was a likely sounding story, and Claudia didn't doubt it for a minute. In fact, she was embarrassed it hadn't been her first guess. In the short time she had actually known Nathan (as compared to the much longer time when he had been nothing more than a name on a series of angry emails), she had come to realize that his single-mindedness when it came to one of his interests was a key part of his personality.

And right now, maybe that could be a helpful thing for her.

"Speaking of cider," Claudia said. "You might be interested in what I've been learning about the marketplace."

She laid out the papers she had gotten from the realtor in front of

Nathan, and he immediately dove into them, even shoving his smoked salmon benedict out of the way when it arrived.

"This is fantastic," he said, once he had finished speed-reading the articles. "Really interesting. But do you think it has anything to do with what's been happening?"

"No idea," Claudia admitted. "But at least it gives me somewhere to start."

They discussed the possibilities, realistic and otherwise, while Nathan finished his meal and Claudia moved the remaining bits of egg around her plate. She was starting to worry about the inevitable discussion about the bill and was composing her arguments when Nathan was struck by a sudden thought.

"Oh, by the way, Carmen mentioned that there had been someone at the marketplace looking for you. I think she said he was one of Betty and Roy's guests? Anyway, she has his card, said he asked for you to give him a call."

"I wonder if it was the same guy she mentioned at the harvest dinner? Betty said he was some kind of serious foodie."

"Maybe he's checking out the marketplace for holding future events. That could be a good line of supplemental income for you."

"Yeah . . ." Claudia wasn't sure she wanted to get into the event business—her few experiences with it so far had been more stress than she typically cared for. But, corporate-speak aside, Nathan probably had a point about the money.

"I guess I should talk to him, anyway," she concluded. "Betty said he seemed nice."

"Right, sure." That seemed to have Nathan worried about something, but before Claudia could decide if she wanted to ask, he changed the subject back. "Hey, have we looked at everything she gave you? I thought there was one more page after the thing about the developer."

Claudia checked again and there was, in fact, another page, so they turned to it. It was harder to read than the rest, having been copied from a densely typed booklet that had been produced for some long-ago historic home tour. The picture at the top was not of the marketplace/barn, but a large Victorian farmhouse, identified as the ancestral home of the Satler family, with their history described in brief. It wasn't clear how much this had to do with Claudia's property, but she read through it anyway, slowly, because in order to share the page with Nathan she had turned it sideways between them.

Nathan must have been a faster reader, or better at craning his head, because while Claudia was still on the part about the sons who fought in World War I, he stopped suddenly and said, "Well, THAT's interesting."

Claudia was about to ask, but he was already pointing to the paragraph below where she had been. She turned the page to face her and read:

*Prohibition posed an extra challenge for the farm, but the ingenious Harmon Satler was not about to be bested by the boys in Washington. He kept producing as much fine cider and brandy as ever, and business didn't suffer. On Saturday nights, the basement of the mansion became a speakeasy for those in the know, and legend has it their facility in San Elmo Bay handled shipping to far-flung parts, with some handy hidey-holes for when the authorities came knocking.*

"Handy hidey-holes," Claudia repeated. "That IS interesting."

"And fun to say," Nathan agreed. "Not to mention plural. I wonder if there are any more compartments like that?"

"That's a good question. I can't imagine where they would be, but I didn't exactly imagine the first one. I guess I had better take a look. I hope I don't find anything too surprising."

"Definitely," said Nathan, though his expression suggested he wouldn't mind a bit of a surprise. "It does explain a lot, though, doesn't it? That compartment looked old, and didn't you even say you smelled apples? It's too small for them to have stored much contraband in, but they could have kept the money there."

"Or the books for the illegal business. You wouldn't want to have those just lying around," said Claudia, who was aware of how much paperwork was involved in any kind of retail operation.

"Exactly." Nathan was starting to get excited about the idea. "It's one thing to have the feds catch you with some apple juice that's gone bad, but something else entirely if they get their hands on all your financials."

Those were probably not the words the twentieth century bootleggers would have used, but Claudia thought they would have agreed with the sentiment. She still had some questions, though.

"But where does Gowan come into this? Those weren't nineteen-twenties ledgers he was taking out of there in the middle of a party."

"Probably not," Nathan conceded. "But based on this, he must not have been the only person who knew the compartment was there. What if someone else had put something in it, that he was stealing?"

"It's possible." Claudia sighed. "Too many things are possible, and none of them make sense."

Nathan reached across the table and squeezed her hand.

"You'll figure it out," he said. "And if not, what's life without a little mystery in it?"

"It might have fewer dead people," Claudia said before thinking. She was so confused by the feeling of his hand on hers that she went with the first thing that came to mind, which was almost never a good idea. She tried to course-correct, but that didn't go well either. "I mean, of course, and thanks. If I never do find out, maybe I can just make something up to tell people? About the secret compartment. Not the murder. Oh, god."

Nathan laughed, and while Claudia had her head buried in her hands, he snagged the bill before the waitress had a chance to set it down. That ended the serious discussion part of the meal, and there wasn't much Claudia could do but to thank him for buying her lunch and try to come up with a reasonable next step.

"I guess I could go over to this house," she said, looking back at the last page. "It says here it's a museum now." There was something familiar about that and she frowned. "I wonder if this is the same historical society Gowan was involved with. That could be interesting, if it is."

"Sounds like a good place to start," Nathan agreed. "I'd come with you, but I left a load of glassware in the autoclave, and I have to get them out and cooling so I can get a batch of the ale going today."

Claudia tried to make noises like that made any sense to her, and they parted on good terms. She wasn't sure she had any more clarity about this part of her life than any other, but for now she decided she could be comfortable with that uncertainty.

There was another reason Claudia wanted to go to the museum, one that she didn't feel comfortable telling Nathan just yet. She wasn't generally very good at directions, but as it happened, she had recently been looking at a map of the area where the museum was located, not out of any burgeoning psychic powers but because Gowan's house was just down the street.

Though she had been surprisingly tempted, Claudia had decided against mentioning to Nathan anything about the promise she had made to Julie. Not that she was worried he would disapprove, or try to stop her—based on his predilection for crazy ideas of his own, she didn't think he would have much standing to object to hers. But she wasn't quite comfortable enough in her intentions to say them out loud, and even the thought had her reaching for defenses against arguments no one had made. Plus, there was no way of explaining her decision without bringing up the fact that Julie was under suspicion, and she knew enough to know that any piece of information shared at the Seagrass Diner, no matter how quietly, was guaranteed to become public knowledge in under an hour. The walls might not have ears, but Claudia suspected there were listening devices in the saltshakers.

The museum was located about halfway between San Elmo and the nearest town of any size, which put it approximately in the middle of nowhere. The houses here mostly dated to the late nineteenth and early twentieth century, when Sonoma County had been an agricultural center providing eggs, milk, and apples to the tables of San Francisco. Larger farms in the Central Valley and beyond had since stolen much of the region's thunder, and its income, and the higher margins of the craft and organic industries were the only hope for many of the historic businesses.

Of course, some had chosen a different path. As Claudia approached the address for the museum, the open fields gave way to an isolated housing development, a pastel island of close-packed stucco homes adrift in a sea of scrubland, built to house commuters willing to take on a multi-hour trip to the city, and the occasional local longing for the suburban experience. Then, as abruptly as it appeared, the mirage of middle America ended, replaced by an orchard of ancient and gnarled trees, heavy with unpicked fruit, where a small herd of deer were grazing on windfalls like they owned the place.

It was in this purpose-built neighborhood that Gowan had lived, when living was his thing, and as Claudia turned her car through the entrance that wasn't quite a gate, but was meant to look like one, she wondered what she was expecting to find here. Getting inside his house was out of the question—there had been quite enough of that sort of thing going on lately—and this didn't look like the sort of place where you could strike up a casual conversation with the neighbors. But she was here now, so she might as well take a look and see if inspiration felt like striking.

Despite the fact that she had the address, Gowan's house proved to be surprisingly hard to find. The roads in the development appeared to have been laid out by someone with a religious objection to straight lines and a personal goal of maximizing the number of cul-de-sacs, and Claudia had never been more grateful for her small car's ability to execute three-point turns.

There was also the problem of the area's near-total lack of cell phone signal cutting her off from the maps she relied on to find anything. That surprised Claudia at first, as out of step as it seemed when compared to the grasping modernity that otherwise described the place, but thinking about it, she recalled there having been some kind of fight over towers and land ownership that was currently working its way through the courts. So she was forced to leave her phone in the cup holder and navigate by the street signs, like it was the middle ages or something.

Eventually, Claudia found the house, located a block away from the entrance in the opposite direction from where she had made her first turn. It was identical to the other third of the houses in the development that had been built to the same blueprints—an oversized block that filled its tiny lot from edge to edge. The curtains on the picture windows were tightly drawn and newspapers were piling up on the front walk, but beyond that there was no indication that the owner wouldn't be coming back.

The emptiness of the house did at least answer one question; whatever the dimensions of Gowan's personal life had been, it was clear he had lived alone. It was a surprising amount of space for one person, but as someone who lived in less than five hundred square feet, Claudia supposed she wasn't one to judge.

Claudia had only been planning to take a look from the car before moving on to her next destination, but a glimpse of movement in the alley by the garage caught her eye. Memories of the previous night filled her mind, and for a moment she considered following the same course of action—namely, getting out of the way and calling the cops. But that carried risks of its own, like having to answer questions about what she was doing in this particular place. And seeing as the middle of the day on a street lined with houses wasn't exactly the same as an empty nighttime hillside, she decided that satisfying her curiosity was worth the risk.

She parker her car a few houses down and approached cautiously. Outside of the safety of the driver's seat, her plan felt like less of a good idea. The street was lined with plenty of houses, but no people, and the weight of her dead phone in her pocket only served to remind her of her isolation. But the sun was shining and the house across the street had a mailbox shaped like a rooster, and under those circumstances it was difficult for the fear to really take hold.

As she approached, it became clear that the movement she had seen around the side of the house had been no illusion. It was a man, dressed in cargo shorts and a short-sleeved shirt despite the chill in the air, and he was bent over one of Gowan's garbage cans, carefully sorting through the contents. He was a distinctly large individual, and for a moment Claudia's misgivings returned in full force. But then he straightened up to stretch a kink out of his back, giving her a clear view of his face, and her worries evaporated.

"Hello, Todd. Fancy meeting you here."

The man had ducked back into the trash can, and he stood up so quickly that he bumped his head on the lid.

"What the—oh, Claudia, hi. Nice day, isn't it?"

One thing Claudia could say about Todd Thompson, he was not subjected to excessive feelings of shame. Which, considering his career and ambitions, could only be a positive thing. He was a reporter for the largest of the local papers, and Claudia had dealt with him in that capacity once before, when a mutually beneficial exchange of information had led to him getting an opportunity to move from covering local events to a front-page byline, and to her narrowly avoiding being shot. Since then, they had developed something of a rapport—Claudia regularly ran into Todd and his husband Brian on the beach where they all walked their dogs, and they had discovered they had things in common, like a love of terrible sci fi movies and a hatred of cilantro. Still, she maintained her policy about reporters, which was still not to trust him any further than she could throw him, and that wouldn't be far. But, something something, the devil you know, and it wasn't like she was going to be able to get away from having a conversation now.

"As a matter of fact, I was hoping I'd have a chance to talk to you," he said, straightening up and leaning on the garbage can like it was a perfectly normal prop.

"You don't say," Claudia said, choosing not to bring up the four messages he had already left on her voicemail. "I don't think there's much I could tell you that's going to be more interesting than what you're going to find in . . . your current line of inquiry."

"What, this?" Todd looked at the garbage can like he was just noticing it for the first time. "Standard procedure. Of course, the police have already been through here, but you never know, they might have missed something. Speaking of which, what brings you here? This doesn't strike me as being your usual stomping grounds."

"Oh, you know, I was in the neighborhood, thought I'd stop by and take a look." Claudia didn't expect him to believe that, but she didn't entirely care. If Todd was going to try to spin a story out of her showing up at Gowan's house, he would have to be as short on leads as she was.

Which, considering his current occupation, she might have realized he was, and she might have anticipated his next question.

"About that latest murder of yours, would you like to share any insights as to what you think happened there?" It was difficult to transition from rummaging through someone's trash to asking tough investigative questions, but Todd did his best.

Claudia was having none of it.

"Of course not. And it's not 'my' murder. I don't have any murders."

The need for friendliness at the dog beach only went so far. Sensing he had crossed a line, and recognizing that he was at something of a disadvantage himself, Todd backed off and softened his approach.

"Of course, poor choice of words. That's me—foot, meet mouth.

Good thing I don't do this for a living. What I meant to say is, I'm sorry you had to find him like that. It must have been a terrible experience for you."

His smile was disarming, but even as she returned it, Claudia remained fully armed. Still, she wasn't going to be able to avoid this conversation forever, so she thought she might as well take advantage of having some control over the situation, and maybe try to do some information gathering of her own.

"Thank you," she said, attempting to apply some charm of her own. "It certainly wasn't anything I would like to repeat. But I barely knew Mr. Gowan; I'm sure it's his friends and loved ones who deserve our sympathy."

Todd responded with a very un-reporter-ish snort. "They would if they existed. I've been looking high and low for anyone who had a good word to say about the guy. Or at least who's going to inherit his stuff."

"No family?" That was interesting. Claudia wasn't surprised that Gowan was single, but it hadn't even occurred to her to think about what else he had in the way of relationships. She probably should have looked into the question sooner—ill-gotten or not, the man had clearly made a good amount of money, and that would be a motive if nothing else.

"None in the area," Todd said. "No spouse, no kids, just a younger sister and a couple of nephews in Montana. I've got some quotes from her in my story tomorrow. She didn't say much, but I don't think they were close."

That was a good amount of information for Todd to have shared with her, and Claudia knew from previous experience that that sort of thing didn't come for free. So she cast around in her memory for what she could offer in return that wouldn't get her name or her marketplace on the front page, but all she could come up with was one that Todd was likely to know about already.

"Speaking of him being unpopular, I suppose you heard about the guy who got in trouble for firing one of his guns? I couldn't believe when I heard that he kept them loaded."

"Oh, you mean Katlen Elliott? Yeah, that guy's not the sharpest tool in the shed. I tried to get him to give me a statement, and he said he wouldn't and then cussed me out, and turned around and wrote a whole post about it on his public Facebook page. I tried to put it in the story, but the editor cut it for length."

"Bummer," said Claudia, who now had the name of the man in question and a place to hear from him in his own words. "I wonder what the cops think of that."

"I'm pretty sure they have other things on their mind," Todd said, leaning into the implications. "There are some other people with holes in their alibis."

Claudia stared at him, uncomprehending, for a minute, until it dawned on her that he was making a reference to Dancing Cow's popular Swiss-style wheel. As innuendos went, that one was pretty weak, and Claudia responded accordingly.

"I wouldn't know about that," she said as flatly as she could manage, wondering how far and wide the news of Julie's visit to the police station had spread. "But I'll take your word for it."

Sensing that she had participated in this conversation for as long as was sensible, plus a bit, Claudia started to turn to head back to the car. Still, character being destiny and all, she couldn't quite resist getting in one last line.

"Anyway, good luck with your story. I hope you don't have to do too much digging for it."

"No worries," Todd said, smiling back sweetly. "I'll go as deep as I need to."

# CHAPTER NINE

As she drove away, Claudia tried and failed not to dwell on what he meant by that. Odds were Todd was just winding her up, the same way she was going after him, but she couldn't help but think he had a lot more capacity to make trouble for her than vice versa. It would be helpful, she decided, if by the next time she saw him, she had something to offer that wasn't already common knowledge.

She wasn't sure she was going to find such a thing at the former home of the family that had built the barn that had become her marketplace, but that was where she was headed. For a moment she was able to get her phone to connect to the network, just long enough to get an idea of how far she was from her destination. If nothing else, she thought, she could recognize the place from the field of gray squares around it.

In fact, it was just a short distance down the road, where after a stretch of orchards, a driveway appeared, with a sign marking it as the way to the "Satler Farm Historic Farm Museum." The sign could have done with a fresh coat of paint, and maybe some repairs from where something seemed to have been chewing on it, but its information was good. Claudia turned and followed increasingly smaller and less-clear signs until she came to the patch of flat dirt she assumed was the museum's parking lot, for want of a better explanation.

The museum itself was the same Victorian house she had seen in the printout, clearer now with the benefit of three dimensions and color. At some point in the past it had been done up in an elaborate gingerbread style, with every window frame and bit of trim painted in one of several contrasting colors, but time had not been kind to the pigments, and most had subsided to various shades of peeling greige. The front porch, which once must have made for a dramatic entry-way, had been redone in concrete, and now stood as half wheelchair ramp, and half storage for mechanical contraptions of indeterminate purpose.

In fact, Claudia realized as she got closer, a lot of the area seemed to be being used for that sort of thing. Next to the parking lot there were three rusting vehicles with what looked like rakes on their fronts, and behind those something that appeared to be a giant funnel on wheels. Claudia wasn't sure what any of them had to do with apple farming, but thanks to Julie she did know a milking machine when she saw one, which was why she was pretty sure that was what was sitting in front of the nearest outbuilding. She wondered if this was the sort of place where people brought the things they thought must be worth something, but would rather not have hanging around the house anymore.

It was the sort of question she might ask someone, if she ever found anyone to ask questions. There was one other car in the lot, an ancient truck that made Claudia's aging hatchback look like the height of auto-motive sophistication, but otherwise the place gave every impression of being deserted.

She tried the house first, but the door was locked, and from the way the windows were blocked by stacks of boxes, she had the impression that it wasn't open for visitors. Back in the parking lot, she considered her options. There wasn't anything so vital she had been hoping to learn here, but she was annoyed to have come all this way and not have gotten so much as an apple for her trouble. She was looking around for some sort of sign at least, so she might have an idea when to come back, when the door to the largest of the outbuildings opened and an elderly man stuck his head out.

"Hi! You're here for the tour?"

"Um, hi. No, actually, I was just stopping by because I had some

questions about the farm and, actually, a building they used to own."
That wasn't the most coherent answer, but it wasn't clear that it mattered, because it turned out it hadn't been a question.

"All right, well let me get the guest book and I can sign you in, and then we can get started."

It was hard for Claudia to guess the man's age—she put it somewhere between seventy and unknowable—but as he wasn't showing any other signs of hearing difficulties, she suspected he suffered more from a loss of listening. But, still hoping there might be some answers to be found here, and not sure what else she could do, she dutifully signed the repurposed wedding book he produced from under a chair on the porch, noting as she did that the most recent name before her own was from three weeks ago.

"Slow season? I've been having the same problem at my business—" she said, hoping to build some rapport and bring the conversation around to the marketplace. But her host was way ahead of her, turning the book around to read her name almost before she had finished writing it.

"Claudia Simcoe, where have I heard that before? You're new, aren't you?"

"Yes, I own the—"

"Oh, you're the one who bought the old barn building out at the coast," he completed for her. "The one that crazy guy was going to turn into a food court or something."

"It's more of an artisan marketplace," Claudia said, aware that she had fully lost control of the conversation.

"Right, of course." If the man had any sense that he had said anything wrong, he didn't show much sign of it. "Everything's so damn expensive there. Twelve dollars for a piece of cheese!"

"We do carry some more specialty products," Claudia admitted. "But if you saw the work that Elias and Julie and their team put into making their cheeses—"

"Oh, Julie, sure Julie. Nice lady. You're here to see the cheese press, then? Not sure what the big deal was with it, but she sure did seem excited about that thing."

Julie's excitement hadn't extended to mentioning it to Claudia, who was hearing about it for the first time.

"Julie is great," she agreed vaguely, having nearly given up hope of learning anything useful from this interaction. "Has she been involved with the museum for a long time?"

"Not very," the man said. "Ten years, maybe? Anyway, you said you wanted the tour? It's seven-fifty, unless you qualify for the student discount."

Claudia admitted she didn't, submitted to the inevitable, and dug into her purse for the full price.

Her host took her twenty and made change from a wad of bills in his pocket. "I didn't think so, but you have to ask. My name's Walter Lilly by the way. I'm here most days, except Monday and Tuesday because we're closed."

"Are you related to the Satler family?"

"Only by marriage," Walter said. "There's none of them left from the actual family. My mother's brother married one of the Satler girls, back in the thirties, and that's how I came to spend my time here. But not enough for them to leave me anything in the will!"

It was clearly a well-practiced joke, and Claudia laughed accordingly. There were a lot of things she could have been doing at that particular moment, and touring a semi-historic house was not high on the list. But she had come far enough that she wasn't sure how she was going to get out of it now and, lacking the nerve to make a run for it while she still had a chance, she decided she might as well stick it out and see if she could get her seven-fifty's worth.

In fact, it turned out that the house itself wasn't on the tour at all. "Problems with some of the floors," was all Walter said by way of explanation, and he seemed to think that was enough. Instead, he led her back the way he had come, to what was either a large shed or a small barn on the other side of the parking lot, where the substantial wooden doors and shiny new locks were the most well-kept things on the site.

The distance wasn't far, but it took a while for them to cover, mainly because Walter was using the time to give her roughly the same history of the farm and its owners that she had already read, slowing his already less-than-sprightly pace to stop and indicate various points of interest along the way, which she might have seen if they still existed.

"Over that way is where they used to have the barn for the horses that pulled the apple carts, before it burned down. There were no horses then, hadn't been for a long time. Mostly what they had in there were the sets for the high school drama department, because old Herb was sweet on their teacher. Rumor had it that the principal set the fire because he was jealous, but I don't know about that."

Claudia had nothing to offer on the point either, and from the size of the trees that had grown up where the barn in question had been, she doubted there was anyone still around who did. While Walter rattled on about thirdhand stories of long-ago scandals, she cast a sideways glance at him and tried to determine what would be the best approach to get him talking about her building.

The talking part wasn't a problem, at least. His patter was neither fast nor loud, but it was incessant, like a water tap with a broken valve. Beyond that, he was an unremarkable man, short and almost entirely bald, dressed in overalls that appeared to be almost as old as he was and which had, she noticed, some rather concerning stains. Claudia was wondering about that when he finished the story he was telling and looked at her expectantly.

"And of course, you'll be wanting to see the tractors."

Claudia did not want to see the tractors. What she wanted was to ask a series of very specific questions about the potentially illegal activities undertaken by the farm's former owners, and how those might have related to their coastal property holdings. But the man looked so hopeful, and no one had been here in three weeks, and who knew, maybe there would be something about this next stage of the tour that would be more enlightening.

So, long story short, she went to see the tractors.

As they approached the building, there was a definite change in Walter's attitude. Not that he hadn't been enthusiastic before, but there was something about the gleam in his eye as he pulled open the door that made Claudia wonder what could be in these sheds that was so interesting, and slightly worried that maybe she didn't want to know.

"And here we are!"

In the short walk across the parking lot, Claudia hadn't built up much in the way of expectations, but whatever she might have imagined, it wasn't this. What looked from the outside like a relatively modest outbuilding—too low for a barn, but wider than what Claudia typically thought of as a shed—opened out into a series of interconnected rooms around a courtyard. And filling them, packed from wall to wall, with only a narrow path down the middle that appeared to be in immediate danger of being consumed, was an enormous collection of what could only be described as Large Old Stuff.

There were spinning wheels and looms, butter churns and bandsaws. A row of rusting plows were lined up against one wall, near a large sign that read "A History of Barbed Wire, 1867–Present," with pieces of said wire exhibited below, tacked to a board. At least half of the items, Claudia had no idea what they were at all, and the print on the instructive cards was too small and faded to see from the distance. To help, some of the displays, like the grape crushing vat, had mannequins standing by to demonstrate their use, in the creepiest way possible.

Walter was still standing in the doorway, displaying the contents of the building with obvious pride. It was clear that Claudia was expected to say something, and gulping loudly and sprinting back to her car probably wasn't going to cut it. So she did the best she could, under the circumstances.

"Wow. This is quite a collection," she said, with absolute honesty. That didn't seem to be quite enough, so she cast around for something to add.

"Is that the cheese press?" she asked, approaching one of the displays. She wouldn't have guessed it at all, if it wasn't for the giant plastic cheese that had been positioned next to it. The item looked more like the product of a teenage dungeon master's fevered imagination than any piece of equipment Claudia had seen at the creamery. An enormous round stone sat on a solid wooden platform with a threaded bar as thick as her arm rising from the stone to a frame above it. A handle around the bar suggested that the threads were meant to raise and lower it, in case the weight of a small boulder wasn't enough pressure for the unfortunate cheese underneath it.

"Yes, it's really something, isn't it?" Walter said, with less enthusiasm than someone might expect from a museum keeper speaking about an absolutely enormous cheese press. "That was Julie's doing. Some cheese place out in Wisconsin was going out of business and they had this sitting out in their front office. Cost a pile to get it shipped here, I'll tell you that. But I guess it was used to make a cheese that made the record in forty-seven, and the board thought that was a good enough reason to have it, even though someone else got the record the next year."

Claudia suspected that expense was at the root of her host's disinterest in the cheese press, and wondered what he had hoped to buy instead. But there were other things she was more curious about, and she finally thought she had an opportunity to get to them.

"Mr. Gowan used to be on your board, didn't he? Was he involved in the decision to get the cheese press?"

Immediately, Walter's face clouded over, and what had been an expression of mild annoyance became something closer to fury.

"No, and he wouldn't have been interested if he was. He was only in favor of things if they went bang or filled his pockets."

If that wasn't an opening to speak some ill of the recently dead, Claudia hadn't heard one, so she took a breath and dove right in.

"You know, I had a weird experience with him just before he died, and I was actually wondering if you could help me figure it out. He was at an event we held at the marketplace this week, and while he was there, he found some sort of secret compartment in the wall and took something out. And I was just wondering, since the building used to be part of the Satler family property, if you might know anything about that?"

"Well, that lying—" Here, Walter seemed to remember he was talking to a stranger about a murdered man and did his best to reign in his emotions.

"There've been rumors about there being some sort of secret spaces in that building, going back to the prohibition," he said. "We tried to prove them, but the owners weren't interested."

"Do you mean Mr. Tolman? I've been meaning to get in touch with him." Some sort of automatic impulse had kept Walter continuing the tour as they talked, and they stopped now in front of the grape vat, where a barefoot mannequin stood awkwardly next to a pile of plastic grapes.

"No, this was long before he came around. After old Mr. Satler died there were some issues with the people who owned the property, and it eventually ended up being bought by some developers." He said the last word in a tone other people might reserve for Satanists, or wasps.

"But someone must have found it," Claudia said. "Gowan clearly knew where it was, and he had a key."

"I'll bet he did." That seemed to be more of an expression of exasperation than an admission of knowledge, so Claudia let it pass without commenting.

"That's just like Clark," Walter fumed. "I can just see him sitting there in the board meetings, chuckling away whenever anyone mentioned the treasure."

"Treasure?" This was a complication that Claudia hadn't even considered up until now.

"That was part of the rumor. The idea was the Satler boys made so much money selling applejack to the speakeasies, they converted it into gold and hid it in the barn, to avoid paying taxes."

"It didn't look like treasure that he took out of the compartment," Claudia said carefully. As intrigued as she was by the prospect of discovering a trove of gold bars in her walls, she was less excited about the idea that other people might show up and try to do the same thing. But Walter was quick to disabuse her of that particular worry.

"Of course not. There was never any treasure; any money they made went right back to the speakeasies. But I guess there was a compartment after all." Walter shook her head. "And of all the people to have found it. It was probably his developer buddies who did the actual finding. He was supposed to be on our side, but every time anyone saw him, he was palling around with one of those characters."

Claudia wasn't interested in whose side anyone was on, but she was relieved to finally get some solid information about at least one of her questions. So Gowan had found out about the compartment from the people who had owned the building after the family sold it, and kept the information to himself, or at least away from his fellow history buffs, for reasons of his own. It didn't get Claudia any closer to knowing what he had taken from it at the time of the party, or why, or who had come by after Gowan's death to commit some light vandalism on her walls, but at least it was a start.

The thought of the late-night invader reminded Claudia of another question she had.

"How many of these compartments were there supposed to be? The one we found wouldn't have been big enough to hide bottles of liquor in it. Could there be others we haven't found yet?"

"It's a possibility, but if there are they wouldn't be for storing the product. That was kept in apple crates with false bottoms. I've heard there are still a few of them around, but we haven't been able to get one for the museum yet. Now, if you found one of those, that's something we'd be interested in."

Claudia agreed that she would keep her eyes open, thought she wasn't sure she would recognize a trick apple crate if she saw one. Still, she could see the appeal of having such a thing in the museum, where the exhibits she had seen so far didn't really seem to have a lot to do with the place, or each other.

As though to illustrate her point, at that moment they passed out of the first shed building into the courtyard, open on one side to the orchards, where a series of tractors that seemed to represent different stages in tractor history, stood under a carport (tractorport?) of dubious stability.

"These," Walter said with obvious pride. "Are our tractors."

Claudia spent the next twenty minutes drowning in a sea of tractor facts, nodding occasionally as cylinder numbers, the relative benefits of wheels versus tracks, and the luxury of optional fenders floated past her head. As Walter waxed poetic about the introduction of lowered seats for orchard work, Claudia thought she was beginning to understand what was behind what she was looking at here. She had had a friend in college whose father had developed a passion for midcentury gas station paraphernalia, and the first time she had visited their house, she remembered feeling a similar sense of disorientation when faced with the rows of signs, oil cans, and an actual, almost-working pump. In Walter's case, tractors were the passion, and the disorganization of the rest of the museum's collection could be attributed to the fact that it wasn't tractors.

"It's clear that a lot of work has gone into this place," Claudia said, when she had a chance to get a word in. "Were you involved in it from the beginning?"

"Before the beginning," Walter confirmed. "Back when old Mr. Satler was still alive, he loved going to sales and auctions of old farm equipment, but his eyesight wasn't so good. He needed someone to come along and drive and read the labels. He taught me more than I ever thought there was to know about the history of machinery in the Californian farm. That's what he wanted to share with the world, and that's what we're trying to do."

"I understand," said Claudia, who almost did. If there was ever a time to put all her cards on the table, this was it. "I feel the same way about my marketplace. The people, their businesses and products—I really think they deserve to have everyone know about them. That's what has me so worried about what Gowan might have been doing there before he died. Everyone keeps talking about how untrustworthy he was, but I can't get any specifics, and I didn't know him well enough to judge for myself."

She stopped for a breath and to gauge her audience. Walter wasn't exactly giving her a standing ovation, but there was a definite sympathy in his expression, along with a wariness that Claudia couldn't quite account for.

"Who was this guy?" Claudia pressed. "And what could he possibly have wanted to hide in the walls of my marketplace?"

There was a pause, and Claudia started to worry that she had overplayed her hand. But apparently the older man was merely marshaling his thoughts, because when he did speak, it was with vigorous conviction.

"I don't truly know the answer to either of those questions, and I'm not sure there's anyone on this side of the grave who does. Clark Gowan was not good at many things, but when it came to dirty tricks, don't think I've ever known anyone who could match him."

He found a stool that had been left next to one of the tractors and sat down, grimacing like he had been on his feet too long. Claudia leaned against a stack of apple crates and gave him her full attention.

"The first time I met Clark was not long after Herb—old Mr. Satler—died. His will was confusing, and the heirs wanted to sell, and we were just trying to get the historical society off the ground. So it seemed like a blessing that here was this lawyer who knew all about property laws and who was as excited about history as we were, who was going to help us get it all straightened out."

"I guess that's not quite how it worked?" Claudia asked.

Walter gave her a look. "Not hardly. At first everything seemed fine, he helped us draw up all the paperwork and deal with the questions from the county. And things started to not go so smoothly with the heirs, so we needed all the help we could get. Clark wasn't anyone's favorite person, but at least he was on our side, or so we thought. That was until the thing with the guns."

"Guns?" Claudia knew that Gowan's story ended with violence, but she hadn't expected that part to come so soon. "How did guns get involved?"

"When Clark was around, guns were always involved. That's what we found out, anyway. He wanted to make the whole museum into a kind of shrine to them, and he had used the property deal to make changes to our charter, so he would have final say on exhibits. At least that's what he claimed, and where were we going to get the money for another lawyer?"

"But he didn't get his way." Claudia hadn't seen a single weapon on the entire tour, so she felt fairly confident in making it a statement and not a question, but Walter answered anyway.

"Not totally. It's a long story, but let's just say the museum ended up a lot poorer, and there are some new townhomes where a beautiful old orchard used to be." He looked out of the courtyard toward the remaining apple trees as though he expected a bulldozer to leap out from behind one of them. "To be honest, I'm not sure that wasn't his plan all along." His expression darkened. "Not that that explains why he kept at it, even after he'd made his money. That's just him being the terrible person that he is. Was. Anyway, I'm nothing but glad he's never going to show up here again."

Driving back to her home, Claudia thought about what she had and hadn't learned. That Gowan was an unpleasant and unpopular man, she had already known, though it was helpful to have some more details. Everything she learned left her more convinced it was going to be vital to find out what he had been hiding in her walls. What she didn't know was how she was going to do that.

Another thing, if she was being honest, was how much time she really should be devoting to the project. This might be the market's slow season, but the holidays were coming, and regardless of what she had promised Julie, there were some things she should be doing that didn't fall under the heading of "investigating a man's death." As a compromise, she promised herself that she would spend the rest of the day doing nothing that wasn't her actual job, a plan that lasted almost as long as it took for her to park her car and get through the marketplace's front door.

"There's a man here to see you." Robbie's greeting was abrupt and unusually nervous, but Claudia didn't have time to ask what was up. Shaking off Teddy's significantly more cheerful hello, she followed the charcutiere to her office, where her visitor was waiting.

The man standing awkwardly in the tiny room didn't look like a tourist. He was wearing a dark gray suit that looked like it had been packed in a hurry, and unpacked in anger, and black leather shoes that spoke more of orthopedic comfort than Italian style. Claudia placed his age at around forty and his origins on the East Coast, because no self-respecting Californian under seventy would wear a tie this close to the beach.

Apparently unaware of the assessment he was undergoing, the newcomer offered his hand and a friendly smile.

"Claudia Simcoe? Nice to meet you. My name's Jim Nguyen. I'm with the FBI."

# CHAPTER TEN

"Nice to meet you too," said Claudia, who couldn't think of anything else. "Are you . . . hmm."

There seemed like there would be a lot of things that would be a bad idea to say to a surprise FBI agent, and Claudia was interested in avoiding most, if not all of them. Finally, she settled on what she thought would be a safe choice.

"Is there something I can help you with?"

"I just wanted to ask you a few questions. Is this an okay place to talk?"

Claudia looked around and thought about that. Her "office" was barely more than a closet, tucked into a corner of the marketplace between Robbie's cured meats shop and Eugene's honeys, with barely enough room for the old office chair and folding desk she had salvaged from her former employer's going-out-of-business dumpster. Lately, she had been making an attempt to clear it out a bit, with the result that it was now technically possible for two people to stand inside, as long as they weren't too large and didn't have any significant issues around personal space. It would not have been Claudia's first choice of a place to meet with federal law enforcement, except that she didn't have any others.

The marketplace was still open, with at least a smattering of customers, and even if she could have turned out one of the vendors from their space, it wouldn't have mattered because none of the shops had doors. The only other option was to suggest relocating to her house, but having Agent Nguyen escorting her across the field in view of a couple dozen pairs of curious eyes, and explaining to him about the geese, was not appealing. Plus, while she didn't seriously doubt his credentials, going to a more isolated place with a man she had just met, entirely on the basis of the (realistic looking, but still) badge he had shown her, did not strike Claudia as the best of all possible decisions.

So, the office it was. Fortunately, the agent was a slender man, and if the close quarters made him uncomfortable, he didn't show it. By Claudia sitting on the corner of the desk, and Nguyen standing with his back pressed against the door, they managed to maintain an almost professional level of distance. The thin light that made it into the room through the one small, high window was supplemented by a single bare bulb mounted on the ceiling, and together they cast a variety of shadows that made the scene either stark or surreal, depending on how you looked at it.

Mostly, though, it was just stuffy.

"I'll be recording this interview, if it's all right with you," Nguyen said, as he placed his phone faceup on the desk. It didn't really sound like a question, but Claudia agreed anyway, because she wasn't sure what other options she had. His first few questions were basic; how long had she owned the marketplace, where had she been living and what had she been doing before moving here, what inspired her to buy the business. (Answers: Three years, San Francisco as a computer programmer, that was a good question—let's say it seemed like a good idea at the time.) He took no notes, keeping a steady but not unfriendly gaze on Claudia's face the entire time she spoke, and even smiled a couple of times at her jokes. Claudia was impressed, but not fooled, and it was almost a relief when he got to the end of his opening questions and there was a subtle change in Nguyen's tone.

"You had an event here two days ago, is that correct?"

"Yes," Claudia said. "A benefit for the Friends of the Library. We called it a harvest dinner, even though we aren't exactly harvesting much around here right now, the grapes were early this year—" Claudia realized she was babbling and cut herself of abruptly. "That is, yes."

"And during this event, I understand something unusual happened, that you didn't find out about until later?"

Claudia had been operating on a kind of a base level assumption that this was going to be about Gowan—after all, if you find the body of a murdered man and shortly thereafter an FBI agent shows up in your office, there's a good chance those things are connected—but she still found herself unnerved by being forced to confront it. As of this conversation, she was now definitely involved in some sort of federal investigation, and everything she had read told her that was a risky place to be.

"A few things happened," she said, trying to be more cautious with her information. "Can you be more specific?"

Nguyen smiled. "I'm not talking about the frog, Ms. Simcoe. My understanding is that a man named Clark Gowan removed one or more items from the building during the party, and you have evidence of that."

"That's true. While we were cleaning up, we found a door to a hidden cabinet in one of the walls had been left ajar, and when we reviewed the security camera footage, it appeared that Mr. Gowan opened it and took something out." That seemed safe, and factual enough. It occurred to Claudia to wonder what sort of interest the FBI could have had in Gowan's murder. After all, this should have been the jurisdiction of the local police, with nothing about it that obviously made it a federal crime. Had Gowan's property crimes really risen to the level of drawing government interest? Or was there something more going on here? Was Gowan some sort of secret agent? A serial killer? A former mobster who had been living in San Elmo as part of a witness relocation program? None seemed very likely, but here she was. The only thing Claudia was sure of was that if Iryna ever found out, they were never going to hear the end of it.

"What did he take?"

"I don't know. It looked like an envelope, or a flat package of some sort. Something small enough that he could hide it inside his coat."

"And you have no idea what might have been in the package?"

"None at all. I didn't even know that compartment was there. It wasn't mentioned when I bought the building, or included in the disclosures."

Any hopes Claudia might have had that that would shake out some more information about her building's history were dashed by the continued immobility of the agent's expression.

"I'd like to get a copy of that video from you, if that's all right," he said.

"Sure, I can do that. The police already have it, by the way." That brought up another question for Claudia. "I actually told them all of this. Does Chief Weaver know you're talking to me?"

"The local police are aware of our investigation."

That wasn't much of an answer, but Claudia didn't know how much more she could have expected. Her role here was clearly as a source of information, not an active participant, which was obviously how it should be. Any concerns she might have about what had happened were nobody's problem but her own, and that wasn't going to change no matter who was doing the investigating.

Still, despite herself, she felt a pang of irritation on the police chief's behalf. Not that they were friends or anything, but in their brief encounter, Claudia had been impressed by Weaver's quiet competence, and it felt unfair that her first big opportunity to prove herself in her new job would be being usurped by a more powerful outside agency. Nguyen didn't strike her as the type to show up and start throwing his weight around, but he was here and presumably that meant he was in charge, however pleasant he might seem.

If Nguyen noticed her distraction, he showed no sign of it. He went on casually, like they were making small talk at a party while they both waited for more interesting people to turn up.

"And you went to visit Mr. Gowan's office on the day after the dinner?"

Claudia confirmed that it was so, and for the next few minutes she abandoned her attempts to satisfy her own curiosity and went through the events of the previous day one more time, trying to keep it as brief as possible without being actively misleading. Not that she didn't want to help, but the spot she had chosen on the edge of the desk was growing increasingly uncomfortable, and she had heard a couple of creaks from the legs that made her nervous.

Finally, Nguyen picked up his phone from where he had set it on the other side of the desk and smiled at her again.

"I think that just about covers it for now. If you find out anything else about what might have been in that package, please let me know as soon as possible. My cell phone number is on the card, and you can also reach me at the Tyler guest ranch. I think you know it?"

Claudia certainly did, and she also knew that Betty was about to get an earful about her guest, just as soon as he ended his interrogation. Now that she thought about it, she realized that his name sounded familiar, that he was the person Betty had mentioned as being a foodie who was interested in possibly holding an event at the market.

And that conversation had taken place on the night of the dinner. Which had happened before Gowan's murder. Which meant that either an FBI agent just happened to have been vacationing near the scene of the crime, or there was more going on here than she had originally thought.

"You aren't really here about the murder, are you?" she said, as realization dawned. "He was involved with something else that you were investigating, and then he got murdered, right?"

Claudia wasn't sure if the expression that flickered across Nguyen's face was irritation with her continued questions or exasperation that it had taken her so long to figure that out.

"I'm not at liberty to discuss an ongoing investigation," he said, in a very federal agent sort of way. "Thank you for your time."

There didn't seem to be any way for Claudia to continue pressing the conversation that wouldn't get her into a really unreasonable amount of trouble, so she followed the agent out of her office, into the blessedly open and fresh air of the marketplace (which only smelled a little bit like cabbage at the moment, thanks to Helen's new batch of sauerkraut).

People were staring, probably because Claudia didn't often go into her office with strange men and close the door, so as she escorted him out of the marketplace she tried her hand at some casual conversation.

"How do you like the food at the ranch, by the way? Betty is really known for her cooking."

That, at least, didn't seem to be on the list of banned questions. This time, Nguyen's smile was completely genuine.

"It's fantastic. As a matter of fact, I'm something of a gourmand myself, and I've been hearing a lot lately about the food scene in San Elmo Bay. So it's been exciting for me to get a chance to have such an authentic experience."

He sounded so much like a magazine writer that for a moment Claudia suspected this was some kind of bizarre long con for a story. But that would be too much to hope for, and as Claudia walked her guest to the door under the watchful eyes of everyone still in the marketplace, she considered the danger of hoping for things.

When they reached the exit, Nguyen stopped, extended his hand, and smiled again. "Please, if you think of or find out anything you think might be important, let me know."

Claudia promised she would, wondering as she did if he knew about her own attempts at investigating. But it probably hadn't been a sincere request anyway; more likely it was the kind of thing FBI Agents said to everyone they interviewed, just in case.

For dinner that night, Claudia had meant to turn some extra sausage and vegetables (from Robbie and Orlan, respectively—anything in the marketplace that was near its sell-by date was generally put up for grabs) into soup, because she felt like it had been a soup kind of day. But she kept getting distracted, first by wondering how bad Gowan's crimes had been to draw the attention of the FBI, then by worrying about Julie being under suspicion and the rash promise she had made to her, and finally ending up in the place she had been avoiding all day, in memories of finding Gowan's body. It took Teddy trying to sneak a bite of sausage off the counter to snap her out of it, at which point she realized she had boiled almost all the liquid out of the pot.

Claudia stared at it for a while, and then shrugged.

"Okay, so now it's a stew."

To complete the confusion, she daubed a spoonful of Julie's crème fraîche on top, and sat down to eat whatever it was, while she thought about her bigger problems.

She was fairly sure by now that whatever Gowan had been getting from the secret compartment must have had something to do with the FBI investigation. Which, in the interests of simplicity, she was going to assume for the time being had to do with the crimes she already knew he was helping other people commit. That would explain the urgency that had driven him to take the risk of doing it during the party; if he knew the feds were closing in on him, he might have wanted to get whatever compromising material he had been storing there under his control before Nguyen or one of his colleagues found it instead.

That even made sense, in a way. After all, if what she had learned was true, the original purpose of the compartment was to store evidence of illegal transactions. Maybe Gowan was such a history buff that he had felt an obligation to carry on the local tradition. Some people liked to dress up in costumes, some people re-enacted battles, his thing was criminal conspiracies.

Which, if it was anything like what had happened, definitely opened up the possibilities for who might have wanted to kill Gowan. Claudia had been operating on the assumption that the likeliest suspects were among the victims of his crimes (a list that, unfortunately, did include Julie, a fact she was going to have to seriously consider at some point). But what if this new development meant his clients were threatened? Claudia didn't know what happened to FBI investigations when the person they were investigating died, but she could at least believe there were people who would be willing to take the chance.

Or maybe it didn't have to be so speculative. Julie had said that in her confrontation with Gowan, he had seemed triumphant; hardly the expected attitude for a man who was desperately trying to keep incriminating documents out of the hands of law enforcement. Maybe whatever was in that envelope wasn't so bad for him as it was for his clients, and he was planning to hand it over in exchange for clemency for himself.

She blew on a spoonful of soup-stew to cool it and considered the possibilities. Presumably, Julie would have mentioned if her ex-husband had been seen anywhere around town, though Claudia supposed it was possible he had managed to pass unnoticed. But would he have been able to do that, and still find out about Gowan getting into the marketplace wall? Claudia had no idea how many friends he might still have in town, but she had to imagine the Venn diagram of people who would have been able to share that news within a few hours of the theft, and people who wouldn't mention to anyone they had seen him wouldn't have a significant overlap.

Now that she thought of it, Claudia was having trouble coming up with any scenario where someone who wasn't already in town could have been the killer, if her theory about Gowan's death being connected to the package was correct. Assuming Gowan didn't inform his killer ahead of time of his intentions, he or she would have had to hear about it no earlier than 10:00 p.m. or so, when Claudia had reviewed the footage and informed anyone in the vicinity of what she saw. If Julie's deductions from her interview with the police were correct, and Gowan had been killed first thing in the morning, that left less than twelve hours for the killer to receive that information, decide what to do about it, get to Gowan's office, and shoot him. Claudia wasn't saying it was impossible to fit some travel time in there, but it did seem like there might be a simpler explanation available.

Claudia dipped a piece of bread into the bowl and watched it soak up some of the residual liquid, and wondered if there was a way to arrange an interview with Gowan's law partner, and try to get some answers out of her. The idea had the appeal of being undeniably direct, but it was somewhat lacking in terms of being something that might actually work. Claudia's connection to the case was tenuous enough for even a normal person to be unwilling to share information with her—a lawyer who was presumably aware by now that her business partner was being investigated by the FBI seemed exceptionally unlikely to be in a sharing mood, even if Claudia hadn't pushed her down a (short) flight of stairs.

She went through the other options—from staking out the law office and seeing if anyone returned to the scene of the crime (probably not a good idea), to trying to find someone with access to the police case to fill her in (worse idea, unlikely to work), to convincing Betty to let her use the ranch's internet system to hack into Agent Nguyen's computer (really, extremely bad idea).

In fact, none of her ideas were any good at all, unlike her dinner, which had actually turned out pretty well. Claudia was congratulating herself for her own ingenuity, and even contemplating taking a picture so she could share her achievement in piling random ingredients into a bowl, when her own foolishness reminded her of an investigative avenue she ought to be pursuing. Because if what she wanted was a simpler answer to the question of who might have killed Gowan, shouldn't she at least be considering the man who had apparently been threatening him?

According to Todd, at least some of those threats had taken place on the guy's own social media, and once she remembered his name it didn't take her long to find them. Katlen Elliot proved to be a man in his late twenties, still living in San Elmo Bay, all information he had left as public on the site, along with everything else. As Todd had said, privacy settings were something he didn't seem to have grasped, along with the concept of self-incrimination, and basic grammar. Wading through the sentence fragments and creative spellings, Claudia was able to tease out the basic gist of his complaints.

It was clear that, in Katlen's mind at least, he was the real victim here, regardless of who else might or might not be dead. His defense of having gotten into a customer's personal gun collection used the phrase "attractive nuisance" regularly and pretty much at random, and his argument for why he shouldn't have been punished for firing the gun, as far as she could follow it, was that firing a gun was the natural consequence of having found a gun, and therefore the only person who was responsible for his actions was Gowan, who had left it there in the first place. Claudia didn't find this line of reasoning very compelling, but most of his friends seemed to, judging by their supportive responses to the post. Some of them went so far as to make comments suggesting that he had taken care of the problem personally. Claudia was fairly sure they were joking, but the fact that Katlen had not contradicted any of them and had, in fact, responded to all of the comments with a laughing emoji was not a great look.

She assumed the police had already seen and recorded the post, but Claudia took screenshots just in case. At this point she wasn't seeing anything that looked like a solid clue among all the ranting, but prior experience had taught her that you didn't always see clues when they were in front of you, and it paid to be thorough.

The rest of his posts were even less enlightening. Claudia spent a while surfing through them, but she only learned that he admired dirt bikes he couldn't afford, never met a factually inaccurate meme he wouldn't share, and lacked a basic understanding of the rules of football. She made it far enough back to find the posts from around the time Gowan had gotten him fired, five years ago, and they were about what she expected; equal parts badly spelled and ill-advised, but lacking any concrete details that would suggest Katlen was anything but an angry and not very smart young man blowing off steam.

One thing that was of interest was the links he featured at the bottom of every post, even the ones that were more than fifty percent profanity, advertising his handyman business. As the owner of a vintage building, it was realistic that Claudia might be in need of handyman services, because it was entirely true. She was pretty sure it was a bad idea to hire someone solely based on your suspicion that they might be a murderer, but on the other hand, there was bound to be something she could find for him to do that wouldn't put her in too much danger. So she followed the link to Katlen's (extremely basic) website, wondered briefly how hard it would be to run some sort of phishing operation to get access to all of his computers, decided against it, and filled out the contact form to ask for a quote.

# CHAPTER ELEVEN

The next day dawned cool and clear, with no sign of rain on the horizon (or in the forecast). Claudia was starting to worry, not because she was such a fan of wet weather, but the longer it went before the rains started, the longer the fire season would be. So every day she checked the app on her phone, hoping for the time when the walk from her cottage to the marketplace became a muddy slog, so at least she could stop thinking about evacuation routes for the next eight months.

But she had other things to worry about right now. Claudia and Teddy arrived at the marketplace a good half hour before opening, but several of her tenants were already there, including Robbie, who was deep in consideration of a clog in the drain under the refrigerator where he kept his fresh cuts of pork. He mentioned he hadn't had any luck so far, adding that he really needed to be getting back to the farm to deal with the sausages he had left on the smoker. Claudia, who could recognize a call to action when she heard one, told him she would deal with it, and he headed for his truck while she went to find a bigger plunger.

Twenty minutes later, she had progressed to a drain snake, and was cautiously optimistic that she was making progress, when she heard the sound of a familiar cough from the entrance to the shop. She looked up to find Nathan standing there, looking more awkward than usual, if that was possible.

"Sorry to interrupt," he said. "Is this a bad time?"

"It's not a great one," Claudia admitted. "But that's nothing to do with you. What's up?"

"Ah, well, I just wanted to tell you." He paused, looked at what

Claudia was doing, and frowned. "Um, I think it actually works better if you turn it clockwise."

"Oh. Huh." Claudia tried it, and she had to admit that the tool did spin more freely than it had been, with an accompanying surge of unpleasantness rising to the top of the drain.

"Thanks. Is that what you came by to tell me?"

Nathan laughed, which Claudia had come to learn for him meant something between a hiccup and a gasp.

"No, just happy to help. I had to do that a lot in the early days of the brewery. What I wanted to tell you is that my credit card just got pwned, and I think it was in person somewhere, because it wasn't the one I use online. So I just wanted to get the word out, there's somewhere around here that's got a security problem.

That was all he needed to say for Claudia to abandon her pursuit of whatever lurked in the pipes, and head straight for the nearest credit card reader. Nathan's slang might be a little out of date, but Claudia was of the same internet era, and if there was a business in the area whose customers were having their personal and/or financial information stolen, she desperately hoped it was not hers.

On first inspection, none of the paypoint stations for any of the shops seemed to have been tampered with, and as she ran through the software diagnostics, Nathan explained what had happened.

"I got a call from my bank this morning, asking if I had just bought a bicycle and thirteen pairs of socks, in Florida. I told them no, so they stopped the charges, plus a few more I saw on my statement. How do you even spend eighty dollars at Taco Bell?"

Claudia didn't know, and she didn't like to think about what would happen if one tried.

"Anyway, it's not a big deal, but it was kind of a pain, and I thought I'd get the word out, because the customer service guy said they'd been seeing a lot more of these lately around here."

"Thanks, I appreciate it." Satisfied, for the moment, that whoever had their security compromised, it wasn't her, Claudia was able to unbend a bit. They were in her office, where she was setting up an extra monitoring program to track any data the credit card readers sent out over the network, just to be safe, and the tight quarters reminded her of what had come up the last time she was there.

"It sure seems like there's a lot of crime going on around here," she said. "Did anyone tell you about the FBI agent?"

They hadn't, so Claudia spent the next ten minutes filling Nathan in on this additional detail in Gowan's surprisingly dishonest life. He agreed that with Julie's information, it did seem fairly likely that that was what Nguyen was after, and also that things didn't look great for Julie.

"Does she need a lawyer? None of the ones who've worked for me do criminal defense, but I'm sure they know some people."

Considering that the sale of Nathan's former company had involved some top-flight corporate attorneys, (apparently to the surprise of the larger conglomerate that was doing the buying, who thought they were going to have an easier time of it than they did) Claudia thought that was a more promising route than Elias's friend. So she thanked him and said she'd suggest it to Julie.

Claudia didn't mention her own plans to help. Somehow it didn't seem like the moment.

Having shared what he had come to tell, and learned more than he probably expected, Nathan eventually noticed the time.

"I should probably get moving," he said. "There's a few more places I want to stop by today, and I have an appointment at four with a guy who's selling an HPLC."

Claudia couldn't imagine what he could want with a complicated piece of scientific equipment, but she was sure she would find out soon enough. So she thanked him again and resisted the urge to ask if he wanted to come over for dinner. (Not because she was afraid of rejection so much as she wasn't sure she had more than one clean plate.) But

Nathan must have been thinking along about the same lines, because as their paths diverged in front of the charcuterie shop, he stopped and smiled awkwardly.

"Hey, so I know you've got a lot going on right now, but there's a new restaurant out on Route 362 I've been meaning to try, and I was wondering if you wanted to go there with me tomorrow night. I know it's short notice, I just heard from a friend that they have a couple tables available. Anyway, it sounds like an interesting place, so I thought you might like it."

"Yeah, okay. I mean, sure, that sounds great. What time?"

They agreed Nathan would come by her house at six, and they would go in his car, which smelled less of dog than Claudia's. She went back to her work on the drain feeling elated, a sensation that lasted almost all the way through the moment the clog fully gave way, soaking her knees in a substance probably best described as "pig juice."

All in all, it was a mixed sort of day so far.

Claudia had gone back home for a change of clothes and a quick shower, and she was drying her hair when there was a knock at the cottage door. Hoping it wasn't another effluent-related emergency, and wondering if she could plausibly make an escape if it was, she opened the door and was surprised to find, for the second time in four days, Kathy Finley on the other side.

When your only interaction with a person has been to accidentally punch them after they hit you with their purse, one might be forgiven for feeling somewhat tense at your next meeting. So Claudia spent what felt like ages (but was probably only twenty seconds) staring at the woman on her step, trying to think of something to say. Ms. Finley must have had a similar thought because for a moment she didn't speak either. Claudia was starting to wonder if this was a leadup to her being sued—for aggravated stair-pushing or unlicensed body-finding, or something—but eventually her guest was able to find her voice and put her fears to rest.

"I hope you don't mind me intruding on you like this," she said. "I just thought I should stop by and apologize for what happened the other day. I want you to know I don't usually hit people when I meet them, it's just that when you told me about Clark I—well, I don't know what I was thinking."

"Oh, sure. I mean, of course, I understand. It's not the sort of thing anyone expects, first thing in the morning."

Obviously, at any other time of day it would be perfectly normal to arrive at work and have a stranger tell you your colleague was dead. Sometimes, Claudia was less than impressed with her speaking ability.

Fortunately, her guest didn't seem bothered by her gaffe. She smiled and agreed, and eventually Claudia figured that she should probably invite her in. Ms. Finley accepted cheerfully, examining the cottage with open curiosity as she entered.

"Clark did say this was a small place, but I didn't realize how small he meant. This really is very small," she said, as though this was something that might have escaped Claudia's attention before now.

"Yes," Claudia agreed. "It's not large at all."

Having exhausted that avenue of conversation, they lapsed into silence for another long moment. Claudia was trying to think of a way to bring up the topic of who might have wanted to kill Clark Gowan, and/or whether such a thing could have been related to her property, but it turned out her guest was way ahead of her.

"I heard about Clark's little adventure at the party the other night. That must have been what you were at the office to see him about?"

"It was," Claudia confirmed. "Do you have any idea what he might have been hiding there? Or why he used the marketplace?"

Ms. Finley sighed. "As for your first question, I have no idea. Clark enjoyed having a lot of secrets, and most of them weren't very interesting. Honestly, I wouldn't put it past him to have come up with some silly thing to hide there, just to know he had it hidden. He loved anything to do with history and outlaws; it probably tickled him to be using the Satler's secret prohibition cupboard."

It wasn't too far off of one of the theories Claudia had already considered and rejected, and she didn't think much more of it now. Maybe in a situation that didn't involve a federal agent and a dead body she would have been more receptive to the wacky hijinks line of reasoning, but as things were she needed some more solid information.

"Ms. Finley—"

"Please, call me Kathy."

"Kathy. What I was wondering is, did you ever have any sense that some of the work Clark was doing might be, you know, a little on the sketchy side?" Claudia didn't really want to come out and say the man was knee-deep in fraud, and for his business partner to have overlooked that, she would have to have either been apocalyptically oblivious, or complicit. But she didn't see a way forward in this conversation without addressing it, and sometimes the only way out was through.

And, in fact, Kathy didn't even seem terribly upset by the implications of the question, accepting it with a wry smile and a couple of extra pats for Teddy as she answered.

"Yes, well, beggars can't be choosers, as they say. The truth is, I took rather a long break from my legal career, of the marriage-and-children kind, and when the marriage part ended rather unexpectedly, I found myself needing to dust off the old law degree and get back to work. But, by the time I had updated my skills and retaken the bar, I'm afraid my resources were fairly well depleted. That's how I ended up sharing the space with Clark. He had an office he wanted to rent out, and I think he thought it looked better to have a second name on the sign. It isn't actually a law partnership in the usual sense of the word. We each have our own business and generally keep them separate. I'm a tax lawyer, in fact."

That was all very interesting, and Claudia wasn't unsympathetic, but she couldn't help but feel like they had strayed from the main point here.

"So you weren't actually involved in Gowan's business," she clarified. "But you knew about it? The allegations, I mean."

"How could I not? There was a while there when it seemed like I couldn't leave the house without someone telling me about it—for my own good, of course. But I had signed a ten-year lease on the space, and there was no way Clark was going to let me out of that for less than all the money I had, and then some. So there was really nothing I could do but grit my teeth and hope he didn't lose me too many friends."

Claudia thought there might be things that were worse than missing out on some party invites, but on that point she held her tongue. It also occurred to her that here was a person whose life was notably improved by Clark Gowan's death, though it seemed like it would be a longshot to convince Weaver on that point. But she did have easy access to the murder scene, which had to count for something.

"Was it true, then?" she asked. "Was Gowan really helping people hide assets?"

"I think so. He never said as much to me, of course, and I don't think he kept any of the incriminating documents around the office." The way she said it made Claudia wonder if maybe she had done some looking. That would be one way to get out of a lease.

"I wonder if that's what he was keeping in that compartment," Kathy went on, like that had just occurred to her that moment. "It's too bad you didn't find it first."

On that point, they were entirely in agreement. "But I didn't even know it was there," Claudia said. "There was nothing about it in the disclosures, and the former owner didn't mention it. I wonder if he even knew."

"I wonder." The knowing look Kathy gave her was clearly intended to convey something to Claudia, but she wasn't sure what. She would have liked to ask for clarification, but before she could, her guest stood up, returning the glass of water Claudia had served her almost untouched.

"I'm sorry, I'm sure you're busy and I've taken up far too much of your time. I just wanted to make sure I got a chance to apologize for what happened the other day. You must have been so traumatized by what you had just seen, and then for me to react like that—well, it certainly wasn't my best moment."

"Of course. And I'm sorry too—I really didn't mean to push you like that. I mean, I didn't mean to push you at all. I mean—" At this point, Claudia decided that her explaining wasn't improving things, and decided to stop. "Thank you for coming by. And I'm sorry for your loss."

"Thank you. You might not believe it, after what I've said, but I really am going to miss that old bastard. He wasn't nice, but he was always interesting."

Kathy left, and Claudia spent a while contemplating that epitaph. There were worse things to say about a person, she supposed, but she wouldn't like to have any of them on her tombstone. She also found herself wondering if there had been another motivation behind that visit. Not that it was so unbelievable that Kathy would want to explain her actions on the doorstep—Claudia had intended to seek her out herself to make her own apologies. But her imagination had taken a suspicious turn lately, and other possibilities kept presenting themselves.

Specifically, the possibility that the person she had just talked to was the killer, trying to find out if Claudia had seen anything incriminating at the murder scene before she was able to get to it. Was it really that unrealistic to think that Kathy could have killed Gowan to get out of a partnership that had become untenable? She had alluded to the end of a marriage being the reason she had needed to rejoin the

workforce at a serious disadvantage; how must have she felt to be sharing a space with a man who was helping other people to screw over
their former spouses?

And what might it have done to her own reputation and business to
have people think she was onboard with what he was doing? If Kathy
had been telling the truth about how breaking the lease would ruin her,
that case of loaded guns in Gowan's office must have looked awfully
tempting.

Knowing what she did now, Claudia might have been tempted by
them herself. The way Kathy had responded to her question about the
marketplace and its former owner only increased her concerns about her
own exposure to Gowan's wrongdoing, and pushed her intentions to
learn more to the front of her mind. The last time she had seen William
Tolman, he had been handing her the keys to the marketplace building
and the cottages and mentioning as an afterthought that sometimes the
drains could be a little temperamental.

She had already left a phone message for Tolman, and sent an email
to the address she had, but so far neither had produced a response. She
tried the number again, letting it ring until the automated voice came
on to invite her, once again, to leave her name and number after the
tone, with no additional information about who she might be leaving
it for. Claudia declined and hung up, unwilling to let the sound of her
questions pile up on some unattended machine.

But she couldn't leave it at that, so she took to the internet to see if
she could do a better job of pinpointing his location. At a previous point
in her life, she might have balked at this sort of quasi-stalking behavior,
but over the years she had come to view the internet as a very large, hard
to use telephone directory, and if someone didn't want to be listed, that
was on them. (That it was nearly impossible wasn't her problem. It had
probably been hard to keep your name out of the actual phonebook too.
She would have to ask her grandparents about that someday.)

At any rate, Mr. Tolman (who had instructed her many times to call him "Billy," which she couldn't quite manage to do, on account of how much he looked like a goat) did not seem to have done too much to lock down his online identity. Within about five minutes of searching Claudia had determined that he was currently living in a suburb of Phoenix, he had tried and failed to start a business selling mobile dog grooming franchises, and his daughter managed a senior center in Houston. That one had a phone number so, after a brief but intense internal battle against her personal disinclination to talk to strangers and a quick check of the time zones, Claudia decided she wasn't going to get anywhere by not calling, and dialed.

"Hello, may I speak to Marcia Tolman?"

"Speaking."

Claudia wasn't sure why she had thought she would have more time before she got to this part, but here she was. With no other options she could think of, she forged ahead.

"Hi, my name is Claudia Simcoe. I'm sorry to bother you at work like this, but I need to get in touch with your father about a building I bought from him, and I can't seem to reach him. Would it be possible for you to give me his contact information, or to pass on a message?"

It was, undeniably, a weird thing to ask of someone in the middle of their workday, and Claudia would have been neither surprised nor offended if the response to her request had been nothing but dead air. So she was pleasantly surprised that the sound on the other end of the line was merely a sigh.

"I would if I could," the younger Tolman said. "You're the one who bought the California place, right? Daddy had such big dreams for that. Actually, he still keeps track of how you're doing; he'll send me stories he finds online about the stores. I think he's really glad you're making a go of it."

That was nice to hear, but Claudia was concerned about the angle this conversation was taking.

"I appreciate that. He did a great job with the renovations."

Plumbing aside, possibly. "But you say you can't get in touch with him? Why is that, did something happen?"

"No. Daddy happened, is all. He's got this new girlfriend, and she's nice enough, but she's an absolute nut for trekking. You know, take off into the wilderness and hike for three weeks to get somewhere you could have flown to in half an hour? So they're off in Nepal, hiking to Everest base camp."

"Everest? Why?"

Another sigh. "Because it's there? Anyway, I'd like to help, but I haven't heard from him since he left Kathmandu, so I can't make any promises. And there were supposed to be internet cafes all along his route, so I'm starting to worry that he forgot his password or something."

Of all of the roadblocks Claudia thought she might encounter in her investigation, she had to admit that "witness lost in Nepal" had not made the list. Not that she couldn't relate—it was a few years now since her own parents had moved to Norway to run a business taking tourists on boat trips in the fjords and she still felt a sense of mild dislocation when they sent her a photo of a reindeer with a caption like, "Two hours of beautiful daylight today!" But at least she was saved from having to explain why her own new career direction seemed to involve so many dead people, as part of their relocation goals had been to entirely disconnect themselves from the news media in their home country.

She supposed that some similar reason could have to do with why she hadn't heard anything from Mr. Tolman, though she couldn't entirely discount the possibility of an avalanche, or yeti attack. But an international recovery expedition wasn't in the cards, so she tried to make the best of what was available.

"Did your father ever mention anything about the lawyer who helped him with the sale? I don't know if you've heard, but he died recently, and there are some questions about his business practices that have me a bit worried." She decided to leave out the parts about the murder, and the secret compartment, and the FBI agent. In Claudia's experience, those sorts of things tended to confuse people, and make them feel less like answering questions.

Fortunately, or maybe not, Marcia didn't seem at all confused by that particular question. "Oh, that guy," she said, and Claudia could almost hear her eyes rolling over the phone. "Yeah, Daddy wasn't crazy about him, but he'd already paid the money, and he didn't know enough people in the area to hire someone else. And it wasn't like he was doing a bad job; apparently the guy knew all kinds of things about the history of the building and he was really serious about having everything done right with the sale. But he just had a bad vibe about him, you know? And he had guns—Daddy hates guns."

Claudia had never gotten a chance to know the man whose market-place dream she had taken over, but she was warming to him more and more. Encouraging or not, though, there was little more that his daughter could tell her about the "bad vibes" except that they had persisted even when Gowan had helped him negotiate a particularly tricky aspect of the zoning. When pressed, though, she seemed confident that there had been nothing in the paperwork that would affect Claudia's right to own the property free and clear, and there had certainly been nothing like that in her father's motivations.

That, at least, was a relief to hear, and Claudia had no reason not to believe it. She had never come up with a clear theory of what sort of threat Tolman might have posed to her business, and unless his daughter was thoroughly misleading her, he didn't seem like the sort of person to use Gowan's illegal legal services. She thanked her new friend for the information and her time, and asked her to let her know if her father ever came back into communication range. Marcia agreed, and Claudia was about to end the call when she interrupted her.

"Oh, and there was one other thing. One time, while he was at the lawyer's office meeting with him, there was a guy who tried to get in,

yelling something about an accident and how the lawyer had ruined
his life. Daddy was pretty upset about that, especially when it turned
out it had to do with the guns, and they were all loaded. After that, he
wouldn't meet with him in his office if he could help it. And I don't
blame him."

Claudia spent the rest of the afternoon back at work in the marketplace, her mind partly on what she was doing, partly on who might
have wanted to do in Clark Gowan, and mostly on wondering if she
had recently tried to hire a handyman who was at best unstable, and
at worst a killer. She assumed it was Katlen who Tolman had seen
threatening Gowan, unless there was another enemy out there she
hadn't heard about yet. The thought that this was someone who she
had invited into her place of business wasn't encouraging, but Claudia's
determination to continue her investigation, and her deep desire to
never again encounter the contents of an outflowing pipe kept her from
writing back to cancel the quote request.

Still, it was a relief to have some options to suspect beyond her tenant and her vet, even if Julie's own account made it clear they would
both have to be on the list. But now she also had Kathy, the not exactly
law partner, and at least one other person with a grudge against the
victim. And it was good to know that her building so far seemed to be
clear of Gowan's machinations, not only for her own sake but because it
made her a less attractive suspect. (Though Claudia had never seriously
considered herself anyway.)

The question now was, what was she going to do next? It would be
easy enough to make a vet appointment for Teddy as a pretext to talk to
Martin Stevens about his potential role, and she should probably find
out a little more about Gowan's personal life, but beyond that she was
at a loss. Which made perfect sense if you remembered that she had no

business doing this in the first place, but Claudia wasn't going to get into that with herself right now.

By the time Claudia locked up the marketplace, the sun was starting to sink low in the sky, and she would have liked nothing more than to settle down in front of her computer with a glass of wine and a variety of search terms to pair with Gowan's name. But Teddy had been getting antsier all afternoon, and as they walked back to the cottage, she bounded ahead with the kind of energy that Claudia knew would mean she would be doing sprints around the living room at 2:00 a.m. if she didn't get some exercise. So, heroically resisting her sofa's gravitational field, as soon as they got through the door, she picked up her warmest sweater and said the words that were guaranteed to send her dog into paroxysms of delight.

"Want to go to the beach?"

# CHAPTER TWELVE

Dinner was pasta with butter and garlic, eaten in front of her computer while Teddy gnawed on her new piece of driftwood and Claudia tried to keep the sand in her hair from getting into the keyboard. (A round of fetch had ended badly.)

In contemplating the lack of glamour in her current situation, Claudia's thoughts turned to her date with Nathan. He hadn't mentioned the name of where they were going, but an online search turned up only one restaurant that seemed to fit the bill. Harry's Barn didn't sound like a fancy restaurant name, but the pictures online of its carefully rustic dining room and the eye-watering prices on the sample menu told her this was no place for jeans and even one of her dressier T-shirts. The problem was that Claudia had worn her only nice outfit less than a week ago, and while Nathan might not care, she certainly would.

Fortunately, she had an expert to turn to for advice, one who was going to be pretty annoyed if she wasn't informed of the event ahead of time. Those things considered, she picked up her phone and texted Betty.

"Going with Nathan to Harry's Barn tomorrow. Do I wear my good sneakers, or are flip-flops okay?"

Betty must have had her phone in her hand already, because her response was nearly instant.

*"What. Omg. That's so great."*

The next line was a series of emojis that made it clear what Betty thought was going to come of the evening, before she got down to business.

"*No flip-flops.*"

"*Honestly.*"

"*You have nice shoes. Wear the green ones. Do you have clothes?*"

"Not really. I wore my best dress for the party."

"*Okay, let me think.*"

There was a pause in the conversation, but the dots at the bottom of Claudia's screen indicated that Betty was typing, and then deleting, a number of things, before finally settling on one to send.

"*Okay. You still have that gray skirt, right? And the denim jacket we found at the thrift shop? Call it vintage, it'll be fine. Plus I've heard that place is drafty. You really have no tops?*"

Claudia thought about the selection in the back of her closet, mostly dating to a time in her life when stretch satin reigned supreme.

"Not really."

"*Okay, there's a new shop just off Main that might have something. Look for a bold print, linen or silk if they have it.*"

"*NO SEQUINS*"

The next morning was a busy one in the marketplace, but by noon things had calmed down enough that Claudia felt like she could slip away for a bit without much trouble. She knew the place Betty had been talking about—a tiny boutique that had opened in what had previously been a bait shop, a couple of blocks from the harbor. When she got there, she was pleased to see that they had kept some of the original decorations, with displays of beaded earrings and delicate necklaces laid out under the posters of fishing lures and the handwritten signs listing the prices for different kinds of worms.

With Betty's edict in mind, she steered clear of anything that glittered, eventually coming up with an ikat-print tank and a vaguely Scandinavian-looking turtleneck in a silk blend, which she thought was close enough. Unable to choose, and feeling more than a little silly for putting so much thought into what might have been just some sort of whim on Nathan's part, she bought both, intending to decide later. It seemed extravagant, but on the other hand, a lot of people probably owned two nice shirts.

As the shop's owner was ringing up her purchases, Claudia snuck a look at the card reader, trying to determine if it might be compromised. Since Nathan had told her about his theft, she had been doing some reading on the subject, and she thought she could spot the most common versions. Based on that, she was fairly confident that the boutique was unaffected, though she also might have wondered what Nathan was doing at a store that sold mostly women's clothing and scented candles.

Since she was out, Claudia thought she might as well take the opportunity to have a chat with one of the other people on her suspect list. She hadn't managed to bring herself to schedule an appointment for Teddy with the vet, partly because she didn't feel right subjecting her dog to potentially unnecessary medical treatment, and partly because her budget really didn't have the room for murder investigation-related vet bills. But Martin had taken to hosting a drop-in Q&A session every other Sunday afternoon in his florist shop, where for a donation to the local shelter, he would answer any reasonable questions about pet care or floral design. The questions Claudia had didn't exactly fit into either of those categories, but there were plenty of things she could ask about dog ownership, and if the conversation happened to work its way around to things like murders and alibis, well, there was a lot of that going around, wasn't there?

She had a little over half an hour to kill before the office hours started—too long to sit in her car, but not long enough to make it worth going back to the marketplace. Her first thought was the cafe, but when she got there she discovered that nearly all the tables were taken by members of the high school PTA, deep in a last-minute brainstorming session for the upcoming Halloween parade. Claudia took one look at the black and orange crepe paper and task charts, and fled before she could be tempted to propose a bobbing-for-pickles station, or something equally inappropriate.

Her second choice was the diner, where the coffee wasn't as good, but the chairs were unoccupied. This time, Claudia took a seat at the counter, ordered a slice of the pie of the day, and hoped for the best.

While she waited for her order, Claudia idly watched the business of the diner going on around her. Three waitresses worked the floor, maneuvering between the tables to deliver what looked like impossibly overloaded trays of sandwiches and waffles, and ringing up bills on their handheld paypoints, all while bantering with each other and their regular customers without ever seeming to look where they were going. She mused for a little while on the nature of expertise and what counted as skilled and unskilled work, until it occurred to her she had a less philosophical question that needed asking.

"Can I take a look at that?" she asked one of the waitresses as she came by with the paypoint. Mildly confused, the server shrugged and handed it over, keeping a close eye on Claudia in case she was up to something funny.

Claudia was up to something, but unfortunately it wasn't at all amusing. Running her fingernail around the edge of the slot for running the cards, she wasn't very surprised to have it catch on a thin plastic cover that had been wedged invisibly into the machine. She popped it out and, holding it by its edges in her fingertips, placed it on the counter.

"You broke it!" the waitress said, horrified.

"Sadly, no." Using the handle of her fork, Claudia lifted the item so she could see the fine network of electronics that ran through it. This was bad news, and she didn't relish being the one to deliver it.

"Someone's managed to get a credit card skimmer on this machine. Is there a manager I can talk to? If it's possible, I think we should look at the others too." Claudia didn't want to say the other part of her suspicion, which was that whoever had been stealing credit card numbers from the diner's customers must not only have had enough access to install the device, or devices, but also to retrieve the data. That limited the list to the employees and maybe some regulars, and there were more than a few reasons she didn't want to announce that too openly.

The manager on site that day turned out to be one of the owners, a woman in her sixties who had the look of having seen everything and been impressed by very little of it. She listened to Claudia's explanation politely at first, and then with increasing concern. Together, they gathered the rest of the paypoints from around the restaurant, turning up two more that had been tampered with and alarming several of the customers. Evidence in hand, and after a quick announcement that the diner would be cash only for the foreseeable future, they retreated to a table in the back, where the owner put her head in her hands and Claudia finished her coffee.

"I'd heard people talking about having their cards stolen, but I had no idea. God, this is just what I need. It took long enough to clean up the mess after that whole identity theft thing. I don't know how we're going to get anyone to come and work here at this point."

"Identity theft?" If Claudia was going to pick a place in San Elmo Bay to be a hive of criminal activity, she wouldn't have gone for the restaurant known mostly for its offering of all-day hash browns as her first choice.

"Oh, it was last year, someone got all our payroll information and got credit cards and things in everyone's names. It was a disaster, took months to figure out. Do you think it could be the same person?"

"It's possible," said Claudia, aware that even for her she was getting into areas a little far outside of her expertise. "You really need to take this to the police."

The woman sighed heavily. "I guess so. I wonder if anyone is even going to want to come in here after all this. I don't know if I would."

Claudia sympathized with her predicament, though privately she thought she might say the same. One thing was for sure: as soon as she got back into the office, she was going to look into some additional security for her on-site electronics, and maybe start some conversations with the vendors about adding background checks to their hiring processes.

She left the diner feeling discouraged and unsure of the point of any of it. It was one thing to say crimes that happened in the same general time and place had a chance of being connected, but combining murder, property ownership shenanigans, identity theft, and stealing credit card numbers was stretching even her imagination. Maybe she just needed to accept that it was a big bad world with a lot of crimes in it, and stop trying to stick her nose into absolutely everyone's business.

She thought about that while she walked the three blocks to the florist shop that shared a duplex with the vet's office, and put her name down on the list for a consultation. There were two people in front of her, so she wandered around looking at the sample bouquets, listening to a man asking about the relative values of raw and grain-free ferret foods while she considered her own approach.

Veterinarian/florist was not a usual combination, and before moving to San Elmo Claudia would have been skeptical of anyone who claimed to have heard of one. But this was the sort of place where people rolled with what life threw at them, and what Martin Stevens had caught was the floral design business he had invested in for his daughter, who had subsequently fallen in love with a rodeo clown and left to follow him around the country. At least, that was the story as she had heard it. Claudia wasn't sure how that version squared with what she had learned from Julie about the money he had lost to the former business partner, or even what the timeline of all of these purported events was.

She had some more time to think about that while a woman talked through her cat's hairball technique in excruciating detail and got a recommendation for more regular brushing. Finally, it was Claudia's turn, and she went in with her carefully thought-out question, which she promptly forgot.

"So, poops. I mean, Teddy poops, well, obviously. But sometimes she doesn't, and they aren't always the same. And I'm just wondering, when should I worry? Or not?"

As questions went, it was neither polite nor sensible, but it was at least genuine. Teddy was the first dog that Claudia had owned as strictly her own, and she had not been prepared for the variety of substances that came out of her. Fortunately, Martin was neither disgusted nor surprised by the question, and gave her a quick summary of canine digestive processes that was pat enough to make Claudia suspect he had answered variations on this question more than a few times before.

She asked a couple of follow-ups, to try and make it clear she was really interested in the subject then, since there was no one else waiting at the moment, paused her departure for some casual gossip.

"I suppose you heard about what happened to Clark Gowan," she said, as though people in town had been talking about anything else for the last few days. "Isn't that just the craziest thing?"

That was probably not quite the right tone to take when discussing a murder, especially when you were the one who found the body, but Martin was too taken with his own grievances to notice.

"Crazy it didn't happen sooner, if you ask me. And you didn't, for the record." The vet might have been a bit more savvy than Claudia was about the sort of things you weren't supposed to say, but she had the sense that he was past the point of caring.

"You know, it's funny you should say that. I don't think anyone I've talked to had a good word to say about him."

"That just goes to show the kind of company you keep. If you were talking to the dregs of society, you'd find plenty of friends of Clark Gowan."

Claudia wasn't sure how she should take that, so she decided to be flattered.

"It sounds like he made a lot of those enemies the old fashioned way. I have to admit, I was worried when I learned about his illegal stuff—he did some work for the guy who sold me the marketplace, you know."

Martin nodded thoughtfully.

"I can see why that would be upsetting. I'd sure think twice before I bought anything if I knew he was involved with the sale."

Despite the reassurance she had gotten from Tolman's daughter, this was not the encouraging sort of thing Claudia wanted to hear. But it did give her the opening she was looking for.

"You had some dealings with Gowan, didn't you? How did you handle him?"

Martin laughed, but not happily. "Badly, in retrospect. I was so sure I had the right and the law on my side, all I had to do was go in and lay out my case and everything would be solved. In my dreams. Between him and a former friend of mine, they ran me in circles until I was out more money than they could ever steal. That was when I learned that the law isn't there for little guys like me. I was lucky to get out of it with as much as I had left."

Claudia knew, of course, that someone could have more than one aspect to their personality, but she still had trouble squaring her image of the cheerful, endlessly patient veterinarian she knew with this furious, bitter man hunched between the stalks of gladiolas.

As if intuiting her thoughts, Martin looked up suddenly and met Claudia's gaze.

"I didn't kill him, though. Not that you would think so, I'm sure."

"Of course not," said Claudia, who had been wondering how much experience he had with firearms, and whether he had an alibi for Thursday morning.

"I said the same thing to the new police chief when she came around. If I was going to kill that bastard, I would have done it long ago, and it would have been something a lot worse than a bullet to the head."

Claudia wasn't sure that was the sort of argument the police found very persuasive, but she didn't see any benefit in pointing that out. What she wanted to do was settle in for a nice long gossip session on the details of Gowan's crimes, past, present, and potential, with an emphasis on who might have reason to worry about him picking up a secret package out of Claudia's wall. But a fresh round of clients had come into the shop, one of them carrying a cockatoo, and she was aware that any attempt to continue the interview would be both unpopular and more than a little suspicious. So she thanked Martin for the advice, promised to do her best to keep Teddy from eating chili peppers in the future, and took her leave, being careful to give a wide berth to the bird, who was making a serious play for a towering floral centerpiece.

Out on the sidewalk, she looked back through the window, so engrossed in the question of whether it was going to be able to pull the entire arrangement down, or would be satisfied with just prying off one of the plastic butterflies, that she forgot which way it was back to her car. Confused and a little embarrassed, she had to stop to get her bearings, hoping that no one was around to see her looking like a lost tourist.

But someone was there, and she was fairly sure he did see her, though Claudia doubted she was ever going to hear about what he thought. From the way that Special Agent Ngyuen was sitting in his rental car, checking his watch and pointedly not looking at her, she got the idea that he had other things on his mind.

# CHAPTER THIRTEEN

"D o you think he suspects Martin?"

"I don't know. I didn't even think he was here about the murder. It doesn't seem like the FBI would be that interested, you know?"

Nathan nodded, his eyes still on the road.

"Not unless Gowan was a mob boss, or maybe a foreign agent. But as it stands, it doesn't make a lot of sense."

They were in Nathan's car, a small luxury SUV that was so much nicer than Claudia's hatchback that she considered asking if they could skip dinner and drive around all night. The leather was buttery, the sound system clear and rich, and as she watched the stars flash by though the moon roof, Claudia reflected that it was a good thing she liked Nathan already, because it would be embarrassing to be thirty-six and dating a guy so you could ride in his car.

She had spent the first part of the ride bringing Nathan up to date on her discoveries, starting with the skimmer at the diner and eventually getting into the murder investigation, because it seemed rude not to mention it. Nathan seemed interested, and less shocked than she expected. If anything, he was a little too into it, and inclined to theories that even Claudia found unrealistic. But she didn't want to be overly negative when he was being so encouraging about her ideas, so she limited her criticism to pointing out that it had been a while since anyone had stored anything important on microfilm, and D.B. Cooper would be much too old to be any of the people involved.

Factual disputes aside, she enjoyed the ride, and was almost disappointed when they pulled into the driveway with a discreet sign that indicated they had arrived at their destination.

It wasn't like most restaurants Claudia had been to. For one thing, she couldn't see it. All that was visible from the parking lot was an elegant garden, where strings of fairy lights illuminated a mix of decorative and edible plantings. The flowers were largely white, which showed particularly well in the low light, and the vegetables mostly leafy greens, the better to fill the space between them.

There was plenty of time to admire the garden design, because the route to the restaurant was a long, winding path which (though flat and wheelchair accessible) was still a little tricky to navigate in the dark in her nice shoes. About halfway along they came across a moss-covered booth under a tree, like a fairy's valet stand, where a server in a denim jumpsuit was waiting for them.

"Welcome," he said as he entered their names into his tablet. "We're so glad you could join us this evening. Would you care for a libation for your stroll through the garden?"

He produced a mismatched pair of cut-glass decanters and two wooden cups.

"Made from our own elderflowers and blackcurrants, grown here in the garden, with or without our housemade gin."

They both opted for "with" and continued on the path in a state of increased bemusement.

"It's just, I feel like I should like it, but I can't shake the feeling that it's all . . ."

"A bit much? I agree." Nathan took another sip from his cup. "Still, this is pretty tasty. And the chef is the real deal. She ran a top place in the city for years, until the rat race got to her and she chucked it all to have her own thing out here." He gave Claudia a sideways smile. "I thought maybe you could relate."

"I do feel like I've heard that song somewhere before," Claudia admitted. "But I didn't exactly come in with anything like—oh, wow."

They had come around the final bend in the path, and the so-called barn stood in front of them in all its glory. And there was a lot of glory.

In theory, the restaurant known as Harry's Barn must have started its life as a barn, owned by some long-ago farmer whose given name may or may not have been Harold. Claudia had no information that would allow her to dispute this, she could only say that her experience with vintage barns had not included much in the way of French doors, or soaring rooflines. The attached, vine-covered pergola was new to her as well, as was the massive stone table next to the entrance, where three more denim-clad young people waited behind a row of small glass bowls full of something green.

The previous greeter must have radioed ahead with their descriptions, because before Nathan or Claudia could say anything, a maître d' peeled off and introduced herself like they were valued but lightly remembered acquaintances and issued each of them a watercress sorbet to sustain them on the trip to their table. Claudia was not very familiar with what it was like to be a rich person, but she suspected she was getting a preview, and wished she had done something more with her hair.

In fact, Betty had been right, as usual. The approach to the restaurant might have been grand, but inside it was definitely more barn than not, with bare wooden walls and a faint scent of alfalfa that lingered in the air. And however much they charged for a meal, Harry's Barn was still in Northern California, where the definition of formalwear remained "jeans without holes" and makeup was an if-you-feel-like-it thing. In this environment, Claudia's new linen top and old skirt fit in easily, and she was fairly sure she caught Nathan sneaking a glance at the reflection of her butt in the darkened windows as they passed, so there was that.

Seated at their table, they barely had time to glance at their menus before a new person approached, carrying what looked like a medium-sized encyclopedia volume (possibly O or F). That turned out to be the wine list, and the woman carrying it the sommelier, ready to discuss their drink options for the evening. Claudia, whose approach to wine was, "sure, I'll have some" had been secretly hoping chauvinism would intervene on her behalf here, but unfortunately Nathan didn't hesitate before waving the book in her direction.

"To be honest, I've never been much of a wine person," he said. "Do you have any beers?"

Far from being offended, the sommelier nodded vigorously. "Of course. I'll have Alex, our cicerone, bring you the list." She turned to Claudia, who had just opened the book and was worried she might have pulled something. "See anything that's interesting to you? Or do you need some more time?"

In the end, they decided that Claudia would have the wine pairings that came with the tasting menu (which was the only option for food; this wasn't the sort of place you could order an appetizer and a salad and hope your friends didn't want to split the check evenly), and a very intense young man who looked like he cut his hair with one of the restaurant's signature salad bowls came hurrying over with a much smaller folder, which he reverentially presented to Nathan. This was the cicerone, which Claudia learned was a beer sommelier, and who seemed to view Nathan as somewhere between a prophet and a rock star. They spent a few minutes discussing the beers on offer, as they related to the dishes that were going to be served, and Nathan made his selections without seeming to give the matter much thought.

The ritual completed, the young man stepped away from the table, then turned back, clutching the leather-bound folder to his chest like a shield.

"I um, I read your book. And I just wanted you to know, people were wrong about it. I think you made some really good points." With that, he was gone, and Nathan was left going red in the face, staring at his empty sorbet glass.

"You wrote a book?" Claudia had thought she knew about all of her neighbor's eccentricities, but clearly there were depths yet to be explored.

"Well, it's really more of a manifesto."

Normally, hearing that on a date would have sent Claudia sprinting for the exit, but she knew Nathan well enough by now that she barely blinked.

"A beer manifesto?"

Nathan nodded. "Pretty much. It was—you know how I told you after I sold the business, I kind of went through some things? So, part of that was I got sort of philosophical, about what beer was, and what it should be, and how the industry had lost its way. And I wrote up this whole thing about it and put it on the internet, and I even found a guy who would print it to sell."

"That doesn't sound so bad." In fact, it barely sounded interesting, as far as Claudia was concerned.

"Yeah, well, I didn't exactly use those words. And I named some names. A lot of names, actually. It didn't go over great. Anyway, after that I decided to go on a trip to Germany that I had been meaning to do for a while, and by the time I got back you had bought the marketplace and I—I kept not dealing with things well."

That part, Claudia knew about. She had barely had the business for three months when she found her every move being challenged by her unseen neighbor up the hill. If someone had told her then that she would someday be sitting across from him while they were served a starter of micro-kale and whipped red lentil hummus in a puff pastry shell, she would have had a lot of questions, not the least of which was what was micro-kale.

There wasn't much time for questions, existential or otherwise, because no sooner had they finished their bites than their server appeared out of thin air to clear the miniature plates and replace them with slightly larger ones, each holding a popcorn ball, like something you might get if there was a house on your trick-or-treating route that didn't believe in packaged candy. What they did not get were utensils, and after a moment of awkwardly pretending they knew what to do, Claudia caught Nathan's eye and they both laughed.

"Cheers," he said, lifting the popcorn ball off his plate. Claudia did the same, and they toasted them above the beeswax candle that smoked and sputtered in the center of the table.

"It tastes like . . . onion? Like French onion soup?" Nathan asked, expressing the confusion they were both feeling.

"Caramelized onion popcorn," Claudia agreed. "It's definitely not something I've had before. It's not . . . bad?"

She couldn't think of anything to add to that, and apparently neither could Nathan, so conversation lapsed as they crunched through their appetizers. It was a nervous-making start to the meal, but fortunately when the next course arrived, with edible flowers pressed onto the surface of a silky bulb of burrata, there was nothing to say about it except that it was delicious.

"One thing I've been wondering," Nathan said, as they both worked to assemble perfect bites of the petals and cheese. "Is what possible reason Gowan could have had for hiding whatever it was in your walls? I can probably think of fifty better places I would store something if I didn't want people to find it, even the FBI."

That seemed like more places than most people would have at the front of their minds, but Claudia stuck to the essentials of his question.

"I've been wondering that too. The best I can come up with, from talking to people about him, was that maybe he got a thrill from using the same hiding place the bootleggers did. Or, I don't know, he wanted it near at hand, but couldn't keep it in his home?" That line of reasoning brought up another question, one that Claudia was surprised hadn't occurred to her before.

"Did you ever see him going into the marketplace while it was empty? Or even after I bought it, before I put in the new security system? I never noticed anything, but you can't see it from my house."

The fact that Nathan had a good view of the marketplace building from the top of the hill had come up before, in other circumstances, which neither of them wanted to get into right now.

"I don't think so," Nathan said, but was interrupted from elaborating by the arrival of their next course.

Heavy white plates with an autumn leaves pattern were set down in front of them, each holding a squat globe of clear orange jelly sprinkled with a light brown powder. After a pause to let them admire it, their server stepped in with an explanation.

"Here we have our gelee of pumpkin, which is topped with a dehydrated latte powder, which gives it that nice earthiness and a bit of acid."

"A latte-spiced pumpkin," Claudia said, nodding. "I think I'm starting to get the hang of this."

Left without instructions on how to eat this latest item, they chose their own paths; Claudia using a spoon to take individual bites while the liquid center pooled on the plate, and Nathan putting the whole thing in his mouth at once. That presented some challenges for speech, and it was a minute before he was able to resume what he was saying.

"What I was saying, is, I don't remember seeing Gowan in particular. But there were definitely a few times when there was a car in the parking lot, and it was always at strange times of the day, like really early in the morning, or just after sunset. I thought about filing a complaint with the city for it being a nuisance, but . . ." He let that idea trail off, looking uncomfortable about the person he had been.

"But you never actually saw anyone going in or out," Claudia said, letting him off the hook this time. "That makes sense, Gowan would have had a key, and he was probably being careful not to be seen. If it was him."

"And then this last time, do you think he was in a hurry because he knew about the FBI agent being in town?" Nathan's question had an electrifying effect on the busboy who was clearing their plates, which rattled in his hands. Embarrassed by their lack of discretion, Claudia waited until he was well out of earshot to answer.

"Must have been," she said. "It's too much of a coincidence otherwise." She was also going to point out that the murder had equally suspicious timing, but they were interrupted again, this time by the waiter to present their abalone liver mousse on fried abalone chips, and deliver a short spiel on the free divers who brought it up from the cold water just off the coast, prying the succulent mollusks off the rocks with a crowbar. Claudia wondered how often the divers got murdered, given what seemed like a lot of opportunities, and then wondered when her brain started working like this.

"It's what makes me worry about the police suspecting Julie," she said, lowering her voice even though there was no one nearby. "Do they really think she would go after him now, after all this time, and when his crimes were finally about to catch up with him?"

"But she might not have known that," Nathan pointed out. "Or she might have thought that wasn't going to be a good enough punishment, and he was about to be out of her reach."

"Oh, come on. Julie? You don't honestly think she would do something like that?"

"No, but the police might. And if they caught her going into his office, they're going to have to think something."

Claudia couldn't argue with that, though she tried to think of a way as she ate her abalone and wondered how it was possible for a mousse to have that much cream in it and still be largely solid.

"Do you think there's another compartment somewhere in the marketplace?" Nathan asked as he wiped a bit of sauce off his plate with a corner of one of the slices of heavily seeded bread from the basket on the table.

"I don't know. I would have said I didn't believe in the first one, until

I saw it. It was kind of small, though, wasn't it? I'd think if you were running a whole illegal business, you'd have more things to hide than that. But I can't imagine where another one would be."

She pushed her food around on her plate as she spoke, trying to visualize the walls in the marketplace while responding to the warning signs from her stomach. Already starting to feel full, Claudia had avoided the bread, and was strategizing how much of the mousse she was willing to leave. Not having been given a menu, she wasn't even sure how many courses were left, let alone what would be in them, so in the end she decided to live in the moment, ate the last bite, and let the future bring what it may.

The next thing the future (or, more accurately, the waiter) brought was a plate of handmade pasta, with noodles that looked like fat worms bathed in a pale orange sauce.

"Local *uni*," their server explained, and went on to describe in detail the ways the overpopulation of sea urchins, brought on by the loss of the otters that were their main predators, was bad for the environment, and how their divers were trying to create a market for the product. Which was all very interesting, but Claudia was starting to think that, of the three people at their table, neither her nor Nathan had been doing most of the talking.

Still, the pasta, like everything else, was delicious. This was by far the nicest date Claudia had ever been on, and she wished desperately she could come up with something to talk about besides a murdered lawyer. While she thought, she reached across the table for the extra dish of grated cheese the waiter had left "in case they wanted it" (a silly question, but whatever) at the same time as Nathan went for another piece of bread and their hands collided near the candle.

For a moment their eyes met and their fingers intertwined, and they both froze in place. A burst of electricity ran through Claudia's body, starting at her fingers and fizzing somewhere near the back of her throat. She wanted to say something or do something—tighten her grip on Nathan's fingers or ask him if he felt it too. But she couldn't quite manage either, and with the silence starting to get awkward, she pulled her hand back and reverted to the only other topic that was on her mind.

"I'm worried about Julie but as much as I hate to admit it, there's something fascinating by the problem of solving a murder. It's like the logic puzzles I did as a kid, but real."

As soon as the words were out of her mouth, Claudia realized it was a terrible thing to say. But Nathan seemed to understand, even if she couldn't tell if he was disappointed or relieved by the return to the conversation.

"I know what you mean," he said, still looking her in the eyes. "You don't want to like it, because someone is dead, and even if he wasn't very nice, that's a bad thing. But that doesn't stop the problem from being interesting."

"Exactly. And, I don't know, maybe it's a coping mechanism? Trying to turn death in to an abstract problem, I mean. I did find his body, and seeing someone who's been shot in the head isn't exactly the sort of thing you just get over."

There was a rattle of silverware near Claudia's ear, which was when she realized that their waiter had come back just in time to catch her last few words. He didn't say anything, just murmured something about the next course being out shortly as he delivered their fresh forks and knives, but from the way he looked at them both, Claudia had the sense they were being judged.

"I don't think tasting menus are very conducive to sensitive conversations," she observed as she watched him go.

"No," Nathan agreed. "The next time we want to talk over a murder, we should definitely go for a buffet."

In fact, inappropriate conversation topics aside, Claudia was starting to reach the point where no style of food sounded very appealing to her. Every part of the meal so far had been delicious, and the servings were small, but there had been a lot of them, and that plus the richness of the food (to say nothing of the generous "tasting" pours of the wines) were starting to catch up to her. She was about to make a joking-but-not-really suggestion that they ask for any remaining food in a doggy bag, when the next course arrived and any notion of surrender was immediately abandoned.

A whole quail, roasted golden brown, sat in the middle of each plate surrounded by marble-sized balls of roast potatoes. Next to the dish was a demitasse of gravy, and another, even smaller, plate with a thimble-sized cylinder of cranberry jelly, complete with ridges from where it had come out of the "can."

It was all simultaneously ridiculous, sublime, and extremely appealing, and even Claudia, who never did that sort of thing, slid her phone out from where she had been hiding it in her lap to take a quick photo.

"It's just, how often do you see a single-serving Thanksgiving turkey," she explained to Nathan, who didn't seem at all bothered by her lapse.

"I think there are chestnuts in this stuffing," he said. "Fresh ones, even."

There was a period of silence as they each found a little more appetite capacity for their early holiday dinners, and Claudia, at least, spent some time thinking about what it was like to have someone to talk to who took her seriously, even when she wasn't a very serious person. (Teddy was pretty good at it, but Claudia couldn't shake the sense that she was judging her, at least a little bit.) But it occurred to her that a person shouldn't spend an entire date talking about her own problems, even if they were as interesting as how to solve a murder.

"How is the pear cider coming along?" she asked, remembering the experimental batch he had shared with her. That seemed like it must have been weeks ago, and it surprised her to remember that it had only been three days.

"It's okay, I guess. Still having trouble with balancing the acidity and the sweetness. I was actually thinking of getting in touch with the people at that museum and seeing if they have any old recipes I could use as a reference. They would have worked with the same kind of fruit we have around here, and I'm thinking maybe they would have some thoughts about how to use it. Why reinvent the wheel, you know?"

Claudia agreed the world was probably pretty well set for wheels, metaphorically speaking.

"I bet Julie could help you with that, if there's anything there. I didn't get the impression that the current museum management is interested in much other than tractor maintenance, but you never know."

That turned out to be an interest of Nathan's as well, so Claudia spent the time until their dessert arrived describing the historical society's collection as best she could. She had made it about halfway through the quail before admitting defeat, but Nathan cleaned his plate, even to the last bite of cranberry sauce. She was impressed, but also a little concerned, especially as the next course arrived—apples seven ways, which was at least three more ways than Claudia thought you could get out of an apple. She made an effort to at least try them all, and ended up thinking that freeze-drying and reconstituting in coconut cream might be a way too far.

The dessert course had come with a half-sized glass of ice wine made in California—a place not known for its freezing temperatures—by harvesting the well-ripened grapes and then freezing them in rented industrial freezers. Claudia wasn't sure how well that aligned with the principles of local, seasonal cuisine, but on the other hand, it did taste nice.

Assuming the meal was over, she was preparing her summing-up comments and thanks to Nathan for the treat, when their waiter reappeared. For a terrifying moment, Claudia imagined it was all about to begin again, but to her relief he was only arriving with the bill, which was presented in a hand-carved wooden box, along with a selection of tiny chocolate truffles and something that might have been a poem.

"This was an amazing dinner," Claudia said, or hoped she did. The wine was really catching up to her now, and she knew the ruby port that had come with the chocolates, however delicate it looked in her suddenly-clumsy hand, was not going to improve matters. As if driven by some psychic force (or, more likely, information from one of the many subtle cameras set around the dining room) their waiter arrived at that moment with a cup of fragrant rose-hip tea, which Claudia sipped gratefully as Nathan finished off the candies.

"It really is incredible, isn't it? I'd heard a lot about this place, but I didn't know whether to believe it. I'm glad you were able to come and try it with me."

He smiled, and in that moment this, and every other decision Claudia had made up until now, felt like it had been a very good idea.

Fortunately, though he had been more enthusiastic toward the food, Nathan's insistence on sticking to beer, and the relatively smaller amount of it he had drunk, meant that there was no problem with him driving them home. The question now was, whose home? Was he planning on just dropping her off at the cottage and driving away, asking if he could come in, or inviting her up to his house? And if it were the latter, what would she do about Teddy? There was no way she could make it until the morning without needing a trip outside. Could she ask him to hang out for a bit at her place while she took the dog out? Was there any possible way to phrase that and still sound even a little bit sexy?

Claudia snuck a sideways glance at her date, trying to gauge his mood, and imagine how he might respond to that sort of request, and found that there were other things to worry about. Nathan had been driving slowly, which Claudia thought had been out of concern for the narrow, unlit country road, but seeing his face, she wasn't so sure. It was dark in the car, but even so, his skin seemed to have an unhealthy pallor, and his expression was distinctly distressed.

"I, um, I think I need to pull over for a sec," he said, as a bead of sweat ran down the side of his face. "Sorry."

He found a place where the shoulder was wide enough to fit the car, parked it, and got out, making it to the shrubbery only seconds before his stomach contents did. Claudia stayed in the passenger seat, listening as the remains of her date's dinner rocketed into the ditch. Part of her wondered if she was supposed to get out and offer him some sort of comfort or support, but another part was more concerned that if she got too close, she might join in.

Finally, when there didn't seem to be anything more to come, Nathan staggered back to the car, doing his best to wipe around his mouth with a crumpled napkin.

"I'm sorry," he repeated. "I'm really sorry."

"It's fine," Claudia said. "Are you okay?"

"Yeah, it's just—I don't really eat a lot of rich food, you know? I mean, my usual dinner is just chicken and rice, or something. I think maybe my stomach wasn't ready for all that." He found a water bottle wedged into the door and took a tentative sip.

"I think I'm okay now," he said, once it was clear the water was staying down. "I'm so sorry."

"It really is fine," Claudia said again. "It happens. Do you want to rest for a bit? I'd offer to drive, but I don't think I can." (As sobering as the recent events had been, there was definitely still too much wine in her system to make it a responsible choice.)

So they sat for a while, in the car by the side of the road, talking occasionally and staring out the moon roof at the stars, until Nathan felt like his system had settled down enough to make it home. There was no question about that now—dog or no dog, this wasn't going to be a night for romance.

They finally made it back to San Elmo, and Claudia was rehearsing her goodnight in her head as they turned up the road past the market-place, and Nathan stopped the car for a second time.

The marketplace parking lot was ablaze with headlights, with people milling around in front of them. One of them peeled off and came running up and waving, and as the figure came closer, Claudia recognized it as Helen Pak.

"We got him! We got him!" She shouted as Claudia rolled down the window. "Come see!"

# CHAPTER FOURTEEN

Helen took off back toward the lights, preventing follow-up questions, so there was nothing for Claudia and Nathan to do but follow her.

The group in the parking lot was mostly familiar faces—Helen's husband Victor and son Brandon, Julie, Robbie, and a younger man who Claudia recognized as helping out in Robbie's charcuterie shop on occasion. The only complete stranger was the man who was sitting uncomfortably on the bumper of Robbie's truck, his hands tied behind his back with a floral scarf. Unsure of where to start with her questions, Claudia looked from one person to the next and hoped someone would start the explaining.

Unsurprisingly, it was Helen who took the lead.

"We caught him trying to break in," she began without preamble. "Well, Robbie caught him, and Julie and I had just left because we were all here late doing inventory. But Robbie had come back because Laurence had locked his keys inside, and he found this guy opening the vent on the roof. So they made him stay there and called everyone, and we came, and when we got here he tried to make a run for it, but he fell off the roof, so I tied up his hands. We tried to call you, but you didn't answer."

Claudia was confused, because she didn't remember turning off her phone. But, sure enough, she checked and there were four missed calls and a text.

"Oh, right," said Nathan, registering her confusion. "One of their things at Harry's Barn is to not have people using their cell phones during the meal, so the whole building is basically a big Faraday cage. Sorry, I thought I mentioned it."

There were some things Claudia might have wanted to say about that, but she left them for later.

"Have you called the police?" she asked.

"Not yet," Robbie said, looking nervously at Helen and Julie. "We didn't know—we weren't sure what you wanted."

"I want to call the police. Let's do that now." Claudia wasn't sure what kind of relationship her tenants thought she had with law enforcement, but she had no intention of taking the independent approach here. Nathan was already on his phone, so she left him to it and turned her attention back to the captive.

"Who are you?" she asked. "And why were you trying to break into my marketplace?"

The man didn't respond, preferring to stare sullenly at the ground. He was older than Claudia had expected—in his fifties at least—and he didn't look like the sort of person who made a habit of climbing around on roofs. He was short and skinny, dressed in a dark sweater and faded chinos, with a poorly kept beard that looked like it had recently been dyed black. He was also the palest person Claudia had even seen—with skin the color of an unpleasant fish filet and eyes so light it was hard to tell the irises from the whites. She was confident she hadn't met him before; it wasn't the sort of face she thought she would forget, even if she wanted to.

"He's not talking," Helen said, by way of explaining why the man wasn't saying anything. "He yelled some at first, but after that it's been nothing. We tried everything to get him to talk, but he just sits there."

Claudia hesitated to ask what "everything" might be in this situation, and decided she really didn't want to know.

"Okay, well the police are on their way, and he can not talk to them if he wants. At least they should be able to find out his name."

"Wait a minute." Julie had been standing to the side, frowning as she contemplated their captive. "I know who he is. That's Donald Newman. I didn't recognize him at first with the beard. What's the deal, Donny? What'd your buddy Gowan have that was worth coming back to town and taking the chance that someone might try and get you to pay some of the bills you walked out on?"

That got a reaction, at least. The man's head snapped up and, apparently seeing Julie for the first time, his lips curled back into something between a smile and a snarl.

"I'm honored to be so memorable, Mrs. Julie. Or is it Ms? I'd imagine you've given up on men at this point."

Claudia wished he had stuck with the silent act; Mr. Newman's voice was no more pleasant than his face. But, having broken the seal, he took to the talking thing with some enthusiasm.

"Last I heard, you were running back to daddy to milk the cows. Did you get tired of people not being sure which one you were?"

Robbie looked like he was perfectly willing to punch the guy, given the option, but Julie didn't need the help.

"Funny. The last news I had about you, you were skipping town after your latest scheme had failed. What did that make, twenty in a row? It's a shame Clark couldn't lend you some brains along with his legal help, though you probably wouldn't have paid that back either. So, what's up? You heard there was an FBI agent in town and decided to turn your life around? Something so small, it probably corners pretty well."

There was far too much in her attack for Newman to unpack in a few seconds, or in his case, probably years, so he latched on to the one thing that seemed to be relevant to his thinking.

"That fed guy's got nothing on me, and he's never going to," he said, then snapped his mouth shut, like he realized he was saying too much.

"Why, because you killed Clark before he could tell him about the business you did with him? That's the rule, right? Whoever talks first gets to make the deal." Claudia hadn't known Julie was so well-versed in federal criminal procedure, but no one seemed to be arguing with her, least of all Newman.

"Clark was making deals, but it had nothing to do with me." He seemed to be relaxing and even enjoying the exchange, though his hands remained tied firmly behind him. Given that, Claudia decided to make another attempt at getting back to the main question on offer.

"If you're so unconcerned, then why were you crawling around on my roof?" she asked.

The man turned to look at her and managed to leer in a way that made him even less appealing, which she hadn't thought possible.

"Clark had some very valuable . . . items in his possession, that by rights should belong to me."

"Yeah, well the marketplace belongs to me, so you can go ahead and explain those rights to the police." Claudia thought those made for some pretty good last words, but it turned out her guest had other ideas.

"Oh, you think so, do you? Well, a little advice, hon. I'm not the only one here with some reasons to be looking for what Clark left behind. And if I were you, I'd be more worried about the bitch who was in his office when he died, and less about a guy just looking for what was his to begin with."

He was looking straight at Julie as he said it, smiling with half his mouth, and he might have been about to elaborate on the point when Julie lunged at him, swinging her purse like a flail. Robbie jumped in to hold her back, and Helen to either help him or join the fight, and in the resulting confusion their prisoner managed to slip his bonds. He dodged under Robbie's grasp and tripped Claudia as he went by, sending her spinning into Nathan, who attempted an awkward catch that landed them both on the ground.

By the time Claudia was back on her feet, Newman had made it to a bicycle and was speeding down the hill. Helen already had her car keys out and was shouting something about catching him, but Claudia had had enough excitement for one night.

"We know who he is, and if the cops want to talk to him, they can find him on their own time. At this point, I don't think there's much danger of Mr. Newman bothering us again."

"Okay, fine," said Helen. "But I guess I need to go and work on my knots."

The conversation with the officer who showed up five minutes later was awkward, but not nearly as much as the identical one Claudia had with Chief Weaver when she arrived. The decision not to chase their escapee was at least given some approval, though not enough to overcome the issues with the fact that they had captured him in the first place. All suggestions that the intrusion was related to Gowan's death were met with a complete lack of expression.

"And he claimed to be looking for something that belonged to him?" she asked after the third time Claudia had tried to rephrase her question about whether Newman could have been in town when Gowan was killed.

"That's what he said," Claudia replied, giving up on her own investigating for the time being. "Except that it didn't sound like it was something that he owned so much as it was a thing he thought he ought to have. You know what I mean?"

Weaver nodded like she understood, which was good because Claudia wasn't sure she was making sense to herself at this point. It was well past midnight, and even though she hadn't been present for the majority of the events in question, Claudia found herself taking the lead in answering Weaver's questions, with all their uncomfortable implications.

There was a phrase about leadership that Claudia had learned at one point, though she tried not repeat it in polite company, involving a fan and a catcher's mitt, which was running through her head at the moment.

"Are you going to try to catch him?" she asked after describing, for what seemed like the hundredth time, the circumstances of Mr. Newman's escape.

"We'll keep an eye out," was all Weaver would say, and Claudia was forced to admit that a failed nonhome invasion was not the sort of thing that generally led to countywide manhunts.

Finally, all the questions that could be asked had, and everyone began to filter out of the parking lot. In the end, the only people left were Claudia and Nathan.

"Um. Do you want a ride home?" Nathan gestured toward his car, as though there might be some other vehicle he would use.

Claudia considered the offer, and the things she had thought the evening would bring. But she was tired, and confused, and already starting to feel like it was going to be a rough morning, and the walk across the field to her cottage seemed like it would be the lesser of two awkwardnesses.

"Thanks," she said. "But I can walk from here. I think I need the fresh air."

"Okay, sure. I understand. See you tomorrow, I guess? Or whenever." He turned and started to go back to his car, and Claudia was acutely aware that this was not how she wanted the night to end. Ultimately, there was only one thing she could think of to say.

"Hey, thanks for dinner. It was great. I had a really good time."

Nathan's smile was fleeting, but hopeful.

"Thanks, I'm glad you liked it. I had a good time too."

The next morning was about as challenging as Claudia had anticipated. As soon as she had gotten home, and dealt with Teddy's more pressing needs, she had drunk several large glasses of water, chased by a generous serving of ibuprofen, but those measures only had so much power against what was, by her calculations, slightly more than a full bottle of wine, to say nothing of the welcome cocktail.

Which wasn't very welcome now, as she staggered to the coffee-maker and tried to remember what the buttons did.

It took a while, but once her blood-caffeine levels had reached the acceptable range, Claudia found herself actually able to contemplate the idea of food. Her digestive system had always operated in the "iron-clad" range, a fact that made her feel a little guilty when she thought about Nathan's experience with their dinner. She hoped he didn't think she was cold or ungrateful for how the evening had ended; she hoped a lot of things.

It was Monday, and the marketplace was closed, but using the spare time to cook an elaborate breakfast was out of the question. Even aside from the technical challenges of getting her brain to work out how to crack an egg, the leftover feeling of culinary inferiority from the night before was too strong and, lacking the energy to learn how to cure her own duck bacon, Claudia declared defeat and found a box of waffles in the freezer.

She did have them with some of Betty's homemade blackberry jam, because what Claudia lacked in cooking skills, she made up for in friends. A spoonful of the shockingly rich Dancing Cow cottage cheese completed the meal—as far from the sad diet ingredient of her child-hood as a rose garden was from a bathroom air freshener.

As she ate, Claudia couldn't help but think about the confrontation between Julie and Mr. Newman the night before. Julie had claimed not to recognize him at first, but was that really believable, considering the animosity that seemed to exist between the two? Claudia had down-played their interaction when Weaver had asked, but it had been hard to avoid the subject entirely. The police chief seemed to have an instinct for being aware of what she wasn't being told, and coming up with questions that were difficult to answer without outright lying. Claudia hadn't wanted to do that, but she also hadn't wanted to paint Julie as the sort of person who flew off the handle at people who insulted and/ or wronged her, and she wasn't sure she had succeeded at either goal.

And maybe she shouldn't have. Claudia had entered into this investigation with the assumption that Julie was innocent, but did she really have anything to base that on, besides the fact that the woman could do great work with dairy products? And yes, she had known her for a few years now, but that was too small a portion of either of their lives for Claudia to say there could be nothing about Julie's character she didn't know.

And she only had Julie's word for it that the conversation at the party that had left her so mad at Gowan was as innocent as she claimed. What if, instead of gloating in a vague way about his ability to get out of trouble, he had been making specific threats to something Julie cared about? Like, for example, her business? Maybe there was some aspect of the divorce settlement that she hadn't told Claudia about, that left her vulnerable to some kind of claim on her property or her income, and with the law closing in on him, Gowan had been desperate enough to play that card? Julie and her father had been investing a lot in the farm and the creamery lately, and Claudia could believe that even a threat to their finances could be potentially disastrous. And if you already hated a man, and you knew he kept loaded guns in his office, and he was about to destroy the dream you had put everything into building, then would it really be that hard to think of taking the next step?

It was an ugly idea, made even less appealing by how plausible she was able to make it sound. Unhappy with the way her mind was working, Claudia looked around for someone else to suspect that would be less upsetting. Unfortunately, her other choices for subjects of consideration were Martin the vet, and Kathy the lawyer—even Walter, harboring a grudge over the mistreatment of the museum. It was amazing to think, really, that one small-town, small-time lawyer could have lived his life in such a way that so many otherwise unobjectionable people might be considered suspects in his murder. Some of them less credibly so than others, perhaps, but it was unavoidably true that someone had killed him, which led her to give more weight to the possibilities than she might have otherwise.

In fact, she was starting to wonder if it was a worthwhile task to try and identify the murderer. Nothing Claudia had learned about Gowan made her think the world was any poorer for his loss, and she found herself feeling a lot more sympathy for the unknown killer than she could manage for the victim. Maybe this was the time to say good riddance, and give her attention over to planning some displays for the holidays at the marketplace. (Was it too late to order reindeer for the roof?)

But that wouldn't do. Someone had walked into that office, picked up a weapon and shot a man in the head. The fact that the victim was openly terrible was relevant, but it wasn't exonerating. And just because the only people she could think of might have had a relatively sympathetic reason to commit the crime, that didn't mean whoever had actually done it did. The dead lawyer seemed to have associated with people at least as unsavory as himself, and it could be their crime she was shrugging off while Julie suffered under suspicion.

That brought her back to Mr. Newman, and what he might have been after crawling around on the marketplace roof. It couldn't have been the package that Gowan had already recovered—with as much as Newman seemed to know about the case, he must have been aware that was no longer on the premises. The most obvious answer was that he was looking for a second compartment, one that had also been used by Gowan to hold another, perhaps even more valuable cache. But if that was true, where was it? Claudia hadn't had much time to look around in the last few days, but she was aware that most of her tenants, and more than a few customers, had been going over the walls in detail and nothing had been found. And if it was there, why hadn't Gowan gone for it at the party as well? After all, he wasn't likely to get another chance like that, with almost every part of the marketplace open to him.

Almost.

Ten minutes later, Claudia was in her office, with her coffee mug in her hand and a smear of jam on her nose. Ever since she had moved in, the patch of floor in front of the desk had been the bane of her existence—just uneven enough that any chair tipped and rattled, but seemingly with no specific spot that was causing the trouble. But she was starting to have an idea about that now, and as she ran her fingers around the area, she thought about what might have happened. As tiny as it was, the room had probably been used as an office for some time—when she bought the marketplace there was already a desk there, or at least a piece of wood nailed to the wall at about the right height to be one.

It was also the only part of the building that could be locked separately from the main space, and it had been on the night of the party. She couldn't remember from her review of Gowan's movements on the video, but she suspected there would be a moment early in the recording where he tested the door before slipping back into the crowd. Maybe if she had noticed that, she could have saved herself a lot of trouble, Claudia thought.

Or maybe not. She had been down here for several minutes now, crawling on her hands and knees while she tried to fit her fingers into anything that looked like it might be a crack in the floorboards, and so far she hadn't come up with anything but three fairly nasty splinters. She was about to give the whole thing up as yet another one of her ideas that sounded better than it was, when she caught a nail on what she thought was going to be a fourth, and worst, splinter. But instead of embedding itself in her fingertip, the slim piece of wood slid up from the slot that had hidden it.

Gently, Claudia pulled on the lever. There was a feeling of resistance, like pressure against a spring, and then at about ninety degrees there was a pop and a section of floorboard, nine inches across, lifted up. Claudia opened it and found a second door beneath it.

This one had a keyhole, and for a moment Claudia was concerned that her investigation was going to be derailed by the need to find a locksmith who specialized in early-twentieth-century locks. But closer inspection revealed that time had been less kind to this compartment than the other, and a frosting of degraded metal around the lock and the hinges suggested a key might not be necessary. Sure enough, with a little effort, the door lifted off in one piece, and Claudia peered into the interior, lit by her cell phone flashlight.

They say that sometimes, when you stare into the abyss, the abyss stares back into you. In this case, it was frogs.

The bottom of the compartment was about a foot down, covered in some sort of dark sludge, on which over a dozen amphibians were resting. They looked to be the same size and variety as Claudia's old friend the toilet frog, though she would leave the positive identification to the experts, if she could find one.

And, thinking of experts, Claudia thought she had better look for one in the field of plumbing first, because while she didn't know a lot about building maintenance, she was fairly sure this much water this close to your foundation was not a good thing. Gingerly, she reached in, to test the depth, and the frogs scattered in front of her exploring fingers. To her relative relief, she found that the water was barely more than an inch deep, though on the minus side, it was also very gross.

Claudia pulled up a bit of the sludge from the bottom, hoping it wouldn't somehow be an important part of the structure. In fact, it was a bit of paper, but the water had degraded it too badly to read anything that might have been written on it.

"Find something there?"

Claudia jumped, which is hard to do when you're kneeling. Chief Weaver was standing at her office door, looking at her discovery with casual interest.

"Sorry to startle you. The door was unlocked, so I let myself in. Looks like you found a second compartment."

"Yes, just now. I was going to tell you, but I don't know how good it is. It's mostly frogs." Claudia was aware that she was babbling, and she tried to will her heart rate to slow back down from where it was working at hummingbird levels. "At least if you find that guy, you can tell him we found it, and there's nothing in it he could use. It looks like the water must have gotten in there a while ago. Maybe once he knows that, he'll stop trying to break in."

"That would probably do it," Weaver agreed. "But as it happens, I'm afraid it won't be necessary. Mr. Newman died last night."

# CHAPTER FIFTEEN

"**D**ied?" Claudia's voice was a squeak, and her heart was just going to have to take care of itself. She pictured Newman as she had last seen him, helmetless and speeding down the road on his bicycle, vanishing into the darkness, and the bottom dropped out of her stomach as she imagined herself as having helped send him to his death. She had disliked the man as much as you could dislike anyone you had only known for fifteen minutes, but that was a responsibility she could very much do without.

"Did he—did he crash?" she asked, wondering what a person's criminal culpability was for driving someone else into traffic.

"Based on the damage to his bicycle we think there might have been a car involved. Did you hear anything that sounded like a collision after he left here?"

Claudia shook her head. "No, nothing. Was he found nearby?"

"Not exactly. As a matter of fact, it would appear he actually met his end in a vintage cheese press. I think you're familiar with it? The museum that owns it has a connection to this place."

"The cheese press at the museum?" Claudia thought back to her tour, when she had admired the giant mechanism and thought how much force it must have been able to put on those long-ago curds. "Oh wow, I saw that just the other day. I was touring the museum," she explained, though she wasn't sure why. Even under the circumstances, it must have been a fairly blameless activity. But it didn't seem like the right response to yet another violent death, so she added, "That's terrible."

"It's not great," Weaver said. "I wanted to ask you, when you saw Mr. Newman last night, did he say anything about that museum?"

"No, nothing," Claudia said. "It never came up. He didn't talk much, actually, and I had the impression that he hadn't said anything at all before I showed up."

She was particularly glad now that she hadn't emphasized Julie's confrontation with this second dead man, and hoped that the others would be similarly discrete. (Or should she hope that? Claudia didn't like to admit it, but there was an uncomfortable correlation developing between men arguing with Julie and subsequently finding themselves murdered.) For a moment she considered putting all her cards on the table, telling Weaver everything she knew and suspected and let the professionals take it from there. But, between loyalty to her friend and a lingering distrust for law enforcement, she couldn't quite bring herself to do it.

If Weaver noticed Claudia's internal struggle, she didn't comment on it, just made another note on her pad and looked back down into the compartment and the soggy pile of paper.

"I'd like to take that, if you don't mind. I can send someone over to pick it up."

"Sure," Claudia said. "I don't need it. Maybe you can reconstruct it or something?"

Weaver didn't respond to that, which, considering the San Elmo Bay police department resources probably didn't extend to TV show–level technologies, was really all that needed to be said. But Claudia did think of one more thing.

"You'll ask them to be careful of the frogs, right?"

Weaver made a couple of phone calls to relay the request for some frog-safe evidence retrieval and then left, leaving Claudia to contemplate her growing selection of problems. The second murder within a week of someone who had shown an interest in her property should probably have taken first place, but she found she couldn't stop thinking about the water that might at that moment be pooling around her foundation. Attempting to distract herself, and since she was in her office anyway, she opened her email and skimmed through the subject lines, looking for anything that needed to be dealt with ASAP.

There wasn't much, but one sender's name stuck out to her as familiar for some reason. The subject was "Your Handyman Job Request," and Claudia was trying to figure out how she might have developed psychic powers and why she hadn't used them for something more useful, when she remembered Katlen Elliot was the man who had been fired for getting into Gowan's gun collection, and her impulse to contact him. She wasn't sure where he fit in with everything that had been happening now, but it was a loose end to be tied up, and no one could accuse her of reaching to come up with an excuse to talk to him.

The email was just two lines, badly punctuated and approximately spelled, inviting Claudia to call to discuss the job in question. The caption below his name offered the only specifics about his business policies: "Advance Deposit Required For All Work. Cash Or Check." and "No Jerks."

Claudia called the number, trying to sound as little like a jerk as possible.

"I think there's some water under my building, and I'm concerned it's the plumbing, because it hasn't rained in so long."

"Mm-hmm," said the voice on the other end of the line, in the tone of a young man sharing his valuable expertise. "It's probably your plumbing. It's been too long since there was any rain for it to be that."

"Right," said Claudia, who was learning how to pick her battles. "So can you come out and take a look at it? I should say, there's a crawl space under the building, but it's not very big."

In fact, the space was so tight that Claudia got secondhand claustrophobia just thinking about it. But Katlen didn't sound concerned.

"Sure, no problem. I can come by and have a look at it tomorrow." He hesitated, apparently not as aggressive as his email signature. "Also, I need a deposit up front. It's a hundred dollars. Can you bring that today? I'd come there, but I've got a job I'm working at in town."

Claudia agreed, though she cringed at the thought of the money. A hundred dollars wasn't a lot in the grand scheme of things, but her finances were tight enough that it was more than she had any business spending on a wild goose chase. (Which reminded her; she had to check to make sure the geese had water.) But at least meeting the man in person would give her a better chance to casually bring up Gowan's murder than she was likely to get over the phone. And she really did need to get the water problem looked at.

The address Katlen had given her was right downtown, only a block from Gowan's office. Given that, Claudia couldn't resist parking a short distance from her destination, so that she could walk by the scene of the crime. (The first one, anyway.) It was the first time she had been back since coming to get her car, and she was surprised at how little the sight of the building affected her. Which was good, because the office was in a well-traveled part of town, and she didn't need to be having a breakdown every time she went to the dry cleaner's, but it did make Claudia worry that she was becoming jaded.

It was while she was standing on the sidewalk, contemplating her own moral failings, that the front door of the building opened and Kathy Finley came out, carrying a pair of shopping bags full of binders. As embarrassed as Claudia was to be caught staring, she felt like it would be worse to be seen scurrying off without saying anything, so she stood her ground and greeted Kathy as she got closer.

"I was just in the area and I thought I'd stop by." Aware that she was sounding like she had come over with a Bundt cake, Claudia elaborated. "I mean, it hardly seems real, finding his body like that. I guess I felt like I needed to get some closure, by coming back to see the place."

(That might have been laying it on a little thick, but this was Northern California, after all.)

Kathy either bought it or was too polite to say otherwise.

"This is just the second time I've been back myself," she said. "The police gave me the all-clear to come in yesterday, but I wasn't able to take being here for long. Obviously, I'm not planning to work out of that place ever again, but I do need to get some of my files. It's going to take a few trips, I don't mind telling you."

Claudia didn't mind hearing it, though she couldn't think of anything to add to the conversation. As it happened, Kathy didn't require much.

In response to Claudia's vague sympathetic noises, she dove into a litany of grievances, from the poor reliability of the internet service at her house to the fact that she was expected to find someone to, as she said, "cope with the unfortunate consequences of Clark's death." When Claudia, confused, asked for clarification, she paused for several seconds and looked deeply uncomfortable before continuing.

"Well, you know, the remains. Not all of him, of course. But there was, it was a bit of a mess in his office. And the police say it's not their job! It's not mine either, but until someone figures out who's responsible for the building with all the ownership nonsense Clark set up, I'm all there is. I don't suppose you know someone?"

Claudia didn't, she regretted to admit. Though, the way things were going, it seemed like she was likely to, sooner or later. That did inspire another line of thinking, which unfortunately Claudia did out loud.

"The historical society is probably going to need that too, after what happened. I mean, the cheese press . . ."

Claudia stopped, suddenly aware that she probably shouldn't be spreading that information around, but it was too late.

"Cheese press? What happened?" Kathy looked more confused than horrified, which made sense. No one heard the words "cheese press" and thought "horrible violent death," though she supposed more people would soon. But Claudia didn't want to be responsible for that, so she kept her explanation as vague as possible.

"Oh, um, well there was a bit of a mishap at the museum. Somebody got hurt. Died, actually." On reflection, that probably wasn't quite vague enough.

"Who was it? Do you know?" Kathy asked, naturally. It might have been a good idea for Claudia to claim innocence, but having come this far, she figured she might as well see if she could get something out of it.

"It was a man named Donald Newman. Did you know him? I got the impression that he was an associate of Mr. Gowan's."

"Donny? Donny's dead?" Kathy looked shocked at the news, but not terribly hurt by it. "I knew him in passing, from when he spent a lot of time around the office a few years ago. He and Clark were thick as thieves back then. That was when they were working on the deal for the museum project—Donny had some sort of in with the developer who ended up with a bunch of the land. I suppose that explains what he was doing there, but a cheese press? I can't even imagine how he would have ended up involved in something like that." She shook her head. "But how did you know him? He must have left town long before you got here."

Subtlety really was not Claudia's strong point. And, in fact, it might be a good thing if certain facts were put into circulation. So she went on.

"He was actually caught trying to break into the marketplace last night. He claimed to be looking for something hidden there, which he said belonged to him. Actually, I wonder if that was what he was doing at the museum. If Gowan was that into hiding things in Satler family secret compartments, it might make sense for him to have used one in their house." She took a breath and then plunged into the second part of her story. "Actually, he was right to be looking in the marketplace, sort of. I found another compartment there this morning. But the water must have gotten into it a while ago—there was something in there, but it was completely ruined."

If Kathy looked a little disconcerted at this sudden rush of information, Claudia wasn't too concerned about that. Two men had come looking for things on her property and died shortly thereafter, and it seemed like a good idea to start letting people know there was nothing left to look for. She didn't know how much gossiping Kathy was involved in, but she wasn't going to miss the opportunity.

"The police took what was there, but I don't think they'll be able to do much with it," she added, to make it clear that there was absolutely nothing interesting in her possession. She might have been laying it on a bit thick, but on the other hand, two dead men.

"Oh. Well, I guess you've been busy." Kathy looked down at the bags she was carrying and Claudia was suddenly aware of how heavy they must be. As if in response, one of the paper handles creaked ominously.

"It's been nice running into you, but I really have a lot to be doing," Kathy said, looking toward her car.

"Oh, right. Sure. Me too, actually. I'm just off to see a guy about the water problem. Good luck with your stuff, and things."

The lawyer thanked her for her concern about her various possessions, and Claudia was left to wonder when and if she would ever learn to communicate like a normal adult.

At least her next conversation should be held to somewhat lower standards, if Katlen Elliot's social media and telephone manners were anything to go by. The address he had given her was another Victorian house, where he was balancing on a very tall ladder while he attached a piece of the gingerbread-style trim to the edge of the roof. She waited until he was finished, not wanting to disturb what looked like a precarious position at best. Claudia had had quite enough of violent deaths for one week.

Eventually, the young man got the piece attached to his satisfaction and, having given it a couple of wiggles for good measure, he started back down the ladder. A few other people had stopped to watch, entertainment being in short supply in San Elmo on an autumn afternoon, but once it was clear the fun was over and no one would be falling twenty feet, they wandered off, and only Claudia was left in the audience.

"Mr. Elliot?" she said, as he prepared to move the ladder to a new location. "Hi, I'm Claudia Simcoe. We spoke on the phone."

"Oh hi, right. Call me Katlen. You've got a job, right?"

He was about what Claudia had expected from his social media profile (though slightly pudgier than his pictures)—a white man in his late twenties, with sandy brown hair that was already starting to recede, a round, open face, and a T-shirt with a picture of an eagle tearing an American flag out of a bear's mouth.

"Yes, the water problem under the marketplace. Are you sure you don't want to take a look at it first? The crawl space really is pretty small."

She didn't notice the implied insult until she had said it, and there was nothing Claudia could do at that point but hope he wouldn't take it that way.

"That's okay, I can handle it," he said, either not noticing or not caring about Claudia's faux pas. "I've been in lots of tight spaces."

"Okay, sure." Claudia was having enough trouble aligning this amiable, cheerful guy with the ranting social media posts about Gowan's death that she was starting to think she had the wrong person.

There was one way to find out.

"By the way," she said, as she fished around her purse for the check. "I hate to ask, but there was something I heard about you and a gun? I just wanted to make sure—I don't want any weapons on my property."

The change that came over Katlen was immediate, and extreme. His brows drew together, and his shoulders hunched, the cheerful young man contorting into an angry troll.

"That was an accident," he said. "Nobody should leave a gun sitting around loaded like that. Anything could happen. It wasn't my fault, but no one is going to listen to me, not when there's some rich lawyer telling them what to do."

That pretty well took care of any hope that he'd learned from his experience. It didn't give Claudia a lot of confidence in the hire, but she already had the check in her hand, and she wasn't sure how she was going to graciously and safely get out of it now.

And he wasn't done.

"It's how it always works, you know? A guy like me can make one tiny mistake and everybody goes after him and wrecks his whole life. But that lawyer guy, did you know he was doing crimes? All kinds of crimes, all the time, and nothing ever happened to him at all. How is that fair?"

"Well, he did get murdered," said Claudia, who didn't entirely disagree with his thesis, but felt like he was missing a critical point.

The reminder did a lot for Katlen's mood, which Claudia was beginning to recognize as being on the volatile side. At the mention of Gowan's death, his scowl cleared and the smile returned, accompanied by a cheerful little laugh.

"He did, didn't he? I guess that's something. Gotta say, though, it's a good thing I was up in Tahoe all that week, or I might be in real trouble."

Claudia gave herself the ride home to beat herself up for wasting time on that dead end—more proof, if anyone needed it, that she had no idea what she was doing. There was probably a reason why regular people didn't go around solving murders in their spare time—actually, there were probably several, and at least one of them had to do with not having the resources or the rights to find out about people's alibis right up front.

She was as close as she had come to chucking the whole thing when she turned into her driveway and found the Dancing Cow van there waiting for her.

"Sorry to bother you," Julie said as she got out to meet her. "Do you have a minute?"

She followed Claudia into the cottage and waited until the door was closed before taking a Ziploc bag out of her purse.

"Do you know what this is?" she asked, looking around nervously.

There was no one else in the tiny house, and nothing out the window but the hillside, ocean, and sky, which made Julie's unease seem particularly unnecessary. For all that, Claudia was expecting to have been handed something particularly shocking or incriminating, but the only things in the bag were a USB hardware security key and a Post-it Note with a series of letters, numbers, and symbols on it.

"It looks like a security key to me," she said, turning the bag over in her hands. "You plug this into your computer, and you can set your passwords to only work when it's connected. It can store passwords and logins, too. Why? Where did you get it?"

Julie looked distinctly uncomfortable.

"From, well, from Gowan's office. It was hidden behind a painting."

Claudia took a minute to process this information.

"You took it? When you broke in? And you didn't give it to the police?"

"I know, I know," Julie said. "It's just, I was there, and I hadn't been able to find anything I could use against Clark, and I was already starting to feel like I'd been there too long. So I was about to go, but when I was on my way out the door I realized the painting wasn't quite flush with the wall. And that made me think maybe there was another secret compartment there, so I looked and I found this taped to the back. I shouldn't have taken it, but I was just so frustrated, and it was the only thing I'd found that seemed like it was anything, so I stuck it in my pocket without really thinking. I know it was a stupid thing to do. But it seemed like the right idea at the time."

"Well, you were right about half of that," Claudia said. She would have elaborated on the point, but another thought occurred to her. "When you were searching, how did you leave the office? Was it already messy, and you put things pretty much where they were?"

"Messy? No not at all. Clark always kept his place neat as a pin, and I left it the same way. I thought he was coming back, you see. Honestly, if it hadn't been for the van, no one would ever have known I was there."

"Huh." Claudia knew that Julie had high standards for tidiness; if she said she had left the office in order, then it had been. And that was not how Claudia had found it, which in itself was interesting. But not nearly as interesting as what was in the bag in her hand.

"How do you want me to help?" she asked, her curiosity overwhelming her better judgement.

"I was hoping you could get more information from it than I could. I know, I know, I should give it to the police. But I don't think they're going to be very trusting of anything that comes from me at this point, and I don't know what they could do with it if they wanted to. But, I thought, you know all about this computer stuff, and maybe you could at least tell me if it really is something important."

"Okay, I guess so," said the crazy person who had taken control of Claudia's mouth. (Who was actually her, of course. However much Claudia wanted to pretend she wasn't making her own bad decisions, there was only one of her there, and she was dying to know what was on the key.) "What's the note? Is that a password?"

Julie nodded. "Yes, you need it to get into the thing once you've got it plugged in. I've got to admit, I did try to use it a little bit. One of the things on there is for an email account, so I tried to go to it, but I couldn't get in. It wanted a code from my phone and I didn't have it."

"Two-factor identification," Claudia said. "For a guy who was hiding stuff in my walls, Gowan does seem to have taken his digital security seriously. Though keeping the password there with it is a weird lapse."

"Isn't it? But that's definitely his handwriting. Lord knows I've seen enough of it."

"Well, it makes things a lot easier for me, anyway. I can take a look at this now, if you like. Do you have some time to hang around and I can see what I find?"

Julie shook her head. "I'd like to, but I've got to go. They're expecting me down at the police station, and I don't want to keep them waiting too long."

"The police station? Why?"

"Well," Julie sighed deeply. "It seems like they're pretty sure I killed Mr. Newman."

# CHAPTER SIXTEEN

Despite Claudia's obvious follow-up questions, Julie didn't have a lot of answers, only that she didn't have an alibi for the time in question because, unable to sleep, she had gone to one of their hilltop fields to look at the view and think, and that, combined with the fact that she had just been seen getting in a near-physical altercation with the victim, was very familiar with the piece of equipment where he had met his end, and had a key to the museum, seemed to be putting her high on the suspect list. But the lawyer Nathan had found for her was going to meet her at the police station, and she was cautiously optimistic that she would at least be sleeping in her own bed that night. (Implied in that statement, and the worried look in her eyes, was an uncertainty about how many nights for which that would be true.)

After that, there was nothing Claudia could do but promise she would do her best with the security key, and as soon as Julie was gone, she did just that.

In truth, she wasn't very optimistic about her chances. There were probably people at the NSA who cracked three of these for fun on their lunch breaks, but she wasn't that kind of expert, and she didn't expect to become one anytime soon. But maybe there would be something she could learn from the contents of the key, even if she wasn't able to go any further.

She plugged it into the USB port on her laptop, with only a moment of anxiety about connecting an unknown device. (It was the sort of thing she was usually cautious about, but even Claudia had trouble coming up with a motive for hiding a drive with a malicious virus behind a painting.) A dialog box popped up, and she entered the password, checking carefully to make sure she had every capital letter and curly bracket right, and wondering again why someone would seemingly be so careful about their security, but not even store their password in a different place.

But it did work, and after a little more clicking around, Claudia found the list of websites and login names that it was storing. The email account was at the top, and while Claudia could understand why that had been the most interesting one to Julie, it didn't hold her attention for very long. An email account was the sort of thing you would expect someone to use a tool like this for; Claudia had been meaning to get one for herself. The next selections were slightly more esoteric but still understandable—an online Bitcoin wallet and a VPN service that she recognized as being the one her old roommate had used to fake being in the UK so she could watch British gardening shows, and then a few of what turned out to be access credentials for several HR management systems, which was mainly confusing.

But it was the next six items on the list that ended up getting most of her attention. At first glance they were unremarkable, just web addresses for sites she hadn't heard of that, when she navigated to four them offered information-free landing pages and apparently nothing else, while the other two had been taken down entirely.

It was possible, Claudia supposed, that the key was just a useless old gizmo, left over from some long-ago technology upgrade project that had gotten stuck behind the painting for some perfectly innocent reason, and everything on it was either pointless or defunct. But other things were possible too, which was why she connected her computer to her own VPN and went to take a closer look.

It had been a while since Claudia had done a port scan on a server, but she still had the tool to do it on her computer and it only took a few minutes to identify the server addresses for the viable websites and plug them in. After that, all she could do was wait while the tool did its job, so she took the opportunity to fix herself a late lunch of the last of a dish of cold noodles she had made from one of Helen's recipes. By the time she got back to the computer, sniffling a little, because she had forgotten how spicy they were, the scan was done and the results were displayed on the screen.

"That's interesting," she said, her hand frozen in the act of reaching for her water bottle.

For all of the servers, the only open ports were to the web and to a secure shell—the encrypted, locked-down way to access a server. And, considering that the web portals had all been dead ends, Claudia suspected that most of their traffic must have been going in that way. Which was, as she said, interesting. There were probably some legitimate reasons to have a server structured that way, but Claudia found it suspicious and, given the rest of the circumstances, she thought that was justified.

She took screenshots of her results and copied the website information, and then sent it all with minimal explanation to a former coworker who had moved into the security field. If anyone was going to be able to identify what she had found, it was Sanjay, and his preoccupation with his interests meant that he was unlikely to find anything unusual about her question.

What she did not do was to try to use the key to access any of the sites herself. If there had been two-factor identification set up on the email account, there was a chance it would also be on the rest, requiring a phone or other device to send the verification code to. And what worried her was what Julie apparently hadn't realized, which was that the email website had indeed sent the code, but it hadn't gone to Julie's phone. Claudia didn't know what happened to a murder victim's personal possessions while their deaths were being investigated, but she could imagine Weaver being interested in someone trying to get into the dead man's email account, if she happened to have his phone on hand.

Having given that some more thought, Claudia reluctantly came to the decision that, whatever Julie might think, she wasn't going to do either of them any favors by hanging on to this item. She was confident that there was no more information she would be able to get off of it, and every minute it was out of the hands of law enforcement was going to make things worse for both of them when that fact eventually was discovered.

On the other hand, Claudia didn't relish the idea of going down to the police station, possibly with Julie still there, and having to explain all of this to Weaver. The police chief had so far shown a total lack of a sense of humor when it came to these things, and it seemed to Claudia like she would end up faced with a lot of uncomfortable questions that she would rather not answer. And frankly, Julie was right—the odds that the local police department would be able to get any more information off the key than she had were slim to none.

On the other hand, the Federal Bureau of Investigation probably had a lot more resources to deal with this sort of thing. And a representative of that agency not only happened to be in town at the moment, but investigating this very case, and if this key represented a way that Gowan had been hiding his ill-gotten gains, then it might be more relevant to him that to Weaver anyway. And what's more, he was staying at Betty and Roy's ranch, which meant that even if things did go badly—and Claudia had no reason to believe that they wouldn't—she would have backup, or at least someone to call Nathan and see if he knew any other lawyers.

She hadn't meant to show up at the ranch right after lunchtime, but when Betty greeted her with a hug and an offer of some leftover chilaquiles, well, Claudia wasn't one to argue with fate. She ate it in the kitchen, filling Betty in on the details of her date and trying to work the conversation around to asking where Mr. Nguyen was.

"He threw up? Oh no, that's awful." Betty tried to look sympathetic, but almost immediately her expression of concern dissolved into laughter.

"I'm sorry, I'm sorry," she said as she tried to collect herself. "All that fancy food, and their special garden . . . Honestly, I've met the chef a couple of times, and she's a nice lady, it's just, did you see the magazine spread they got last month? Eight pages and the cover about how this is the future of restaurants, like they're the first people ever to figure out that plants grow in the ground. But I really am sorry your date didn't turn out as awesome as it could have been. Still, it's a story to tell your grandkids, right?"

"I don't think we're exactly at the grandkids point yet," said Claudia, who wasn't sure she ever would be. "And anyway, probably nothing would have happened, what with the guy breaking into the marketplace and stuff."

Betty had heard the outlines of that event, because news travelled fast in San Elmo, and it travelled even faster in her direction, but she pressed for details and Claudia supplied them as best she could.

"And then he goes and dies, of course. Why do people keep dying on me? Is it my deodorant?"

"We've been meaning to talk to you about that . . ." Betty raised an eyebrow at Claudia as she pulled a tray of mini carrot cakes out of the oven and put another one in. "Seriously, though, he didn't just die, someone must have killed him, which makes two people in a week. And in that cheese press, ugh. That's not funny."

"Well, humor is subjective," Claudia began, but stopped when she saw Betty's expression. "Sorry, sorry. I know, it's pretty bad. That's why I'm trying to tell everyone I can find that the papers in the second compartment were ruined, and the police have them anyway. With any luck, that should mean that no one thinks I have anything they want. Speaking of which . . ." Claudia had found the opening she was looking for, and she took the bag with the hardware key out of her pocket. "Is that guest of yours around here somewhere? I have something I think he might be interested in."

There was an argument, of course. Betty was supremely unimpressed by Claudia's sideline as an investigator, with her point of view being that there were plenty of people around who did that sort of thing for their jobs, and Claudia should leave it to them.

"But I am," Claudia pointed out. "Who's a better person to get this than an FBI agent? I'm probably even going to get Julie mad at me, for not doing what she asked."

"I can't believe Julie would really do all that," said Betty, who had a longstanding business relationship with the cheesemaker. "It doesn't seem like her at all."

Claudia picked up a fried tortilla strip and used it to scoop the last of the egg yolk from her plate. "I wouldn't have thought it either. But after what Gowan helped her ex-husband do to her, I think she must have felt like this was her last chance to get him." She looked up from her plate, her eyes bright and shrewd. "And now Weaver thinks she killed both men, and if we don't do something soon, the real killer might never be found."

Betty rolled her eyes so hard at that that Claudia thought she might pull something. But she also made a show of squeezing the block of cream cheese she had just taken out of the refrigerator, before sighing and setting it down on the counter.

"Okay, well, that's going to need to soften before I can make the frosting anyway. I guess if you're determined to be a crazy person, at least you can do it where I can keep an eye on you. It's not like he's going to leave us a bad review or something." She started to lead the way out of the kitchen, then stopped and turned back with a more serious expression.

"This whole thing, you're assuming Julie didn't kill him, right? And I don't think she did, either, but how do you know?"

"I don't," Claudia admitted. "But if she goes to prison, who's going to make next summer's burrata?"

They found Agent Nguyen alone on the patio, where he had taken his lunch, and despite the fact that he had just finished a meal that featured some of the best of Julie's cheeses, Claudia didn't think she was going to get very far with that argument with him. But she was here now, so there was nothing for it but to try her best.

"Agent Nguyen? Sorry to bother you, but you said I should get in touch if anything more came up that was related to Mr. Gowan and the things he had stored in my marketplace. And there were a couple of things, so I thought I'd stop by."

Even that didn't make him look more than politely interested, but he indicated the chair across the table from him, and Claudia took a seat. Betty remained in the doorway, radiating disapproval, but not about to miss a minute.

"I suppose you heard about my finding the second compartment," Claudia began. "I'm sorry there was nothing useful in it. I'm having someone come and look into the water problem, but I guess that doesn't help you, at this point."

Nguyen confirmed that the future state of the compartment wasn't very much in his interests.

"Chief Weaver mentioned it to me earlier—she said they were going to try and see if they could get anything out of what was in there, but she didn't sound hopeful. Is that all?"

"Not quite." Claudia pulled the bag with the key and the note out of her pocket and laid it on the table in front of him.

"It, um, it was found in Mr. Gowan's office. Before he died. According to the person who found it, it was hidden behind a painting."

"I see." Nguyen took the bag and examined its contents through the plastic. "I take it you were not the one who found it?"

"No. The person brought it to me, because sh—they thought I might be able to get something out of it. But I thought it would be a better idea to bring it to you."

The agent nodded. "That was correct. But it would have been even better to have taken it to the police. They're the ones investigating the death, not me."

"Right, of course." There was no way Claudia was going to get into her reasoning on that point. "Can you take care of that? Or do you want me to take it back and bring it to them?"

The bag vanishing into his pocket like a magician's trick was about all the answer she needed.

"I can handle it," Nguyen said. "Why don't you fill me in a little more about how you came to have this . . . item."

Claudia wasn't entirely sure what her rights were here, but she decided to press them.

"I'd rather not. It was given to me with an expectation of confidentiality. If you need proof for court or something, there's probably a way you can get it."

"Probably." The agent seemed more amused than offended. "Well, I appreciate your cooperation, as far as it goes. And please, if you happened to come into possession of anything more along these lines, I would strongly recommend you hand them along, to me or to the local authorities. I'll be in town until Wednesday at least."

Claudia registered that both for her own information, and also that it was a good for Betty and Roy to get the business. Which raised another question for her, and she didn't see any reason not to ask.

"Does the FBI always put you up in places like this?" asked Claudia, who might have been considering a career change.

That got a rueful smile. "Not hardly. I was supposed to stay in the motel in town, but it closed suddenly and I had to scramble. It was this or the golf course, and my bosses definitely aren't authorizing that kind of cost."

"That makes sense." For a place that was so dependent on tourists, the San Elmo Bay community was surprisingly resistant to giving them places to stay. Other than the ranch, and scattering of bed and breakfasts, the main options were the aforementioned luxury golf resort, and a motel near the fishing port that had been built in the fifties and slowly decaying ever since. It was mostly slow at least, but a couple of weeks earlier it had closed suddenly, when the exterior staircase fell off the building.

"Well, I hope you've had a nice time," Claudia said, as it gradually dawned on her that the more time she spent here talking to Nguyen, the more likely she was to say something that get her into real trouble. But she couldn't resist trying to get just one more answer to something that had been bothering her.

"By the way, I was wondering—what was it that made you come after Gowan now? It seems like he had been doing his thing for a while. Did something happen?"

"The agency has a variety of criteria for prioritizing cases," he said, meeting Claudia's eyes with a serious gaze that gave nothing away. "On occasion, the process can take some time."

"Of course, I understand." And then feeling, inaccurately, that she had very little left to lose, Claudia took a gamble. She didn't want to let on that she had gotten a look at the contents of the key that she had just so responsibly turned over to the appropriate authorities, but the fact was that she had, and ever since seeing it, questions had been forming in her mind. She couldn't ask all of them, but there were things that kept coming up, offhand comments in passing conversations—credit card skimmers, tax problems, one person after another who had their identities stolen—that took on a different texture with that new information.

So she went ahead and asked.

"When you are making that kind of decision, if there were a lot of other crimes going on in an area, might that, theoretically, make you look more closely, maybe bring the most obvious one to the forefront? Just, you know, in terms of things that could happen."

The agent's poker face was good, but it wasn't perfect. There was just the barest flicker in his expression—it might have been nothing more than some momentary discomfort, but Claudia knew no one got gas from eating Betty's food.

Instead, she was sure she had just gotten some useful information, though what exactly it was would take some figuring out. In the meantime, she figured she had pressed her luck far enough.

"Anyway, I'm sure you're busy," she said, standing up abruptly. "Thanks for your help. With getting the key to the police, I mean. I mean, the item."

Claudia felt like she had probably incriminated herself enough for one day, and she was ready to go, but this time it was Nguyen who had a final question for her. He folded his napkin and set it on the table, then focused on her with a piercing and surprisingly eager gaze.

"I heard that you went to Harry's Barn? What's it like?"

Back in her cottage, Claudia was sitting on her couch with her third cup of coffee and trying to get her head around the things she did and didn't know. There was a lot in the second category, so she started with the first.

Two men were dead, one shot in his office first thing in the morning, and one crushed by a historic cheese press some time in the night. Both were deeply unpleasant men, and both had been interested in the contents of some secret compartments that no one had told Claudia were in her building. (And both had raised the ire of Julie, but she wasn't going to get into that just yet.) There were plenty of other people who had a reason to hate the first victim, among them her vet, Gowan's fellow lawyer and tenant, and her new part-time handyman, whose alibi she should probably check out, though Claudia had no idea how she would do that. She supposed she could even add the museum curator to the list, who Gowan had come so close to depriving of a place to store his precious tractors. But what did any of those people have to do with Mr. Newman? According to Kathy, he had been involved in the shenanigans around the museum deal, so there was that. But that had all happened years ago—why wait this long to get revenge? It came back to the same question Claudia had asked Nguyen: why now?

And that brought her back to her guess, and his response. There was criminal activity going on in and around San Elmo, more than was usual for a town its size, and things that had nothing to do with creative paperwork around property assets. Was Gowan involved somehow in a larger criminal conspiracy? Was that what Newman had meant, when he said he was looking for something valuable? Claudia had not had a lot of dealings with organized crime, but she supposed that if you were able to return something to them that could otherwise expose their operation, they might be willing to compensate you for it.

Or they might kill you.

Claudia shook her head. She was getting to be as bad as Iryna. Mobsters putting out hits? What was next, a coastal cult that had killed both men as a sacrifice to their sea-lion god? People got their credit cards skimmed and their identities stolen all the time—those were just the hazards of the modern world. And if a man who had made his living helping others defraud their nearest and dearest had finally made one enemy too many in the same town that had had a run of those kinds of crimes, was that really so hard to believe?

Or was her problem more that the most believable version of that scenario involved someone she liked? Julie had as much reason to hate Gowan as anyone, had had a confrontation with him not long before he died, knew about the guns in his office, and had, in fact, burgled that same office that night. She was also the person in town with the best and most intimate knowledge of the cheese press—who else would have that as the first thing on their mind when they were looking for a way to kill a man? True, her asking Claudia to help her solve the case didn't necessarily fit in with the theory, but that was assuming she actually thought Claudia was capable of doing something productive on those lines. What if she hadn't, and her real takeaway from Claudia's previous investigatory experience was that she could be trusted to throw suspicion on herself, drawing it away from Julie? That could even explain why she had handed off the security key; maybe she had hoped that Claudia would be caught with it, or do something stupider than she already had.

If so, then Julie was both far more devious than Claudia had ever given her credit for, and a completely different person than she knew. And while she could bring herself to accept the former, for Claudia, the latter idea remained a bridge too far. She might not be the world's greatest judge of character, but even at her least perceptive, Claudia thought she was better than that.

Which still left her with several rational options, but she couldn't manage to get herself interested in any of them. Instead, she kept coming back to the security key, and the look on Agent Nguyen's face when she asked about the other crimes. There was something there, she thought, something just out of her reach that almost made sense. She closed her eyes to try to chase the phantom of an idea, but it kept slipping away until, finally, she fell asleep.

By the time she woke up, the autumn sun was low in the sky and Claudia had a charley horse in her calf. Trying to straighten it out, she overbalanced and fell in slow motion off the couch, tumbling to a stop next to the coffee table, where Teddy came to helpfully lick her face.

Eventually, she managed to extract herself, and she was thinking about how living alone had some advantages, like not having anyone around to see you when you did things like that. Then she went to the refrigerator and discovered one of the downsides, which was that when you were completely out of things to eat for dinner, you had no one to blame but yourself. Normally, in a situation like this, Claudia would come up with an excuse to drop by the ranch and help Betty out with her leftovers, but even under normal circumstances, twice in one day was a bit much, and she didn't think she should be going back there right now. And since delivery wasn't exactly in her budget, there was nothing for it except to put her pants back on and go to the store.

The grocery options in San Elmo were limited, and most people went into one of the larger towns further inland for the bulk of their shopping. But that was at least half an hour each way, and Claudia didn't have the patience for an expedition right now. So, as happened more often than she cared to admit, she made her way to the small market in the center of town to check out their current freezer selection.

There were two frozen pizzas in her basket, and Claudia was considering the wisdom of the vegetarian enchiladas when she heard a familiar voice.

"Busted! I can see the headline now—Organic Foods Doyenne Caught In Dalliance With Preservatives. It'll be the scandal of the week, if we have one without any murders."

Claudia didn't need to turn around to know she had run into her favorite member of the local media, but she did anyway, making a quick check of his basket on the way.

"Hi, Todd. You're in an awfully good mood for someone who's buying three different kinds of gluten-free crackers and a bag of prunes. Having the saddest party ever?"

That came out meaner than she had meant it, but the reporter didn't seem to mind. In fact, he laughed like it was the best joke he had heard in years. Claudia wondered what had brought on this outbreak of cheer, and she didn't have to wait long to find out.

"Maybe I will have a party, now that I think of it. And you'll have to be invited, considering this was all your doing to start with."

"It was?" Claudia asked, worried about what she could have done this time.

"Well," Todd said, lowering his voice and leaning in conspiratorially. "I shouldn't be telling you this, but it's only fair. You remember when that woman got killed in your marketplace a couple of months ago?"

Claudia admitted that she was able to recall the incident.

"Right, so at the time you came up with something about this cult guy she had maybe had a run-in with in the past. And that didn't turn out to be anything, but when I was following up on that lead, I managed to find out some stuff. You know how there was the guy who was running it, the one who went to jail and moved to Humboldt after he got out?"

"Serenity Icono Bartok," Claudia said. (It was the sort of name that stuck with you.)

"So, he's going by Gentleman Mo now, but yeah, that's the guy. And it turns out he hasn't been being so much of a gentleman lately. In fact, he's gone back to his old ways."

"Another cult?" Claudia was starting to wonder if it was even possible for her to think of something weird enough to not have it happen.

"Kind of. But this time he's dropped the whole love and light thing and gone straight for telling people he can teach them to make themselves rich with his special system."

"Which is?" Claudia was starting to get an idea, but she wanted to hear him say it.

"A nice combination of visualization, positive thinking, mantras, and credit card skimmers they've been installing at businesses up and down the coast. I'm still working on the details, but I've gotten a couple of former members to talk and I'd like to round up a few more. The guy is pretty litigious, so I want to make sure I've got all my Ts dotted and my Is crossed."

Claudia was impressed. "That's quite a story. I'm impressed you've managed to get so much so quickly."

"Yes, well, I had some luck." Todd's attempt at modesty was undermined by the extreme self-satisfaction in his expression, but Claudia didn't begrudge him it. She did have one more question, though.

"You mentioned the credit card skimmers—were they doing any business in identity theft also?"

Todd shook his head.

"No, just the skimmers, I'm pretty sure. One guy even stole a laptop, and Mr. Gentleman chewed him out for that something terrible. It's part of this whole mythology he has, where—" Realizing that a couple of other shoppers had overheard their conversation and stopped to listen, Todd finally managed to rein himself in. "Well, you'll just have to read the article to find out. It's going to be like nothing else you've ever seen."

That, Claudia could well believe. She repeated her congratulations and promised not to tell anyone about the story before it was published. (Politely ignoring the possibility that there wouldn't be much point, because he would have told them already.) Todd thanked her again for the tip and said that in exchange, he wouldn't out her shameful pizza habit and they parted on friendly terms, despite some frustration on Claudia's side. For a minute there she had thought she might be getting somewhere with the idea of Gowan being involved in some sort of criminal conspiracy, but she wasn't sure she could see him getting mixed up with a cult, or how she would find out any more if he was.

As she paid for her groceries, absentmindedly adding a bag of powdered mini donuts from the bakery stand by the register as they were being rung up, she wondered how a person went about trying to get themselves recruited into a cult, and if Betty would consult on the outfit.

# CHAPTER SEVENTEEN

Claudia was microwaving the enchiladas when the texts started coming in. By the time she figured out which jacket pocket she had left her phone in there were already four of them, all from Sanjay, and increasing in urgency.

*Where is this from*
*What are you getting into*
*Seriously, do you know what you're doing?*
*I'm going to call*

It was the last one that got Claudia's attention. Sanjay was famous among their former coworkers for his hatred of talking on the phone—any voicemail left for him would generally lead to a response by text at least a week later. So the fact that her phone was ringing either meant he had found something very serious on the list she had sent him, or three years was long enough for a person to undergo a complete personality change, vis-à-vis phone conversations.

"This list you sent me, are you crazy?" he said as soon as Claudia picked up, confirming it was the former.

"Yeah, probably. What is it?"

"It's a lot of trouble, that's what. Where did you get it?"

"That's a long story. Basically, it's all from a hardware security key that a friend of mine found and wanted to know more about. If it helps, I didn't access any of the accounts."

"That's good. But maybe you want to tell this 'friend' of yours that they should be less curious."

Sanjay clearly didn't think the friend existed, and Claudia wasn't going to bother explaining.

"Okay, so now that you've got me all interested, what are they? I recognized the email and the Bitcoin locker, but that's about it."

"Yeah, those are fine. And there's a couple others that would be normal if . . . you seriously don't know what these are?"

"Seriously." Claudia remembered now that Sanjay had always had a flair for the dramatic, and she was starting to get annoyed. "That's what I was hoping you could tell me. Sometime this month, if possible."

"Okay, okay. It's just—fine, anyway. Basically, what you've got here is all the account information for someone who's in business selling stolen identities on the internet. Forum accounts, online black market passwords—whoever had this was taking their security seriously, which is why I am a little worried about you having it."

"Well, if it makes you feel any better, the FBI has it now."

"Huh. Better than nothing, I guess. Anyway, your friend or whatever seems to have been busy, because they had accounts at several marketplaces, including some that have been closed. You're sure they don't know you have this anymore?"

"Pretty sure." Claudia didn't want to explain that the former owner was currently in a place where security keys didn't matter much. "Anyway, thanks. Sorry to bother you with this. We should catch up sometime when it's not, you know, about crimes and stuff."

"Sure, definitely." Sanjay still sounded distracted, and Claudia didn't blame him. She had expected that her new way of life would mean she would end up drifting away from her old friends and colleagues, but this wasn't quite what she had envisioned. Still, there was one more question she had to ask.

"You said identity theft. Is there any chance the person was also selling stolen credit cards? Like what you might get using one of those skimmer devices."

"Nah, different market. It's crazy the level of specialization there is out there. I can send you some websites if you want to read up on it. Just information, I mean."

Claudia said that would be helpful and, after she had reassured him another time that she wasn't in immediate danger of running afoul of an international cybercriminal mastermind, Sanjay ended the call with what sounded like considerable relief.

Claudia was less comforted. She had expected the hardware key to have something on it that wasn't quite aboveboard, but nothing she learned seemed to make sense with anything else. Why identity theft? Why keep the password in the same place as the key? If he had access to all of these sophisticated online resources, what was Gowan doing hiding papers in Claudia's walls and floor? How many crimes could one man commit? Where did he find the time?

Or . . . fragments of conversations and unconnected ideas started to float back into Claudia's mind. A personal recommendation, the problems of a small business, a criminal who told his friend he wasn't in danger of prosecution. Suddenly, all of the disparate pieces of information were like one of those posters Claudia had gone cross-eyed staring at in third grade, that looked like they were just random swirls of dots until you focused on them just right, and a rabbit popped out at you.

But the figure that was forming in her mind's eye was no bunny. If she was right—and she had no reason to believe she was, but no reason not to—the person she was picturing was desperate, dangerous, and in too deep to stop at anything now.

And there was another image, one of Julie trying to get into an email account and not being able. Claudia had been worried Julie might be in trouble if the 2FA notification went to Gowan's phone, but now it occurred to her that it could be a lot worse if it hadn't.

A call to Julie's phone went straight to voicemail, which wasn't unusual, but it was still worrying. The cell phone signal was so bad out at the farm that mostly Julie didn't bother to charge it until she was in the car, but in this case, Claudia would have liked some more commitment to connectivity.

The next thing Claudia did was call the creamery, hoping against hope that Julie was there, or even better, had been put safely in jail. But the phone kept ringing, past the point she would have normally expected it to go to a machine, only to have Elias pick up, sounding annoyed.

"Julie? No, Julie isn't here. She had to go to the museum, some kind of emergency. You want me to take a message?"

"No, no message." Claudia's mind was racing. "Elias, you're going to think I'm crazy, but Julie might be in real trouble. If you hear from her, tell her not to go to the museum. I'm heading there now; I need you to call the cops. Tell them, I don't know, tell them something. If I'm wrong, I'll deal with it."

"The police! Let me tell you about the police." Elias clearly had every intention of doing just that, but Claudia didn't have the time."

"No, I'm leaving now. Call them, please."

It only took her a couple of minutes to find her shoes and grab her coat, but Claudia was already worrying about Elias's reliability to raise the warning. He might pass on her message, or he might get distracted by his own grievances and end up ranting to some poor dispatcher until they hung up on him. She needed a backup plan so, on her way out the door she stopped and texted to Nathan.

*Julie at the museum. Trouble. Call the police.*

There was no way of knowing what Elias had meant when he said Julie had just left—his grasp of time was as vague as his command of English.

But Claudia had reason to believe she wasn't too far behind; Julie might have a head start, but she had further to go, and probably wasn't taking the curves at fifty miles an hour. Claudia pushed the hatchback to its limits and beyond, and the little car responded with squealing tires and a disturbing smell that Claudia hoped wasn't the transmission.

There was a chance, of course, that all this was for nothing, and she was going to get to the museum and find an emergency meeting to decide what to do about a skunk family in the basement. Which would be fine, as far as she was concerned. Because if what Claudia suspected was right, there was a murderer out there who thought Julie was holding a key piece of evidence that they would do anything to get back.

A scattering of raindrops appeared on her windshield as she rounded a corner on slightly less than four wheels, and Claudia tried to focus on what she would do when she got where she was going. In her hurry to leave, she hadn't brought anything that she could use as a weapon, and while there might have been something in the car that would count, she didn't want to spend the time it would take to look for it. So it would be down to the element of surprise and what counted as her wits, and she just had to hope that Nathan had managed to get through to the police.

She was past the housing development before the rain started coming down in a serious way. As much as Claudia had been hoping for the change in the weather, the timing was not great. In the long dry season plenty of drops and dribbles of oil had built up on the surface of the road, forming a thin layer that was beginning to lift off and float on top of the water. There were a couple of close calls, but Claudia managed to keep the car under control, right up to the moment she turned into the museum driveway and just kept turning.

Claudia managed to maintain the presence of mind not to slam on the brakes and settled on screaming a variety of swear words, none of which had much effect. The hatchback ended up sideways across the parking lot entrance, its bumper firmly stuck under the sign that said trespassers would be towed.

"Good luck with that," Claudia muttered under her breath as she climbed out the passenger door.

The Dancing Cow van was alone in the parking lot, which at least answered the question of whether Claudia was the first one there, though not in the way she would have liked. She would have thought the manner of her arrival would have ruined any chance she might have had at surprising anyone, but as she approached the shed, she could clearly hear voices coming from inside. Two of them—and one was Julie's, to Claudia's relief. She couldn't make out the words over the rising wind, but neither sounded happy, and the non-Julie voice rang with increasing desperation.

"Tell me where it is. This is your last chance!"

"Or what? I can't tell you anything if you shoot me." Julie's words sounded defiant, but there was a tone to them that Claudia recognized. (She knew from experience that it was very hard to make defiance sound convincing when someone was pointing a gun at you.)

The main door to the shed was standing open, the crime scene tape that had been stretched across it broken and floating in the wind, but inside the lights were off. Claudia pressed herself next to the wall and peered through the crack by the hinges, hoping she didn't cast too much of a shadow.

Julie was standing in the middle of the room, facing Claudia, her hands held up like someone had told her to keep them there. Between her and the door there was another figure, short and squat, holding something at chest level that was aimed in Julie's direction. Claudia couldn't see her face, but she didn't need to. If the familiar voice wasn't enough, there was still the fact that Kathy Finley was carrying the same tote bag she had used to hit her with.

"I can make you talk," she was saying. "I have ways. This is quite a museum you have here, you know? Got a lot of options. I'm not using the cheese press again, though. You know that handle sticks, right? It's a huge pain."

"I'll be sure to look into that." Julie was looking around her now, probably hoping to find something she could use to defend herself, but from her spot in the middle of the room she was too far to be able to reach any of the displays easily. But her searching eyes passed over the door, and in the darkness Claudia thought she saw a flash of awareness cross her face.

"You're sick," she said, taking a half step further back into the room. "You need help."

"What I *need* is for you to stop messing around and tell me where you put my property. Otherwise, as soon as I'm done with you here, I'm going to go to that farm of yours and I'll do whatever it takes to find it."

It might have seemed absurd, this petite, middle-aged woman threatening torture and murder, but Claudia didn't feel much like laughing. There was a crude certainty in her threats—even if Kathy wasn't actually able to carry them out, she believed that she was, and that was danger enough.

There might have been some intent in the way Julie was drawing Kathy further from the door, or it might have just been luck, but they were now far enough into the barn that she couldn't even see the entrance in her peripheral vision. It was still a risk, Claudia thought, but it was now or never, particularly as far as Julie was concerned.

She waited for a moment when the rain got heavier, the clouds blotting out what little light was coming from the night sky and then skirted around the door and into the shadows on the other side, hoping the squelching from her shoes wouldn't give her away.

In front of her, Julie had lost her temporary control of their movements, and was being driven back, toward the barbed wire display, as Kathy kept up a steady stream of threats to her and her family. There were terms she was using that even Claudia hadn't heard before, and she had once dated a paramedic who wrote horror novels in his spare time. She felt terrifyingly exposed standing there by the door, only about twenty feet away from such violent fury, not to mention the gun.

But she wasn't the one who was in trouble, at least not yet. Julie had spotted her as soon as she came inside, and though she was doing a masterful job of not letting on that she saw her, she was bound to expect Claudia to do something to help, and soon.

A plan would have been useful here, but Claudia didn't have one, so instead she picked up one of the tools that had been left leaning against the door and hoped for the best.

Seeing her approach, Julie focused on her attacker and raised her voice.

"As soon as I tell you, you're just going to shoot me anyway. If you want to know what happened to your thing, I need to get some kind of guarantee from you."

Kathy laughed, a sharp, barking sound.

"The only thing I'm guaranteeing is it stops with you if I know where to look. But thank you for confirming that you do have it." She shook her head. "It's that kind of poor judgement that's been your problem all along. I remember Clark talking about how hopeless you were when he was doing your husband's case. And I'm not saying I haven't made mistakes myself, but at least I've learned from them."

"That might be true," Julie said. "But I'm not about to get hit in the face with a shovel."

Kathy turned just as Claudia swung, catching her squarely across the cheek. The gun went off, but the shot went wide, and before she could fire again, Julie tackled her at the knees. That sent Kathy flying into Claudia, who was already overbalanced from the swing, and all three of them hit the ground in a heap.

Between them, Claudia and Julie should have been able to contain the much smaller woman, but Kathy had the strength of desperation and, frankly, the gun, and their tentativeness about the latter must have been enough for her to employ the former to kick herself free and get away.

She didn't head for the front door, possibly because Claudia was lying in the way, instead darting toward the back, making it out into the courtyard before Claudia and Julie could get to their feet. Over the sound of the rain, they could hear the sound of a tractor starting, and by the time they were at the doorway it was already vanishing into the orchard.

"I think she has a car parked down by the road, I saw one there on the way in. Come on, we can take my van," Julie said.

"There's a problem with that. I kind of blocked the driveway on my way in."

Julie turned and looked back out the front door.

"Okay, so not that. But we have to stop her."

"The police—"

"Did you hear the things she was saying, threatening my family? We can't let her get away."

"We won't," Claudia said, suddenly resolved. "You try to get in touch with someone, I'm going after her."

She took off on foot, ignoring Julie shouting something behind her. There was no time to be arguing tactics now.

The tractor wasn't moving very fast, but thanks to the heavy mud that both slid under and stuck to her shoes, neither was Claudia. Still, she stumbled ahead, as the vehicle disappeared into the gloom, hoping for a break that would allow her to make up some ground. It was easy to follow where it had gone, at least, thanks to the deep tire tracks in the only tractor-sized path through the trees. Claudia tried running in them, between them, and on the grass next to the path, but nothing seemed to help her speed. At this point, she thought, her best hope was that Kathy would have trouble finding her car keys in that bag of hers, and she could catch up to her then. (Ideally, without the gun being a factor. She had forgotten about the gun.)

Claudia slipped and squelched on, wondering how she had managed to get herself into this situation, and how she was going to get herself out, when help came from an unexpected direction. There was a low rumble behind her and, turning to look, Claudia saw a hulking shape loom out of the darkness. A moment later it resolved itself into one of the other tractors, with Julie in the driver's seat, her hands gripping the giant wheel on both sides.

"Get on! It took me a minute to get it started or I'd have been here sooner."

The tractor was not exactly a two-person vehicle, but Claudia managed to wedge herself onto one of the rusty fenders in what was almost a stable position. (Her jeans were a write-off, but that was the least of her concerns at the moment.) The increase in speed wasn't tremendous, more like a slow jogging pace, but it was enough that Claudia thought she could see them drawing closer to the other tractor ahead.

"This is the fastest one in the collection," Julie explained, intuiting her thoughts. "And the most valuable. Walt is going to kill me if anything happens to it."

"Yeah, well, you should be used to that by now. I'm sorry I didn't get to you sooner—I should have figured out that it was Kathy a long time ago."

They were closing the distance, but not very quickly, and there was plenty of time to talk while Julie steered the tractor under the dripping trees.

"I'm just glad you made it at all. And it's more figuring out than I did. How did she know I had that computer thing, anyway? That's what she was looking for, right?"

"Right. Unfortunately, I think it was because you tried to use it to get into the email. When you did that, it sent a code to her phone that you were supposed to enter, and she knew someone had it, and that person was still alive. I think until then she probably thought Newman was the one who had gotten it. The FBI has the key now, by the way. I'm sorry, but it really seemed like the right thing to do."

"I understand. It's what I should have done in the first place." The rain had plastered Julie's hair to her head, but she showed no signs of discomfort beyond occasionally wiping the water out of her eyes.

Of course, she had the seat, Claudia thought, as a tractor part dug into her calf.

Trying to ignore the discomfort, she went on. "I don't know for sure, but my best guess is that Gowan stole the key from her, because he wanted to use it to make a deal with the FBI. That would be why the password was with it. He must have installed a keystroke logger on her computer or something to get it, so he would be able to hand over some solid evidence of her crimes."

"What crimes? What could she have done that was so much worse than him?"

"Large-scale identity theft. And murder, but that came later."

"Her? How? And why?"

Claudia ducked to avoid a branch that hung over the path, nearly losing her balance in the process.

"For the 'why' I'm going to guess money," she said once she was fairly sure she wasn't about to tumble off into a ditch. "She mentioned having been through a divorce that left her in a pretty bad way, and she may have felt like she didn't have a lot of options. And the how would be easy. She mentioned to me that she has been doing tax work for a lot of the small employers around town, which somehow must have involved her getting access to their HR services providers. She could claim a legitimate reason to get into their systems, collect everyone's tax information, and then spread out the sale of it over time to make it harder to track the source."

"That happened to me! And I paid her to help me straighten it out!"

"Yep. Get them coming and going. Of course, most of her victims wouldn't be right here in town—that would be too risky. But she probably made more from the victims she took on as clients than from selling their data in the first place."

"Despicable," said Julie. "And Clark knew about it, but instead of stopping her, he kept it quiet for his own benefit."

They had travelled about half a mile at this point, and the gap between the two tractors had noticeably closed. Claudia would have been worried about Kathy overhearing their conversation, but the sound from the pair of vintage engines made it a nonissue. The gun remained a definite issue, though.

"Right. I don't know if he was blackmailing her, or just keeping it as insurance for a situation like this, but she found out, probably around the time he stole her security key."

"Or he might have told, just to taunt her. That's the sort of thing he would do. Clark thought he was smarter than everyone, and he thought everyone should know it."

"Huh. Well, that would be pretty dumb. Anyway, however it happened, she went ahead and shot him, and when she didn't find the key when she searched the office then, she figured she would have plenty of time to look for it later. That's probably why she was so shocked to see me there when she arrived in the morning. Whatever her plans were, I didn't suit them."

They were close enough to the other tractor now that they could make out Kathy's figure distinctly, struggling with the gears and occasionally looking back. She must not have liked what she saw, because the next thing she did was to dig through her bag, and before Claudia could say "I think she's going for the gun," she was proven right by the sound of a shot.

Claudia ducked, as best she could, but Julie was surprisingly unconcerned.

"I doubt she can hit us from this distance. I got a pretty good look at the gun, and I think it's one from Clark's collection, some kind of revolver. Like an Old West gun, but smaller. I can't imagine it's very accurate."

That was not sufficiently comforting for Claudia.

"But she still might miss missing us," she pointed out, hanging on to the front of the tractor with one hand and the fender with another as she struggled to keep herself low without falling off or catching her jacket in the wheel. "And we need some kind of plan for when we do get close enough."

Another shot rang out, and Claudia thought she heard it hit a tree somewhere to her right.

"Well, it's a revolver, isn't it? That means she only gets so many shots before she runs out of bullets. And she's already used three. They all have six, right?"

"I have no idea. I'd Google it, but I don't have any free hands right now."

"And she took my phone. I guess we're just going to have to hope, then." Julie was taking the situation entirely too calmly for Claudia's liking, to the point that she wondered if her friend was suffering from some kind of shock. Or maybe it was just a case of having faced the potential of being shot at close range, their current level of danger seemed manageable by comparison.

Still, Claudia appreciated Julie's optimism, as well as her tractor-driving abilities, and hoped that both would be enough to see them through. Unfortunately, Kathy must have figured out the thing about the bullets around the same time they did, because she stopped firing and was looking around, possibly seeking a place to make a stand.

"I think we're going to need to split up," Claudia said. "When she stops, or we get close enough, I'll get off and come around from the side. She can only shoot at one of us at a time, and maybe we'll get lucky." She thought for a moment more. "I wish I'd brought the shovel."

Julie didn't argue with her plan, which Claudia took to mean she wasn't able to come up with anything better. She didn't relish the idea of leaving the relative protection of the tractor and trusting her life to the unreliability of a vintage handgun, but at this point there didn't seem to be any other options, if they wanted to stop a two-time killer from escaping free and clear.

As had happened so often lately, Claudia turned out to be completely wrong about that.

They had been out in the rainy, unlit night for long enough that her eyes were fully adjusted to the dark, able to pick out the pale windfall apples on the ground and the shape of Kathy's head as she huddled over the tractor's steering wheel. So it came as a shock when they rounded a curve in the path and were confronted by the sudden illumination of a pair of headlights.

"This is the police!" said a disembodied voice from somewhere behind the spots in Claudia's eyes. "Drop your weapon and step away from the tractor."

# CHAPTER EIGHTEEN

The backseat of the police car was not very comfortable, but it was dry and quiet and no one was shooting at her, so Claudia considered it an upgrade. The initial encounter with Weaver had involved a lot of shouting, mostly from Kathy, who was trying to convince the police chief that she was the victim, being chased by a pair of out-of-control murderers bent on killing her and framing her for the other deaths. That hadn't gone over well, partly because, and Weaver pointed out, it was Claudia who had relayed the message that brought her to the museum, but mostly because Kathy still had the gun. So she was in the chief's SUV, in handcuffs, while Claudia and Julie remained uncuffed in separate patrol cars that had arrived later. From that, Claudia intuited she was in some amount of trouble, but not the maximum quantity.

Leaning back in the seat, she closed her eyes and listened to the sound of the rain on the car roof. There were a lot of things, Claudia thought, she could have done differently. But Julie was alive and a killer was in custody, and that had to be worth something. It was to her, anyway, she decided. Sometimes, all you can do is your best.

There seemed to be a lot going on outside, and after a while Claudia started to wonder if she had been forgotten about. Eventually, she dozed off, sleeping fitfully until the car's front door opened, sending a blast of cold, wet air into her face.

"Sorry about the delay," said the policeman. "The chief is going to want to talk to you later, but I just need to get a statement from you now, and then we can take you home. I understand there's an issue with your car?"

There were so many things that Claudia wanted to ask, and explain, and try to excuse, but something told her this wasn't the time. Possibly it never would be.

So all she said was, "Yes, I think it's going to need a tow truck," and waited for the questions.

As tired as she was, Claudia didn't get a chance to sleep in the next morning. Weaver was on her doorstep at eight-thirty, ready with her notebook to ask all the questions Claudia had already answered, plus a few more. Claudia tried her best to justify her decisions, and not get Julie in any more trouble than she probably already was, but she didn't think she was more than partially successful at any of her goals.

It didn't help that she had woken up still groggy, with a splitting headache, like a hangover without having had the fun. The last thing she wanted to do was to complain about it to the chief, who must have been up for hours longer than her and seemed to be suffering no effects at all. But it must have showed, because after Weaver had her go over her reasoning for why she thought Julie might be in trouble one more time, she set down her notebook and studied her face.

"Shock can manifest in a variety of ways," she said, conversationally. "Sometimes it can take a while for all of the effects to become apparent."

Claudia flushed.

"Thanks. I mean, I'm okay. I wasn't really in that much danger, not compared to Julie."

"I wasn't talking about last night. A couple of months ago, you went through a similar situation, didn't you? Only that time, you weren't in control of what was happening."

Claudia didn't know what to say.

"I, um, yes, I guess so. What do you mean?"

Weaver closed her notebook and got ready to leave.

"You've been making some unusual decisions lately. Ones that I think might not be typical for you. I hope you can see now how they have the potential to put the people around you in danger."

Claudia was quiet for a minute while she thought about that.

"Okay," she said. "But why are you telling me this? I mean, how do you know?"

There was a flicker of a smile on Weaver's face. "Sometimes, even cops can know things."

Claudia braced herself for a further lecture on leaving police work to the experts, but it didn't come. Instead, Weaver seemed to lose interest in that line of conversation, reaching into her briefcase to pull out an unmarked folder.

"Incidentally, you might be interested to learn that we were able to retrieve some information from those papers you recovered from your floor. It appears that some of them were, in fact documents relating to certain bank accounts where Mr. Gowan was holding some off the books assets."

"Of course. Well, that explains why Newman was so interested in getting at them. I guess whatever Gowan got out of the first compartment is long gone, though. My guess was that it had to do with what Kathy was up to, but if she got them then we'll probably never know."

"You would think that, wouldn't you?" Weaver was more relaxed than Claudia had seen her, leaning back in her chair and giving every appearance of enjoying the mug of nuclear-grade coffee, which was the only way Claudia brewed it. Claudia wasn't sure if it was a ploy, the relief of having a suspect in custody, or if the chief just enjoyed doing a bit of showing off, but it was a nice change.

"As a matter of fact," she went on. "There was an envelope matching that description in Ms. Finley's bag when she was arrested last night, which contained some additional documents related to her crimes. It seems that after she had retrieved it, she hadn't been able to find an acceptably secure way to dispose of the papers. Possibly the fact that my people had confiscated the office's shredder was part of the problem."

"She had it in her bag the whole time?" The whole idea was absurd, but there was one part that particularly stuck out in Claudia's mind. "She hit me with it!"

"That's very likely. It's a shame it didn't come out then. Would have saved us a lot of trouble."

"No kidding." Claudia would have liked to dwell on that possibility for a little longer, but something else that Weaver had said suddenly stood out to her. "Wait—you said only some of the papers from the second compartment were Gowan's. What were the rest?"

"As a matter of fact, that was what I wanted to tell you." Weaver took a folder out of her own bag and spread out some photocopied pictures on the table. "It looks like there were some older documents that may have belonged to an earlier owner of your building in there. Once we confirm they have nothing to do with the case we can return them to you, and I thought you might want to make some arrangements to try and have them restored."

"Wow, yes, thank you." Claudia wasn't even sure where to start with that, but as she examined the faint and spidery handwriting in the images, she was determined to try. She had never been much of a history buff, but it was hard to resist the allure of a secret that had been right under her feet.

Thinking about history and its fans reminded Claudia of another question she had that she still lacked an answer for.

"Speaking of the secret compartments, I was wondering if you ever found out anything about the missing page in the disclosures about the marketplace? I think I mentioned it to you—I haven't been able to reach the realtor to get an answer."

An expression passed over Weaver's face that Claudia couldn't quite identify.

"We were able to get in touch with her, and I'm afraid we haven't gotten a satisfactory answer to that question. But it doesn't appear to have much bearing on our case, so the information has been forwarded to the FBI."

Claudia wondered what Nguyen was going to do with that. Maybe at least it would give him an excuse to make a return trip to try more of Betty's food. She wouldn't have minded continuing that line of conversation, but Weaver stood up and resumed her briskly professional manner.

"That's all for now, I think. We may have some more questions for you in the future, so I hope you'll keep yourself available."

"I'll be here."

Claudia could have, and probably should have, left it at that, but there was one more thing she needed to ask.

"Did you know it was her? The identity theft, the murders, all of it? Did you already know she did it?"

Weaver stopped on her way out the door and started to say something. Then she seemed to think better of it, and nodded.

"I would have."

Once again alone, Claudia reflect on the conversation and wondered if this was an opportunity for her to do some serious self-examination. But she didn't want to, and anyway, she was already late for work. So she found her shoes (under the couch, where she had kicked them the night before) and Teddy's leash, and headed off to continue being whatever she was.

Everyone in the marketplace already knew some or all of what had happened, and most of them were surprised to see her there. Only Helen, who had never met a workday she didn't show up for, seemed to think it was a natural thing to do.

Julie was nowhere to be seen, though the assistant cheesemonger who was manning the shop assured everyone she hadn't been arrested again, which was a relief. The handful of customers who happened to be in on a midweek fall morning were more than a little interested in their conversations on the subject, but Claudia decided there was nothing she could do about that at this point. If she was going to end up being known as the owner of Northern California's Murder Market, then so be it.

A cluster of the vendors had gathered around her in front of Iryna and Carmen's stand, where she had stopped to ask how the sales of their new pumpkin pie pierogis were going and had gotten drawn into providing a more detailed account of the previous night's adventures.

"How did the police officer find you?" asked Iryna, who was hanging on every word.

"Nathan called 911 and I guess he was able to convince them it was serious, because they actually put him through to Chief Weaver. I don't know what he told her, but it made her decide to come out personally." (She left out the part about Elias's simultaneous call, which had resulted in some people from the county visiting the farm for a wellness check, to his extreme outrage.)

"She tried to get into the parking lot first, but my car was blocking it," she went on. "And that's when she heard the shots, and the noise from the tractors made it fairly easy to find us."

"It's a good thing she did," Carmen said, in a dry tone that made it clear that she didn't share her wife's enthusiasm. "You could have been in a lot of trouble there."

Iryna dismissed her concern with a wave of her hand.

"Oh, they would have been fine. After all, she was almost out of bullets. Did you do the counting thing? You know, 'was that five or six'? I would have."

"It wasn't exactly the moment for movie references," Claudia admitted, to Iryna's disappointment.

"So, I get why she killed the lawyer, and why she wanted to kill Julie.

But what about that other guy, the one we caught breaking in?" Helen asked, looking worried. "Was it because we let him get away?"

"I don't think so. Not exactly, anyway. Gowan and Newman had collaborated on their crimes in the past, so when he showed up in town after the death, talking about how Gowan wouldn't have gone to prison, and he had something so valuable, she must have figured he knew about the evidence that implicated her. She may have thought he had the security key too, when she couldn't find it in the office, but when Julie used it after he died and Kathy got the alert on her phone, and she knew it wasn't him, because he was already dead. And that's when she must have figured out it was Julie, because she was the only other person who had been in the office before Kathy had a chance to search it."

"I can't believe Julie would do all that," Carmen said. "What was she thinking?"

"I understand it. After what that guy did to her, she had to do something," said Helen.

Carmen was having none of it. "She didn't have to do that. She's lucky to be alive."

"Aren't we all?" Robbie joked. "Personally, I'd like to have a go at driving one of those tractors. I wonder if they'd consider giving classes?"

The conversation turned to the group's varying experiences with different kinds of farm equipment, and Claudia was about to excuse herself to get back to work when there were three thumps and a clanking noise from somewhere below their feet. Claudia was just about ready to give up and join the circus, when Robbie remembered something.

"Oh!" he said. "I forgot to tell you. A guy showed up this morning just after we opened. He said you hired him to check out a water problem under the building, so I went ahead and let him into the crawl space. I hope that was okay."

Claudia might have pointed out that all of the events of the last week could have been avoided by keeping random strangers from accessing various parts of the building, but she didn't have the energy for that right now.

So instead she said, "Thanks, I guess I'd better check on him" and went to do that.

The only access to the crawl space was a hatch at the back of the building, about the size of a medium-large raccoon, covered by a metal door. Claudia got there just as Katlen was emerging, squeezing through the hatch like too much toothpaste coming out of the tube. His clothes were caked with mud and there was a scrape on his arm. Given the conditions she had apparently left him to work in, Claudia fully expected to have another encounter with his temper, but in fact he couldn't have been more cheerful.

"Found your problem!" he said as soon as he got himself free. "Bad seal on one of the sink drains. Doesn't look like it did any real damage, though, you had some luck there."

"So that's where it went," Claudia said, but he wasn't listening.

"But the other thing, did you know you have a lot of frogs down there? Like, a lot of frogs." As Claudia admitted to having some knowledge of this, he went on. "So, I was thinking, because if we take away their water they're going to be in trouble. But I could build, like, a little area for them where that compartment used to be, in the floor. I could even put in a window or something, so you can see them."

He was positively beaming at the idea, and he must have interpreted Claudia's look of confusion as relating to that because he added, by way of explanation, "I really like frogs."

There wasn't much Claudia could say to that, and before she had fully processed what she was agreeing to, Katlen was wiggling his way back under the building, saying something about some boxes down there he was going to bring out, and then he'd get right on the new project. Claudia didn't doubt that, though she did wonder how she was going to frame frog sanctuary construction as a business expense on her taxes.

The thought of taxes drew her mind to other things, ones that she didn't want to get into right now, so she stepped away from the building to a spot where she could see around the side of the hill to the ocean beyond.

The rain had stopped, but she had the impression it was thinking about starting again, so she took the time to breathe in the damp air and watch the clouds building over the water. Closer in, a hawk was perched on the power lines, its feathers puffed out to try to dry them between the storms. She wondered if it knew it was just going to get wet again, or if it cared, then looked back up at the sky to try and judge how soon, while she thought about her own decision-making process.

"I think I just hired an assistant frog-keeper," she said to the clouds.

"Well, it's a good idea to delegate."

Claudia turned around to find that it wasn't the weather that had answered her, but Nathan, coming around the corner of the market with his hands in his pockets.

"They told me I could find you out here. How are you doing?"

"Okay, I guess. Thanks for calling the police for me."

"Anytime," Nathan said, then frowned. "Actually, I hope I don't have to do it again. But if you need me to, you know, I will."

"That's good to know."

They stood there for a minute, just far enough apart that it would be awkward to get closer. Nathan was wearing one of his very soft-looking sweaters, and Claudia realized that there was nothing she wanted more at that moment than to run over and bury her face in it.

But she was fairly sure that would frighten him, so she decided on a more conventional approach.

"Hey, um, are you doing anything for dinner? Because I've got a couple of frozen pizzas, and Betty gave me a carrot cake."

Nathan smiled, and his eyes lit up in a way that made Claudia think maybe she should have tried the sweater thing after all.

"Sure," he said. "Pizza and carrot cake sounds amazing. I'll bring some of my new batch of cider."

Claudia was trying to think of a way to suggest they might also watch something on streaming in a way that wouldn't sound like a euphemism when there was a rattling sound from the direction of the building. They turned in time to see Katlen squeezing himself out of the hatch, then reaching back in to pull out a pair of wooden crates. The slats were dark with age but apparently still in good condition, if the amount of force Katlen was able to exert on them to drag them into the daylight was anything to go by.

"Check this out," he said, obviously pleased with his discovery. "They were all the way in the back corner, practically buried under some old sacks. I thought for sure there would be something in them, they're so heavy, but they're empty. What do you figure they are?"

Kneeling next to the first one, Claudia's mind reeled with the memory of her conversation with Walter at the museum and his tales of the myths and legends of the Satler family. The box was about two feet across, a little shorter than it was wide, with an open top and handles cut into the sides. She tried lifting it, and it was definitely weightier than its material and dimensions would suggest, with an oddly bottom-heavy feeling.

Claudia took a deep breath.

"It's an apple crate," she said. "And I'm not so sure it's empty."

At an earlier time it might have taken her a while to locate the mechanism, but by now Claudia thought she was getting the hang of this, and it was only a matter of a few minutes before she was able to get her fingernail under the lever concealed in one of the snugly-fitted bottom slats. Pulling on it revealed that the bottom wasn't composed of slats at all, but a thin board cleverly engineered to look like multiple pieces, which came up as one. Underneath, packed in tightly together and shining in the cloudy afternoon light, were a tidy collection of slim gold bars.

Katlen's mouth dropped open and he made a kind of a gurgling noise, and Nathan let out a low whistle. Claudia stood in silence for a while, unable to put the various thoughts in her head into coherent words.

"Well," she said at last. "That's something."

# ACKNOWLEDGMENTS

This book, like all books, would not have been possible without the work of many people, most of whom are not me. Thanks go to my wonderful agent Abby Saul, for her patience, support, guidance, and more patience, especially when I email her things like "what about giant mosquitos," to my keen-eyed editor Dan Meyer for believing in these books and helping to bring Claudia's adventures to the world, and to everyone at Seventh Street and Start for all their great work.

I am also grateful to my friends and family for being with me, at least in spirit, through this crazy year of endless March. And to Cameron, for his depth of knowledge on all things technological and for being the person with whom I would most like to ride out a plague.

To Laurie Sheehan and all the members of the MWA NorCal Zoom writing squad for providing a lifeline of fellow writers and helping to keep me on track when all the days ran together, I offer an on-mute thumbs up and an apology for every time I picked my nose on camera.

And to the researchers who kept the work on mRNA therapeutics alive for so many years, against a world of doubters, I offer my sincere thanks and appreciation.